My Most Chosen Friends

My Most Chosen Friends

by

Robin Alston

British Library Cataloguing in Publication Data
A catalogue record for this book is available from the British Library

ISBN 0-9550993-0-7
ISBN 978-0-9550993-0-4

Typeset by Amolibros, Milverton, Somerset
This book production has been managed by Amolibros
Printed and bound by T J International Ltd, Padstow, Cornwall, UK

For the friends I loved. And for those
who said, 'All's fair in love and war.'

Acknowledgements

Thank you, Jenny, for cheerful support, encouragement, and the big chair by the PC. Thank you, Peter Gordon, Sybil McNair and Grey Eyes for wise words on medical matters. Thank you also to Kenneth Laband, author of *Colonial Postscript*, who, with Lennox Honeychurch provided a glimpse of life on a faraway island. I am also indebted to the late Clifford de Feu for his notes on a wartime journey. Last but not least *muito obrigado*, Chico Ramos, for showing on the cover of this book three of my chosen friends.

Chapter One

A black eye, a real shiner and bruised lips. It was no way to come face to face with God – in this case my headmaster. It was no use trying to conceal the damage, and it was Miss Peedie, the matron, who spotted it, who got hold of me and frogmarched me to him. I froze as she pushed me across the vestibule to the holy of holies, to his dark, book-lined study with a worn rug on floorboards that objected every time you trod on them. The Peedie rapped on the door, it swung back and I was done for. I knew it. I blew hot, then cold, and trembled. I was not brave.

'Young Master Hartside, sir! Just look at him! Bin i' the wars, you little devil, haven't you!'

Headmaster W. A. C. Connor, usually known as Whack, rose from behind his desk.

He was tall, and his head was too small for his bony, skeletal body. His nose was long and sharp, barely fleshy enough to balance his pince-nez.

Hands on hips. Interrogation. 'Ah, young Hartside! Are you going to tell me a pillar in the colonnade stepped down and struck you? Because your futile imaginings will not seduce me, no matter how clever. I've heard your stories before.'

He turned away. 'Thank you, Miss Peedie, that will be all.'

She left as I steadied myself, hand on the back of an antique chair. Then he surprised me by plumping down into his own chair and resting his hands on the desk. His voice turned a shade warmer. I controlled my trembling.

'Now, Hartside, are you going to tell me how you came by those bruises? They must be very painful.'

I nodded. They were.

1

'I take it some good friend of yours decided you were not very nice-looking and sought to give you…shall we say…a facelift? If that is the case, Hartside, I need to be told. You know perfectly well I will not tolerate violence in this school. Who did this to you?'

I shook my head.

'I will ask you again. Why were you struck, and by whom?'

Again I shook my head. I said nothing and just concentrated on the two glass jars on his desk, one labelled humbugs and the other gobstoppers. I'd seen them once before. If Head was pleased with you he gave you a choice. There was no offer going this time. I just concentrated on gobstoppers.

His voice softened.

'See here, lad, it may surprise you to learn that I was once a boy…yes, a long, long time ago, and I had an occasional scrap. So you see, I understand. These upsets can happen. To put matters straight the truth must come out.' A pause. 'I am waiting, Hartside.'

It was Thomson who had done it. I sloshed him one but he was bigger and stronger than I was. We set about each other in the dorm with an audience looking on and cheering. But I lost out and then he swanked about how he was taught boxing at prep school. I wouldn't have hit him – that was my mistake – but he had tried to steal the records for my gramophone – and not for the first time.

'Hartside, I have not got all day. I insist you tell me.'

Much as I disliked Thomson I was not going to rat on him, there'd be no peace if I did. Anyway, I was not a telltale. I refused to answer.

'In that case, you give me no choice. If you will not say you will have to pay. Truth, above all, Hartside, truth is our only guide as you must learn. Better by far that you learn now. I cannot respect a boy who will not tell the truth.'

He picked up his cane from the corner of the room. I knew well what was to come. He bent me over the antique chair, pulled down my trousers and began. The worst of it was I had not got a fat bum and six of the best had me groaning with each swish and strike. He did not hold back. I tried but could not stop my tears. When the beating ceased he would not look at me and his voice was nearly a whisper.

'Pull up your trousers, boy!'

Then he lifted the phone. 'Matron? Come through, please. Take Hartside to the nursery and tell Sister to do the necessary.'

Pop Wilkinson, a big lad, was the first to greet me when Sister had seen to me in the sickbay. I emerged still nursing a very sore bum.

'You poor bugger!' Pop exclaimed. 'Bastards!'

He was my new friend, a senior in Penn, the same house as mine. His language was rough but he had a good heart. He placed a hand on my shoulder and his black eyebrows converged. A hint of menace.

'That Thompson,' he growled. 'If he does you again just leave him to me.'

I fancied he was pretty useful with his fists himself, but he did have a friendly streak and he wanted to show it.

'You like a surprise?'

I nodded.

'We can do it.' A nod of conviction, and a whisper. 'I got a packet of ten. From Bert. Craven A.'

I sensed what was coming. The friendly bit was tinged with a touch of urgency. 'You got a tin of Heinz in your locker and one of those…y' know.'

A wink. I knew what he meant. A whip-cream walnut.

So that was it. Pop was trying to make amends for Thompson's bullying and the beating from the head. I said I did have a tin of baked beans in the locker where I kept my stodge. But only the small size.

'Okay, kiddo. Half an hour. Behind the school house and we'll go HV.'

So it was arranged, as it had been before. Across the Japanese garden, past the science block and the swimming baths, over the wooden bridge and down along the bank of the canal to the cinder track. Then, skirt the cricket field and head on past the meadow with cows to our secret hideaway. HV. Happy Valley. Just the place for a smoke on a Saturday half-day.

The beating I received from the head happened a year after I had arrived at Whitworth School. I had come via a small day school near my home forty miles away. Here, I was a boarder in Penn house together with a group of other lads. I was in the fourth form now.

'Splendid educational institution!' That's what my dad rather pompously called Whitworth. He knew. He had been a pupil here when he was a boy, with his brother. Two boys together. They had also been in Penn. William and Harry. Their names were in the 'old scholars' book.

'It will do you the world of good,' my dad said. 'Knock the corners off you'.

Whitworth was run by the Quakers – The Society of Friends. He said they were good people. They were religious. They believed in God so I would get a fine education, a good springboard for university. At the time I did not know that God believed in education. Or universities. And certainly not in beating boys' bums.

Dad said the school opened as long ago as 1780, and the main buildings had been built as a branch of a foundling hospital. When I arrived I was barely eleven and was homesick. I cried myself to sleep many a night under the bedclothes in the dormitory where the water in the drinking jug froze. The whole place felt cold and especially when the north winds got to us and fairly whistled through the colonnades and corridors.

Whitworth was in the North Country, a monumental pile of grey stone buildings on a hillside staring blindly over damp farm fields and the village of Whitworth-by-Moorside. It took me all of a year to learn the school ways, drilled into line by bells and whistles and compulsory outdoor sports.

The chums I ganged up with were also in Penn. Pop Wilkinson, Squirt Fountain, Walter Fearndale, Squeak Whiting, Mortimer A. V., and Jack Emslie. There were others in the house of course, but I was not especially close to them. They were Pee-wee Smith, Snottie Bell, Jeff Plowright, Cumberland, Sandy Bamford, Jim Appleyard, Art Wilson and Parnell.

In all, the school held about 150 boys and, quite separately, almost the same number of girls. They were housed in joined-on but separate quarters to us and we were not encouraged to recognise their existence.

Turning the blind eye was not easy because they were visible at various times and places. The heart of the school was the central block containing the big library, and on either hand were two identical two-storey blocks for the girls to the left and us boys to the right. Our block contained, on the ground floor, a very large dining hall, while above were some of our dormitories. Far below were the cellars where we stored our trunks. These blocks, both for the girls and ourselves, were joined to classrooms by curved colonnades. Above ours was the boot room, and above the girls' colonnade was an arc of cubicles, each containing a bath. We were allowed a supervised bath once a week.

The classroom buildings faced each other across a wide expanse of smooth, sloping concrete, which was known as the Green, and these buildings were called the East Wing (for us boys) and the West Wing (for the girls).

Above the Green, stretching east and west, was a terrace with benches along the wall and at the lower end of the Green was the Japanese garden with trees, vegetables, rhubarb, and berries. It was a very large garden, which extended to the canal and the open meadows beyond. It also enclosed small plots where those with green fingers were encouraged to practise their gardening skills. There were also quite a number of adjacent buildings housing the nursery, art rooms, craft workshop, the assembly hall with the masters' studies below, the meeting house, masters' houses, and the gymnasium with the chemi labs above. Also the laundry, the girls' houses and the barns and sheds of the school farm, with its dairy herd, its hens and milk pasteurisation plant. We were almost a self-supporting community and might well have been inmates of a monastery. Our one ear to the outer world was *The Bulletin*, a digest of news in the form of a single sheet of quarto pinned to the main notice board between our colonnade and the door to the geography room. The items of information were supplied by Jumbo Liddington, the deputy head, who taught history and was also my housemaster.

Sometimes his choice of subject was augmented by a line or two from the lads in the wireless room. They had earphones and loudspeakers. They listened in and were able to pick up snippets of news and sometimes even the latest jazz bands in faraway London.

It was in the summer term when two items in *The Bulletin* attracted my attention. The first was about the biggest ship in the world called the *Queen Mary*. It would be launched by the Queen herself. The second item was sports. Fred Perry was pronounced champion at Wimbledon.

From that time forward he was my hero and tennis became my favourite game. There were other items I did not understand so I usually appealed to Jack Emslie for advice. He was one of the gang, about my age but really very, very old and wise.

'That bit there,' Jack noted with a touch of authority in his voice as he pointed to a paragraph in *The Bulletin*, 'it's about Germany. And Hitler. He's a Nazi of course. Nazi means leader, it's politics, like we have a leader. The Prime Minister. Ours is a decent sort, but my dad says Hitler is mad.'

I was not very interested in Hitler or Germany. I was glad I was not a German. I was relieved to be safe and secure with my friends behind the school gates in the windy spaces of our work and play.

Chapter Two

Walter Fearndale was my second best chum, after Pop. He was a good talker. He passed round gossip to us like sharing a fag, and he usually made us pay for his news. It was no surprise when he said he had a bit of something and we were to meet him in the cellars. They were that dark, forbidden place beneath the dining room. Our private hideaway.

Walt's gossip this time was about the girls.

'I tell you,' he confided, 'it's true. Scout's honour.'

'Scout's balls!' replied Pop. 'They'll never let us mix wi' t' lassies.'

Squirt Fountain agreed. 'Course they won't. It's not cohensive here, never will be. Not the Quakers, and they don't...well, y' know...'

He broke off, blushing darkly.

'You mean co-education,' corrected Jack. 'We're not a co-education school, never have been.'

'Nearest we ever get to the birds is Sunday meeting,' said Cumberland. He added, 'There's that gangway between us, and the birds. Like no-man's land.'

'It's called an aisle,' said Jack.

Walter was impatient. 'If you'll just listen. What I know is that we are going to be allowed to mix with the other side. There's to be an announcement.'

'They'll not allow that. Bet you a tanner,' exclaimed Pop.

That made Walter laugh. 'Okay, Pop, you're on. Anyone else?'

I thought I'd better say something. 'Pop's right. We can look, like everyone does. But that's all. If we got close up they'd never trust us.'

There was silence while we had a think. Everyone knew we fancied the birds. I reckoned the whole school fancied someone over that side.

I turned to Walter. 'Just wishful thinking, Walt. It's been like that ever since my dad was here.'

It became clear that a few pennies would be passed across the bay. In the end I reckoned Pop would win, or lose, two shillings and ninepence. A small fortune to most of us, and especially to Jeff Plowright, who liked to chum along with us but seldom offered an opinion. He was a shepherd's son.

I was always puzzled as to where Walter obtained his bits of news. We did not have long to wait.

The assembly hall, called Fairclough Hall, seated at least 300 boys and girls with an aisle between. There were plain oak benches, polished, straight-backed honest benches, crafted I guessed by honest, straight-backed Quakers in times long gone. On most Saturday evenings the hall was crowded with boys on one side of the stepped aisle, the girls on the other, all chattering and twittering like a dawn chorus. Normal practice was the lantern lecture, but on this particular Saturday there was no screen showing slides of the pyramids or the Himalayas. No ancient visiting lecturer. Instead, only the boring sight of masters and mistresses seated on the stage and facing the restless company.

The girls' side was occupied by several of their teachers including the headmistress, Ma Neatly, and her deputy, named as Arabella Joy in the school brochure but usually known to us as plain A. J. In fact, she was far from plain.

Facing our crowded benches were some of the masters, led by Whack. They included Sarki Stan, Tashy Watts (French teacher), Pisc Long (maths and geometry), Clubby Nash (art), J. Seagrave (English), Bill Rodgers (master on duty, swimming and sports) and Jumbo Liddington.

Whack rose to his feet and raised a hand to silence the chattering. 'This evening,' he began, 'we have a change to the normal programme. We are gathered here for an important announcement, which, as I see it, will bring a change to the long and happy tradition of our school. To tell you about this change I hand you over to our deputy head of girls, Miss A. Joy.'

Miss A. J. rose to her feet smiling. She was tall and slim and could have been mistaken for one of her seniors as she was wearing the same school uniform that the girls wore – dark navy gym slip and a pale blue blouse. Mortimer A. V. once said she probably wore pale blue bloomers as well.

She inclined her head, a token of unspoken thanks to Whack, then turned to face us.

'Good evening to you all! It is super to see you here, all together like one big family. I apologise that there is no slide show tonight. Instead, Miss Neatly and the headmaster have asked me to give you some important news. It concerns both the East Wing and our West Wing.

'I have to tell you that it has been agreed by the board of governors and also by our committee of management that on Sundays after our meeting for worship there will be what I call "walking together as friends". And I want you all to pay careful attention to this. Any girl who is related by family to a boy on the East Wing will be allowed to walk with him on the Green for an hour or so.'

She turned to Ma Neatly and Whack for confirmation and added, 'This means, until the dinner bell. Yes?'

Ma Neatly nodded, but Whack simply looked ahead, expressionless, as if he had not heard what she was saying.

'Similarly,' A. J. continued, 'any boy who is related by family to a girl on the West Wing will be permitted to walk with her in friendship on Sundays…'

Unexpectedly there was an interruption and before he could be prevented Mortimer A. V., who was sitting next to me, jumped up and asked, 'Even if it is raining, Miss? It often rains on Sundays.'

Whack looked like thunder. He opened his mouth but nothing came out. A. J. quickly said, 'What is your name?'

'Mortimer A. V.,' he replied unabashed. Then he sat down as those around him started nudging and whispering.

A. J. said, 'Well, Mortimer A. V., that is a fair question and one we had not addressed. I think the answer must be probably not if it is raining.'

There followed a wave of more murmuring and whispering on both sides of the hall. When it subsided A. J. continued.

'Those of you who have studied the history of our school will know that this change we are proposing is far from new. The very first scholars who came, and they came by horse and cart all those years ago, were Barnaby and Mary Aird. They were brother and sister and were allowed to walk together on occasion. And so were scholars who followed them. The practice ceased, however, in the mid-nineteenth century, when our Victorian forebears pronounced it to be quite improper. Friendships were supposed to happen only after schooldays were ended. We take a different view today. Cousins as well as brothers and sisters will be allowed Sunday walking together.'

She paused, then said, 'If any of you have queries or doubts about Sunday walking, please see your form mistress or your housemaster.'

My chums around me were smiling, but when Whack rose there was not even the suspicion of a smile on his face. He said, 'Thank you, Miss Joy. That concludes this meeting. We will now have a few minutes' silence.'

Perhaps it was more of a stunned silence than a Quakerly vote of thanks to God. Then Whack got to his feet again and looked across to the row where I was sitting. He glowered. 'Single file, and no talking on the stairs. Mortimer A. V., tomorrow before meeting, 9.30 sharp. My study!'

Whatever that command might mean for A. V. it was clear the announcement made by Miss Joy would put all of two shillings and ninepence into Walter's pocket. He had won his bet and we all lost.

Chapter Three

I was not particularly keen at first and I told him no. The day was heavy, overcast with grey clouds obscuring the sun. There was heat, as if it rose from below the earth and prised out warm smells of sweet grasses and moss to mingle with the acrid mist that floated up from the canal like steam.

Early summer. Two summers before A. J.'s surprising announcement about walking with the girls. Walter wanted me to go with him to watch senior school cricket, our first XI versus the lads from Archbishop Perrow's Grammar in Burneston. I wasn't keen. I wanted to play my gramophone because I had a couple of new Parlaphones I had brought from home. In the end Walter was too persuasive and I gave in.

'They have a tea break in the pavilion, Johnny,' he told me, his eyes sparkling with mischief. 'Sandwiches. And if we keep a lookout when they go back on the pitch maybe we could…y' know!'

I knew all right and it wasn't a bad idea, though I was far from sure that we'd get a chance to steal a few, or a bit of the cake that was usually supplied with lemonade for the teams. All the same, in the end I changed my mind and said I'd go with him for a bit to watch the match. He had a way with him and it was hard to refuse.

So it was that we walked together down to the cricket, across the wooden bridge, over the cinder track and through the gates. There were no stands or seats, except the few in the pavilion, so we lay in the grass behind the white boundary line. The pitch looked miles away and the players were like little model figures. There was still no sun, but the warmth in the grass made me feel quite sleepy as I listened to the occasional cries from the players.

Walter seemed far from sleepy, and at first I did not know what he was up to. To be accurate I did not know what his hand was up to, but I was jerked very wide awake when I felt it against my trousers. We wore shorts and I became aware of his fingers gently undoing the buttons at the front. I was shocked and pushed his hand away – but it stole back and I heard him murmur, 'Johnny, Johnny, it's all right, no one can see.'

His fingers advanced again.

'Walter, get off!' And again I tried to push his hand away, but he persisted. He had turned towards me and was lying on his side, very close. He whispered, 'Johnny, you've done it before, c'mon, tell me when you last had a little toss.'

I still did not realise. His fingers began to touch me. It felt very nice and I grew excited. I held my breath, and I did not prevent his more insistent touching and a warmth began to wrap round my thighs. More urgently now he grasped and sent waves of pleasure through me that grew more and more intense and I found I could not hold back. I wanted to push him away but realised I couldn't, the feeling was so sweet. I surrendered completely. A smile, half triumph and half disbelief moved across Walter's face. He knew then that I had not done it before.

'I can show you, Johnny boy,' he said, flushed and excited. And he nodded. 'You're glad you came after all, isn't that right, Johnny?'

I nodded back. Oh yes, it was suddenly so very right. But as Walter reminded me later, we never did get those sandwiches.

It was while I was enjoying a smoke with Pop in Happy Valley that he told me he didn't believe walking with girls would be allowed.

'Just a bit of talk, Johnny. Daft promises to keep us quiet.'

He did not trust promises, nor did he reckon much of birds. He did not care for them. They were a different sort, always whispering and giggling. But then, that was Pop. He blew a smoke ring and I watched as it spiralled away on the breeze. A big nought, a zero like the nothing he felt for 'birds'.

'Any road up,' he observed, 'you don't fancy the birds, Johnny, do you?'

I was not going to answer because I didn't want to fall out with Pop. The fact was, I did see girls, mostly in my dreams. Now, my dreams were changing…becoming real to me and that change was accelerating after the announcement in Fairclough Hall. I quite liked the deputy headmistress, A. J. If I'd had a big sister I hoped she would have been like her.

Pop repeated his question. 'Get on! You're not daft on birds, are you?'

I did not tell him, but I had seen a girl across that no-man's land and there was something about her that drew my attention. She had seen me as well and when she realised I was looking she looked back. Our eyes met and when they did I was surprised and half-scared. I turned away quickly. Sure enough she was not in my dreams, she was real, with shiny dark hair, black as the liquorice strips you could get at Ma Coltart's. It was long hair, straight and down to her shoulders. In that swift glance there was one other thing I noted and that was her forehead. It was pale, and wide and higher than you might imagine. It made her look very intelligent.

It was some time later when I decided I would like to walk on the Green with her. I often thought about that time with Walter two years ago in the cricket field and it was fresh in my mind even now. Of course, you couldn't do it with a girl, but you could do walking up and down. Except I couldn't because my dark lady wasn't a relation, not my sister, not even a cousin.

I'd given Pop half a packet of a fag I liked called Sweet Afton, and he offered one of my ciggies back to me. He said he wanted to talk about soccer, not girls. He said, 'You're a daft dreamer, Johnny, but I know you can draw quite good. Next term you could make a drawing of our team and put it on to the notice board for the house matches. Better than a list of names like the others do.'

The smoke with Pop had confused me. Soccer was a term and a holiday away, so why go on about it now? I decided I would do whatever he wanted. But I would rather we had talked about the girls. Especially the one with the dark hair. I guessed she was about my age.

Pop wasn't very brainy, and was slightly below me in class. He was 4B and I was in form 4A, mainly because the English master, Seagrave, liked my essays, and because I was quite good at art. But Pop did seem quite keen on reading and paid a lot of attention to the big notice board, and especially the weekly *Bulletin*.

'See what it says now, Johnny boy? It's about war.'

'What war? There isn't any war.'

'Well, there could be. They say the German air force is twice what we've got. If they attacked us we'd lose and never recover.'

I didn't want to think about it, and was surprised when it cropped up in our meeting for worship of all places. Meetings were held every Sunday, 10.30 a.m. to 11.30, and the whole school, including masters and mistresses, had to attend.

These meetings were held in the big meetinghouse by the school gates. We trooped in to take our places, row by row, on the brown benches, the girls on one side and us on the other with no-man's land in between. It was not easy, sitting there very still in silence for an hour. The masters and mistresses had nice blue cushions to sit on but we had only the wood benches. I often got a numb bum.

Silent worship, it was called, but sometimes a master or mistress would get up and speak. Jumbo Liddington with other members of staff sat at the front facing us. He stood up. 'Friends,' he intoned, 'you are probably as sad as I am to hear talk of war by our politicians in Parliament. If we are to believe them, Germany is now being placed on a war footing. Their soldiers and airmen are in training in great numbers, and armaments are being produced on a scale hitherto unheard of.

'In spite of this, we all hope peace can be maintained. Talk of war does nothing but darken our days. How much better it is to follow Christ's teaching and arm ourselves not with guns but with the props and stays of peace as declared as long ago as the nineteenth century by the early Quakers. They set out their faith in writings called *Advices* and I would like to read to you one advice.'

There was a good deal of shuffling and coughing as he took a small book from his pocket.

'Their testimony, friends, was crystal clear. They wrote, "We are called to live a life that takes away the occasion of all wars. Do you faithfully maintain our testimony that war and the preparation for war are inconsistent with the spirit of Christ? Search out whatever in your own life may contain the seeds of war. Stand firm in our testimony, even when others commit, or prepare to commit acts of violence." '

He ended by adding, 'We are advised to bring into God's light those emotions, attitudes and prejudices in ourselves that lie at the root of destructive conflict. In our worship today let us think on these words of good counsel.'

He sat down, and we sat uneasily, in some discomfort. I hoped we looked as if we were listening intelligently, but I for one was gazing across to the other side to where tree branches scraped against the big windows, and where, among the rows of girls, I could just make out the one with the dark, shiny hair.

Chapter Four

*J*une and a clear sky, day after day, a dazzling, cloudless blue with the heat from the sun hammering down. It warmed the old stones of our classrooms, which fairly bounced back the heat in the still air. Our legs and arms turned brown. We burned for a whole month.

My kid brother Richard – known as Paddy 'the next best thing' – came to Whitworth School at the beginning of that stifling summer term. Two years younger than I was, he was a gifted tennis player, having been taught by Dad to hit balls from the age of three. As he grew older he honed his skills and I thought he could become a county junior.

Because he was so talented, Paddy and I were allowed a special privilege. On Wednesday and Saturday afternoons we could play on a proper court, the red shale court in the garden behind the school inn. We counted our luck and all went well until – without warning – disaster struck.

I'd arranged to play a couple of sets with Paddy and was alarmed when he did not appear. I searched, and asked everyone around until, eventually, I tracked him down in matron's office. To my alarm she was applying a swab to staunch the blood from a deep cut on his brow.

'What on earth happened to Paddy, matron? I've been looking for him everywhere.'

She straightened up. 'Nasty cut, probably should have a couple of stitches. We'll have to see.'

He winced but said nothing.

'So what have you been up to, Paddy?'

Matron said, 'A nasty fall, I should think.'

I doubted it. Paddy was far too surefooted. He was agile. And I was right. Half an hour later, when a plaster had been stuck in place on his brow he told me all about it.

'It was that big boy,' he said. 'I hate him, I hate him!'

There were lots of boys bigger than Paddy. 'Which big boy?' I asked.

'Don't know. He pinched my racket and when I tried to get it back he hit me with it…here, right on my head!'

For a moment I thought he was going to cry.

'Did you get your racket back?'

He nodded.

I said, 'But which big boy was it?'

'I don't know him, he's a fifth former I think, and he's just a bully. Someone said he was Thomas, or a name like that.'

The light dawned. 'Paddy,' I said, 'his name wasn't Thomson, was it?'

He considered for a moment. 'Well, it could be. He's very tall. They said he's always pinching things…'

So, that was it. Thomson for sure. Up to his tricks again.

I felt very angry. It wasn't fair, especially as Paddy was a new boy – he'd not even been at school a whole term.

'Well, don't you worry, Pad. Just keep your racket locked away for a bit, and let matron see that cut again in a couple of days. We'll see about Mr Thomson.'

And so we did.

The small garden for boys was supposed to be looked after by fourth formers and older lads, but no one seemed to bother very much, except Walter and me. We'd planted a lot of seeds in the spring and much to our surprise flowers had begun to show. We were pleased but we realised there would be more to do before we got a full show. That 'more' was weeding. A lot of it. We left it until evening, after prep, when the day had cooled a bit. There were lavateria, red dianthus, some lupins and nasturtiums. The sunflowers would come later.

As we worked around the plot I told Walt about Paddy and how Thomson had tried to steal his tennis racket, and hit him.

'You going to do something about that?' he asked. 'Because if you are, I'll give you a hand, Johnny. Thomson's always stealing, he's just a thief and a bully.'

We did more weeding, then Walt said, 'We're going to need water here, the sun's drying them out.'

So it was. The soil felt hot. Dry and crumbly. A wonder the weeds or the flowers grew at all.

Across the path that led down the centre of the Japanese garden and just beyond the sundial, there was the girls' garden. It was larger than our plot and more colourful. There were two girls working there.

'See that?' said Walt. 'I think they're watering. They've got a can. Maybe we could...'

I said no, we couldn't. Walt knew perfectly well that we were not allowed anywhere near the girls' garden. I looked across and they did seem to be watering, but it was not easy to see properly because the sun was low now and blindingly bright.

Then I looked again and, with a shock stood rooted to the spot. One of the girls was blonde and the other, as far as I could tell, had very dark hair. It was *her*. I was certain.

'What are you staring at...you've gone pale. You got sunstroke?'

It was her, I was sure. I said no, I had not got sunstroke. 'But you're right. We'd better get some water, d'you think they'd give us a can?'

There was no more to be said. A quick look round and we crossed the path and stepped over to the edge of the girls' plot.

I noticed her hair was different...put up in a kind of bunch, a ponytail.

The blonde girl was startled. 'Hey, you boys can't come here, it's not allowed.'

Walter said, 'We know, we know. But we need some water, our flowers are dying for want of a drink. Have you got water in that can?'

I felt I was dying for want of another look, a closer look. Then Walter, in his practised, persuasive way said, 'Honest, we do need some water. By the way, I'm Walter. This is Johnny.'

The late sun was spinning like a web of gold behind her head but I think she smiled...her eyes seemed to smile, then she looked down and coloured slightly.

She said nothing, but the other girl grinned, then the four of us just stood staring at each other. The blonde girl said, 'All right, but you'll have to be sharp about it. I'll fill the can.'

She did so and before we humped it away she added, 'I'm Liz. Liz Cowley. This is my friend, Anne Rigby.'

So – that was her name. Anne. I said, 'Hello!' No reply, but she looked up and smiled again. I said, 'Your garden, it's…it's much brighter than ours.'

She raised a hand, uncurling her fingers and showing her soiled palm as if giving a wave. It was like a small flower unfolding in the sun. Then she simply nodded and I felt a sudden happiness opening inside me.

Chapter Five

$\mathcal{W}$alter said, 'It's probably going to mean telling a few porkies.'
We were discussing the girls, Liz and Anne, and were
in the hut known as the old bicycle shed, on Back Lane
near the farm buildings. I never knew how it acquired that name because
no bicycles were kept there, it was simply a store for bits of broken
furniture and a moth-eaten settee. As a hideaway the shed was an
alternative to the cellars, but we kept quiet about it. Only Walt and I
went there. Ever since Walt had introduced me, at the cricket field, to
those heart-stopping pleasures we had practised together whenever
we could. It was a secret we shared. We would do what we wanted to
do together, and it became the bond that cemented our friendship.
We grew hungry for our pleasures and shared them with a breathtaking
seriousness.

On this visit to the shed we were not doing it. In fact we were talking
about the two girls we had met in the garden. Walt surprised me by
asking if I was struck on Anne.

'The one with the dark hair,' he said. 'I reckon she might fancy
you. Are you struck on her?'

I countered by saying both girls seemed super and that it would be
a treat to get to know them.

He asked me again. 'Well, supposing we could, which one is it you
fancy?'

I was embarrassed and did not want to answer him. What I felt was
a private feeling, but of course Walt had guessed right. If it had come
to a choice it would be Anne.

Walt had a strategy. 'First we've got to find a way of getting a message
to the girls. They may not want to see us again, but if they did,' he
paused, 'the only way, Johnny, would be walking on the Green.'

The Sunday walking up and down had only just begun. About ten boys, it seemed, had sisters or cousins on the West Wing, and they had appeared two-by-two last Sunday doing their promenade. They were closely observed by half the school peering from classroom windows.

Afterwards I said to Walt, 'It's all very well, but even if we could get a message across it would be no use because I don't have a sister or cousin over there, and nor do you.'

'Leave it to me, Johnny. Sandy Bamford's got a sister. I'll ask him to pass a message to her.'

'But what if he refuses?'

'Well, if he won't play, I've another plan. Maybe I could get a note to her. You could write it in your own fancy way and she could hand it to Anne or Liz. What d' you say?'

I didn't think it was a very good idea, as it could be dangerous. 'Supposing someone finds the note – the staff might get their hands on it.'

'Possibly,' said Walt impatiently. 'But you think of a better idea, then.'

I would certainly have a serious think. I was determined to get in touch with Anne.

It was Pop who called us all together. A total of ten, when we went down to the cellars. He spoke first.

'Johnny…Walt and me have sworn we'll do something about it. We've got to teach that boy Thomson a lesson.'

Squeak Whiting, who knew nothing of the situation, jumped up and down and shouted, 'Yeah! But why pick on Thomson?'

'Because he's a rotter,' replied Pop. 'You ask Johnny boy. Thomson fair clouted him when he first came here, and now he's done the same to Johnny's kid brother, young Paddy. Stole his tennis racket. We've got to stop him thinking he's the boss.'

The others murmured their assent. Several suggestions were put forward, and I agreed that something had to be done. Jack Emslie advised caution. 'We ought to go steady,' he said. 'Y' see, if we start a scrap it could get back on us and we don't want that. It could come to a real fight and then others would join in…the masters would be sure to get wind of it.'

Bamford said, 'A fight's okay, we'd win, there's more of us.'

That was true, if you included Plowright, Jeff Cumberland and Art Wilson. They were big lads. Finally we decided to leave it to Pop, with Jack still advising caution because Pop started muttering about kidnapping Thomson.

I agreed with Jack and that's what I told Walt the following evening when we went down to the garden again. I was hoping Anne might be there in the girls' plot, but there was no sign of her. There were two other girls I'd never seen before. They took no notice of us. I asked Walt if he thought Pop was really going to carry out his threat. I said, 'I mean it's all very well but where could we take him? There's really nowhere and we'll probably be found out whatever we decide.'

Our washrooms were two floors up, above the changing rooms where we kept our sports clothes, and alongside the communal shower bath with its walled and tiled area. In the corner a flight of stone steps led up to the washrooms with their rows of solid wooden partitions bearing mirrors and pegs for our towels. There were big windows above the hand basins and they looked out over 'the area', which was the entrance to the school's front door. That gave me the idea. My plan had nothing to do with Thomson and I only hoped it would work. There were three school houses across the main road and they contained bedrooms for some of the senior girls. They went out through 'the area' every night, with clothes over their arms and one girl usually carried a small can. We often watched from the windows and it was generally assumed that the can contained farm milk for their goodnight cocoa.

The three houses were called Holm Park, the Garden House, and Newsham. Walt told me that Liz Cowley and Anne were in Newsham along the road towards Back Lane and the farm.

What I had to do required careful timing. In the washrooms on the chosen evening I got Walt to keep watch and as soon as he signalled that the master on duty had gone to the boot-room door, which led to our dorms, he gave me the agreed signal. I then opened one of the windows above the hand basins and got ready. Straining forward and with a thumping heart I waited until I saw Anne and Liz step down from the school front entrance and start to walk out across 'the area'.

Then I dropped the blue envelope out through the window and saw it flutter down. I didn't see it land because Walt gave me a frantic signal to indicate that the MOD was returning, so I never saw whether the girls picked it up.

The letter inside was, after all, not difficult to write, but I had thought about it a long time.

Dear Anne,

If you could agree to become my cousin we could walk together on Sundays. That's if you would like to. RSVP. Please leave your reply under the big stone by the lupins in our garden.

For safety I just signed with the letter 'J'.

Chapter Six

*P*op said 'Have you got that rope?'

Squeak nodded. 'Course! Got it from the farm. No one saw.'

So the plan was hatched and Pop persuaded Plowright, Cumberland and Wilson A. J. to help.

To kidnap Thomson was not a good idea and I suggested that instead we should send him to Coventry, but I was out-voted. The others said that a bully like him should be given a taste of his own medicine. He had tried to steal my gramophone records more than once, so that was the starting point. He was told that my records were now kept in a trunk in the cellars. In fact they were stowed safely in my locker. The plan was that he would be told to go down to the cellars, open up the trunk and help himself to what he wanted. He took the bait. What he didn't know was that several of the gang were already down there waiting for him. When he came face to face with them he immediately realised it was a trap and tried to make a run for it. There was a short struggle, but, strong as he was, he was no match for them. They tied his hands and feet, and, to keep him quiet, secured the posh scarf that he wore with his jerseys and fastened it securely round his mouth. His hands were then tied with a length of rope to his feet so that he was totally unable to move. They then propped him up against the trunk he had thought to plunder.

'Done a right good job,' declared Plowright. 'Trussed him up like a turkey, he'll nay get outa that!'

I was then invited to tell Thomson why he had been trussed.

'Listen, Thomson, we don't mean you any harm but I'm fed up, and so are the others, because you keep stealing things which do not belong to you. You've no right to do that and you've got to stop it. If you don't there'll be worse to come.'

Pop said, 'We're going to let you stay down here to think on.'

'And get back your senses,' added Squeak. 'You went and hit Paddy and you hurt him bad till he was bleeding!'

Thomson made muffled muttering noises.

'We're leaving you to think about it,' added Walt. 'You're here for the night!'

We left him, crept quickly away and pulled the cellar door shut behind us.

'He'll go without his supper,' said Pop. 'But we'd better get him out after prep. We can't keep him there all night.'

Walt and the others agreed. But it didn't quite work out that way.

The following morning at breakfast Whack strode to the lectern in the big dining room to start the day, as was his custom. Usually he read a short passage from the New Testament. This time, however, there was no reading.

'You will all be concerned, as I am, to learn that one of our boys has gone missing.'

There was an audible stirring, a whispering, a rumble of excitement from the rows of tables, followed by an expectant hush.

'He did not appear for his supper last night, nor was his bed in dormitory three slept in. The missing boy is Forbes Pelham Thomson, Lower Five. We suspect that for some unaccountable reason he has run away.'

The response from the tables was a great clattering of spoons and a thunder of stamping feet. Whack raised a hand. 'It may be that, although we had never expected it, he has been unhappy. We thought perhaps there had been a bereavement in his family and he made for home. However, I have ascertained that is not the case. I am therefore appealing to you, all of you this morning, to tell me, or your housemaster, of anything you believe might have given rise to his absence. He could have met with an accident and if that is the case we must act without delay. Meanwhile I have informed his family, and the local constabulary of the situation.'

With that, he stalked down between the rows of tables, strode from the room – and left 130 boys open-mouthed.

Whack's announcement hardly surprised me, or the other members of the gang. We were scared stiff. The fact was we had not been very clever. As we had agreed, after prep, Pop with Plowright and Wilson A. J. had gone to the cellars to bring Thomson back up into the daylight and free him.

'Buggy me!' declared Pop, 'we couldn't do it. When we got there the cellar door was locked, we couldn't open it!'

What must have happened was that a master, probably John Rodgers on his rounds, passed by and noticed that the cellar door was slightly ajar so closed it, locked it and took the key away with him. We were now in a fix. If we didn't own up…well, Thomson would moulder away, starve. 'Probably get eaten by rats,' prophesied Squeak.

We told him to stop talking nonsense. I said, 'If we can't get Thomson out soon the police will be all over the school. There will be interrogations.'

Obviously, the longer he was locked away down there the worse it would be for us. Sooner or later we would have to confess.

Walt said, 'Yes, and tell him *why*! Whack ought to be told that Thomson has been stealing things and bullying young kids.'

That was true, but I did not believe it would help us very much. Pop was striding about. 'Who's going to tell Whack? One of us will have to…but I'll not do it!'

'Me neither,' chimed Wilson A. J. 'Plow and me, well we didn't plan it. We helped just because Pop asked us!'

They turned to me. 'It's not fair,' said Walt, 'but it all started with your brother Paddy. Couldn't you go and tell Whack? You could speak for all of us.'

I decided I would go to Jumbo Liddington rather than Whack, and confess to him. As my housemaster I hoped he might present our case to Whack in a reasonable light and make a plea for clemency. There was not much hope for us but I had to do it, and it was urgent.

In the history class, before Jumbo launched into the Romans, I put up my hand. 'Please, sir!'

'What is it, Hartside?'

'Could I have a word, sir?'

'A word about what?'

'It's private, sir.'

He stared at me very hard. After a pause he said, 'I see. You have something to tell me. Two minutes then, next door. The rest of you…textbook, chapter five. The Emperor Severus in Britain.'

We stood in the empty room where the cleaners kept their brushes and mops.

'Well, Hartside, what is it? Hurry up, I haven't got all day.'

Summoning my courage I told him about Thomson and the cellar. I was not sure, but I felt I could trust him. He had always seemed friendly, and especially to those of us in Penn. I glanced up. He raised his eyebrows. 'I thought you were one of the more sensible boys. I see that I was mistaken.'

I wished the ground would open up beneath me. He said, 'And just how did this stupidity happen?'

I told him everything. He said, 'You realise this is very serious? I shall want all your names. The headmaster will have to be informed before the matter goes any further.'

'Yes, sir. But it's not fair, sir. Thomson is a bully, hardly anyone likes him…'

'That's enough, Hartside, I want no excuses. Get back to class.'

My heart fell. There was real trouble ahead. I knew Whack's way of teaching you a lesson. The other masters did different punishments, rounds or copying out. Rounds meant you had to run round the Green, and it could be twenty times. Copying was usually lines from the Bible. But worst of all was being 'gated'. That meant no buying tuck at Ma Coltart's, and you couldn't go to the school inn with your mum and dad if they called to take you out at half term. As if that wasn't bad enough, I remembered Jack Emslie warning that for a really serious misdemeanour you could be expelled.

Thomson was released and taken to his house, which was Fox, and given a severe lecture by 'Pisc', his housemaster. We were rounded up – all of us, Pop, Walter, myself, Squeak, Plowright, Cumberland and Wilson A. J. We were then sent to the meeting house where the big double doors were locked behind us and we were left to sit there for half an hour. If we were expected to feel contrite and ask God's forgiveness I didn't. It felt cold. Staring across to the rows of empty benches where the girls sat in Sunday meetings made it worse. I thought of Anne. Anne in the garden when she waved and smiled. I wanted to get down to the garden and look for her reply to my letter under the stone by the lupins.

In due course Whack appeared, accompanied by Jumbo Liddington. They stood before us side-by-side. Walt whispered 'Tweedle Dum and Tweedle Dee!' It was no joke. Whack looked like thunder.

'There are absolutely no excuses for your deplorable behaviour,' he began. 'You should all be thoroughly ashamed of what you did to Pelham Thomson. You cannot be allowed to take the law into your own hands. If punishment is to be given it is the sole prerogative of staff members. I have to tell you that after meeting with the master on duty and others, I have seriously considered expelling the lot of you.'

He paused to allow his words to sink in.

That was going too far. No one had actually committed murder. The lecture continued. No one was to be sent home, but punishment there would be. We were all to be gated for three weeks and given ten rounds apiece. After the inquisition Squeak complained that he would rather have been sent home. None of us welcomed being made to run those rounds. The intention was clear. We were to be shamed. We would be watched by girls from their windows in the West Wing. If Anne saw me…what would she think? Would she ever want to walk with me? I sensed there would be worse to come. And there was. After the meeting for worship on Sunday I was sorting my records. I had decided to cheer myself up with a little music. As I was opening my gram and dusting the turntable, Walt come up.

'Don't look now,' he said. 'You won't like what you see.'

I had no idea what he was talking about. 'How about something cheery?' I said. 'I've got "Chicago". American trio.'

He said, 'Okay. But d' you see what I see?' He pointed out of the window. There were quite a number of couples walking up and down on the Green. 'Over there, Johnny!'

They were turning to walk back up towards the terrace. It was Thomson and they were holding hands as most couples did. He was walking with Anne, no mistake. Anne, with her hair done back in that ponytail, and wearing a summer dress, a gold colour. I did not want to believe my eyes, but sure enough, that was Anne. She was laughing, and so was Thomson. Walter looked at me, shaking his head. 'You know why he's doing this? To get back at you.'

'No, it can't be that. He couldn't know I wanted to go with Anne.'

'Probably noticed you looking at her. But heck, Johnny, what if he really is related to her?'

There was no more 'Chicago'. I put my records and the gramophone away. I decided I would go down the garden to see if there was a message under that stone.

Just before Sunday evening reading in Jumbo's house I slipped quickly down to the garden and lifted the stone by the lupins on our plot. But there was no note. No letter from Anne. I was sure there would have been one, and I was bitterly disappointed. Either she had not found my letter in 'the area' or, worse still, she had got it but chosen to walk – of all people – with Thomson. I just couldn't believe they were cousins. Two days later it was Walt who came to my aid. He had asked around, and the story was that Thomson and Anne were *not* related. Their mothers, it seemed, had known each other. They were neighbours and friends. That was the connection.

Chapter Seven

*P*op drew my attention to *The Bulletin*. Re-armament in Germany was gathering pace. German troops, led by Hitler, had marched into the Saar – wherever that was – and appeals by the League of Nations went unheeded. Britain was to get more aeroplanes and in the next two years the RAF was to be three times its present size.

I turned aside from *The Bulletin* and, as I did so, my eye was caught by a new notice that had been pinned below it. It was headed 'Dancing Classes', and read:

> For senior boys who would like to learn dancing, weekly classes are to be held in the gymnasium below the science block. Those wishing to join should sign their names, and class, below. Numbers will be limited and tuition will be restricted to boys in class 4B and above. Senior girls are also being invited to join.

The notice was signed A. J., the deputy headmistress, so the idea must have originated in the West Wing.

Pop was quite sarky about it. 'I bet it's the birds who asked for the classes!' He pulled a face. 'You don't want to sign up for that, Johnny. You'd be better off going to the Wireless Society, or even joining Nat Hist.'

I told him I was going to sign on. There might be a chance that Anne would be there. Before the list was taken down I counted fifteen names.

To concentrate on lessons was becoming difficult. Anne was ever present in my mind, and I envied Walt who had wasted no time in contacting Liz Cowley and gaining her agreement to walk with him.

＊

The boy called Parnell was in the same class as I was. He was a bit of a loner. Out of class he spent most of his time roller skating on the Green or working in the craft workshop. He was sullen and often in trouble, but he gained unsought-for popularity when his craftwork bore fruit. He produced what came to be known as a 'waistcoat scooter'.

It consisted of a flat board like a sledge, but in place of metal runners underneath it ran on four roller-skate wheels. Two were fixed at the rear and two more at either end of a wooden bar that pivoted right and left for steering the thing. The idea caught on and the school staff allowed other scooters to be made. Performing on them was simple enough. You pushed the scooter ahead, took a run and flung yourself flat onto it and shot swiftly down the slope of the Green. You made a ninety-degree turn at the end of the run, otherwise you would shoot through into the Japanese garden.

I was determined to try it, and one evening borrowed Parnell's scooter. It was exciting. Your chin was literally inches from the ground as you sped along. I started a bit too quickly, gathered speed and at the last minute could not manage the sharp turn left and shot down into the garden, only coming to a halt when I crashed into the sundial, fell off the thing and rolled away hitting my head and trapping my left arm. It was extremely painful, but I clambered to my feet, picked up the scooter and started to limp my way back towards the Green. As I did so I suddenly realised she was there. There in the girls' garden, hands on hips, staring. It was Anne. I stopped and stared back.

She said, 'Are you all right?'

I could only nod a yes.

'You came an awful cropper…you've hurt yourself!'

I found my voice. 'No, really, I'm all right. Just couldn't stop.'

'You've hurt your wrist!'

I shook my head, and I felt a fool. My whole arm was very painful but I was not going to admit it. I looked across to her and I knew what I was going to ask.

'Did you get my letter…under the stone?'

'I did, yes, I did. I wanted to reply, but someone might have found it…and I didn't know how to get a letter back to you.'

31

We stood in silence, both of us tongue-tied. I burned with embarrassment.

Finally, I said, 'Thomson, I saw you with him. Is he really your cousin?'

She coloured and looked away. 'I sort of knew him when I was little. Our mothers were friends. It was his idea.'

'If you're struck on him…'

'No, I'm not.' She looked straight at me, a really serious look, and I heard her say, 'If you want to I'd much rather walk with you.'

My heart leapt. I felt dizzy and stupid all at once and an awful pain was shooting through my arm and wrist. I looked straight back at her and with a shock saw her eyes were a most beautiful golden brown. I stood still, wordless. My head was thumping and I thought I heard a bird singing, then all the birds in my head were singing, scattering a shower of notes as if they fell from the sky, and then my knees gave way and still hanging on to the scooter I no longer saw her eyes as I stumbled and sank to the ground.

I heard her voice: 'Oh! Oh you *have* hurt yourself, you've cut your head!'

The school nursery was where you were sent if you got chickenpox or measles. When I came round I found myself sitting in the day room. Sister Dewhurst and John Rodgers were standing over me. I heard Sister say, 'We'd better get that head of yours cleaned up, it's a nasty cut and there's bruising. Then we'll get you to X-ray. I think you may have a broken wrist.'

Rodgers said, 'Hartside, you've been very foolish, you want your head examined as well, though I doubt they'd find much brain there…what did you think you were up to? When you've cleaned him up, Sister, I'll get him across to X-ray. The cottage hospital in Ferniehill.'

Sister nodded. She looked quite concerned. Rodgers said, 'I think you'll find, Hartside, that your foolishness will put an end to those scooters. They will no longer be allowed, they are obviously far too dangerous.'

His words only made me feel more wretched, and if the scooters were to be banned I would hardly be the most popular boy in school, more like the most unpopular…in Penn, in my class, in the dorms, everywhere. I tried not to think about it, and kept my mind on Anne with her lovely eyes, and the way she had looked at me, so serious. She it was who must have gone over to Rodgers to get help. Best of all I recalled what she had said. We could walk together as 'cousins'.

I returned to school with my left arm in a sling and my wrist in plaster. A greenstick fracture. Pop was not inclined to be sympathetic. 'Silly bugger, Johnny! You should have learned the thing proper. Better watch out for the lads with the scooters!'

Luck seemed to have deserted me. The following Sunday it poured with rain. There was no walking on the Green. I would have to wait another week – and hope that Anne would not change her mind.

'Crumbs!' yelled Squeak. 'Look at *that*! Holy mackerel!'

We were filing through the colonnade on the way to the dorm when we suddenly came to a halt. Everyone started shouting and pointing to the terrace.

It was white all over and the entire surface as far as the centre-library steps was covered. As I gazed a chamber pot from a dorm window came hurtling down, then another, and another. They exploded and shattered into fragments on the asphalt. It looked as if every jerry had been thrown from window after window and smashed to bits below.

My chums broke ranks and tore across the terrace, kicking and then picking up fragments for closer examination. Some of the lads were hooting with laughter and cheering, until Rodgers emerged and we were ushered back into line and marched up to bed. Sure enough, there were no jerry pots to be found. There was usually one under each bed. If the other dorms were the same as ours at least one hundred must have been hurled from the windows.

As far as I knew, no boy had ever been expelled from school. But now the finger was pointed. The boy was named. It was Parnell, the popular inventor of the waistcoat scooter. It was disclosed that he was the culprit. He had flown into a rage because of the ban on scooters and taken his revenge by destroying 'school property'. I felt desolate. It was my fault. If I had not crashed that scooter and got them banned Parnell would still be with us. We gave him the best send-off we could devise. We had no flags to fly, so we fastened bath towels, and face

33

towels of all colours, to the handles of brushes and hung them outside the washroom windows.

For two days no one spoke to me, except Walt and Jack. 'Could be worse,' Jack said. 'You're lucky the scooter boys haven't set about you.'

Chapter Eight

'Left foot, right foot, in alternation!' she called. 'Now, Gracie liebling, we are to commence, please!'

The music began, with notes from Gracie at the piano for our first dancing lesson in the gym. On arrival I counted fifteen boys and about twenty girls. We assembled on either side of the floor and sat down on the benches, which had been set against the wall bars and beneath the looped climbing ropes. The vaulting horses, hair mats and other gear had been cleared away to the far end.

Before the class began Arabella Joy looked in, accompanied by Helen, the school's head cook. Some comic said it was Helen with the face that launched a thousand chips. She was a very pretty woman. I couldn't figure out why she had come to the gym, unless it was to act as supervisor.

A. J. clapped her hands for attention. 'It is very gratifying,' she began, 'to see so many of you here. I would like to introduce your teachers, Miss Voss and Miss Gracie. They have a dancing school at Rawdon and it is very noble of them to come all the way up here. You should consider yourselves very lucky boys and girls. Dancing, as I am sure you know, is not difficult. This is ballroom dancing and I am sure you will enjoy it. Righty-ho, Miss Voss, over to you!'

With that cheerful introduction, she left and Helen the cook took her seat by the door. I stole a good look at our teachers. Gracie, at the piano, had a mop of reddish hair. She wore specs, had a plump face and hot complexion and very bright lipstick. Miss Voss had blonde hair, which was plaited and wound round in a bun. It looked like a large pastry cake. When she spoke she had a funny accent.

With Cumberland, Walt, Wilson A. J., Mortimer A. V. and the other boys I stared across the floor. Second from the left she was there sitting beside Liz Cowley. All the girls looked pretty nice in their summer dresses, yellow or blue. Anne wore yellow. She smiled and gave a little signal with her hand. I signalled back with my right hand – my left arm was still in a sling. Apart from Anne and Liz I did not know any of the other girls.

'We begin!' called Miss Voss. Then she rapped out, 'Each boy take a girl and stand opposite! To learn is simple. This is called the foxtrot.'

Several boys spluttered with mirth, made their hands like paws and pretended to be foxes.

'Halt!' shouted the Voss. 'Not animals! And we have too many girls. Six of you go out…we change places when I say.'

There was a fluttering among them and some argument, until the Voss strode across and singled out six girls. They retired to the far end of the hall and, with evident displeasure, sat down cross-legged on the mats.

Fifteen boys and fifteen girls then rose to their feet and advanced to the middle of the floor. Walt positioned himself opposite Liz and I did the same opposite Anne.

'Gracie liebling, for a moment wait! To start, each boy places hands on girl's shoulders. Girls do the same. Now, girls, step back six paces, left foot, right foot alternating, and boys do six paces forward in time to the music!'

She nodded across to the piano. Hardly had the first notes begun when the Voss clapped her hands and shouted, 'Halt!' She then marched across to me.

'You are one arm only – you cannot do this. Go and sit down.' She turned to Anne.

'You also, please!'

To my surprise Anne replied, 'Thank you, but we can manage, I think. One arm is enough.'

The Voss looked astonished. She said, testily, 'Later for the holding you cannot, one arm is not good.'

Anne stood her ground. 'I know, but could we try it, please?'

Summoning my courage I joined in. 'It is not impossible and we *would* like to try.'

This seemed to give the Voss pause. Then she stared hard at us and barked: 'For this time only I will allow it. The rest of you, notice, please. They are positive and that is good. Always positive for dancing.'

Gracie's head appeared unexpectedly above the piano. 'Yes, you see,' she piped up. 'In dancing you must always be positive!' And she added cheerfully, 'That's the ticket!'

We began again, left foot, right foot, the girls stepping back, the rest of us treading forward. Anne looked directly at me, pursed her lips, raised her eyebrows – and winked. My right hand was on her left shoulder. I gave it a little squeeze as we moved off. I recognised the tune. It was on one of my gramophone records. It had a nice lilt and made you want to dance.

For the next part of the lesson we had to get closer. I put my right arm around Anne's waist and pulled her gently towards me. My left arm in the sling got in the way.

'No you don't,' she whispered. 'You can't. Not allowed!'

I looked down the line and saw Walt and Liz were holding on tight. We were back to arms' length. 'Tell you one thing,' I said. 'On Sunday there will be no more rain. The sun is going to shine.'

'You have arranged it?'

'Of course!'

She smiled. 'Good. After meeting I'll come to the end of the terrace.'

We stepped along to the rhythm and learned to do a right turn, then a reverse turn, and I felt we were doing quite well and hoped Voss was watching. Next time, she said, we would learn the waltz.

When the lesson ended, Helen, who had supervised our progress, called the girls to the door, and Bellerby, the science master, appeared. The girls filed out and he made us wait until, many with a backward glance and a wave, they disappeared. He and Helen then spoke together for a while before he ushered us out and back to the East Wing.

That night in the dorm after lights out Walt wanted to talk about the dancing lesson. He stole across to my bed and tried to climb in beside me.

'Walter, no! There's no room. My arm!'

'Put it above your head, under the pillow.'

I didn't, but he put it there for me and eased his way under the bedclothes.

That night was the first time but not the last time that Walter came to my bed. This was summer with blazing days and sultry nights, which seemed to encourage warmth, affection and a physical languor and longing. Everything spoke of love. In the Japanese garden there were small trees, but also some giants, beech and elm. They towered above our plots, their heavy boughs and branches bending low as if to watch and listen in the still air.

I was right when I had boasted to Anne that Sunday would be sunny. I woke early and lay awake listening through our open windows to the familiar humming of the pasteurisation plant in the farm below. I was impatient, and eager to walk with Anne, but the meeting for worship came first. Just an hour, but it seemed much longer, and I was glad when Ma Neatley rose to her feet.

'Friends,' she began, 'yesterday I was driving back to school after a meeting I had to attend. And I was so forgetful. I took the wrong turning. At the crossroads I made a left turn when I should have gone straight on. I reached home safely of course, but it started me thinking. In life there are many crossroads. We see several roads which lead in different directions but…which one should we take? We may see one which looks to be the right one, it is green and sweet as a country lane. It's easy to chose that route and off we go quite cheerfully. But alas, after a mile or two the road breaks up. There are big holes and even boulders barring our way. Clearly the wrong road, and it makes you realise that appearances can be misleading.

'The older ones among you will know those lines of Shakespeare's. The Prince of Morocco is seeking Portia's hand in marriage, and to win her he has to pass a test…to choose the correct casket of three that are placed before him. One is lead, one is silver and one is gold. He chooses the wrong one, as the message inside the casket tells him:

'All that glisters is not gold,
Often have you heard that told.

'Alas! He made the wrong choice, he took the wrong road. Perhaps he should have chosen the casket of lead, with its message:

'Who chooses me must give and hazard
All he hath.

'That was the way our Lord Jesus chose. He chose the hard and bitter road. He gave His life and in so doing He gave us a map to help us choose the right way.'

✷

She appeared as she had promised at the far end of the terrace by the girls' colonnade, and began to walk. I waited by the library steps until she was at my side. I took her hand. She smiled and said, 'Hello! Do I call you John or Johnny?'

I heard her, but could say nothing. This was Anne with her hair tied back with a gold ribbon that matched her eyes. She was wearing a blue dress this time, bare legged and with sandals. We joined the other couples walking.

'Have you lost your tongue?'

'Sorry! I was just, well, I was thinking it's been a long time, I mean it seems a long time…'

She squeezed my hand. A reassuring squeeze. 'Is your wrist better now?'

'John,' I said. 'But sometimes I'm called Johnny.'

'I like Johnny. It's more friendly.'

'Yes. The plaster is coming off tomorrow, I think.'

'No more scooters?'

I found my tongue. 'The dancing class! Did you like it?'

'Of course. Except Miss Voss. I think she is German.'

We reached the end of the Green and turned to walk back up towards the terrace. I was sure we were watched. Masters and mistresses, I supposed, eyeing the scene, trying to judge if the walking with friends was going to be a success. I didn't think I was doing very well. Ma Neatley's 'sermon' had got to me. I could only think of choices…'all that glisters is not gold'.

I said, 'Were you at the meeting? I didn't see you there.'

'I saw you, you were listening very hard to Ma Neatley.'

We turned again at the bottom of the Green by the big trees. They were watching. They were listening. They approved of the walking. And of Anne.

'The trees like you,' I said.

She offered that very serious look, and shook her head. 'You say such strange things, Johnny!' Then she laughed. 'I expect it's with crashing on the scooter, and hitting your head.'

I said I would explain another time.

'Next Sunday?' she said.

'Yes, next Sunday.'

For the first time in weeks the sky turned as grey as the weathered walls of the school. Gone was the sunshine flashing on the cupola above the East Wing and turning the weathervane to gold. It was Sunday after the meeting and it was dull, dull, dull. Worst of all, the rain came and there was no walking on the Green. I was bitterly disappointed.

From the classroom window I could look across to the West Wing, and I was sure I could see Anne sitting there at her window. It must be Anne, I told myself. I waved, and I think she waved back. I thought…if we can't walk and talk we could still be in touch. I opened up the window as wide as I could, got out my gramophone, placed it on the sill, wound it up and chose a record.

My loudest one was 'The Charleston'. Even if Anne did not hear it cheered me up a bit. Walt came through to listen. He was miserable too because he could not walk with Liz. Then half the class came in…Pop Wilkinson, Cumberland, Mortimer A. V. and lots of others. They started jumping around and Wilson A. J. leapt onto a desk and started trying to tap dance. They were making an awful din, so I tried to quiet them down and played one by Rodgers and Hart that I really liked. Then Squeak Whiting burst into the room.

'Rodgers on the prowl,' he yelled. 'Too much row, you'll have to stop!'

'It's not a loud one,' I replied.

Squeak persisted. 'No! Honest, it's not just you, Johnny. Thomson's up in fifth right overhead and he's playing *his* gram!'

So, that was it. If Anne had turned him down he would get his own back by trying to drown me out. He probably had a bigger record collection than mine. Cumberland made one of his rare observations. 'He doesn't learn, does he? We could pinch his records, that would shut him up. After all, he tried to steal yours, Johnny.'

I said no. It would only cause more trouble. Before a debate began, as Squeak had warned, Bill Rodgers appeared and closed us down.

Chapter Nine

T he latest item in *The Bulletin* reported that there would be conscription in Germany and that the air force there was called the Luftwaffe, and a high-ranking soldier called Goering was to be in charge. I stepped into the wireless room because I knew several of the older boys listened in to the news there. Sometimes a notice went up: 'No Entry. Keep Out!' I suppose that was sensible because the wireless boys played about with high voltages. Owen Hardwick – a senior boy who was in charge – said I could stay for a few minutes. He was listening in with headphones and writing in a notebook. Presently he removed the headphones and I asked him what he had been writing.

'Stuff on Germany. A report says Hitler is getting more submarines built. In reply Baldwin has announced it's a time of emergency so we have to have more bombers and more pilots trained. Then there's stuff I didn't quite catch but something about an agreement with Germany. Hitler will be allowed to build five battleships and fifteen cruisers, and some aircraft carriers and destroyers!'

I asked Owen if he was going to pin his stuff on the board outside. He said, why not? Then I had to go. It was the day for those rounds.

There was one good thing, the rain was so heavy the girls on the West Wing would scarcely be able to see us. Round followed round, I got stitch, the pace got slower and we all began to tire. It took us forty minutes to complete the rounds, after which Rodgers sent us through to the showers to get soaked all over again. Even Pop, who was really tough, was complaining. 'It gets your ankles…not like on grass.'

The odd thing was that running on the Green never hurt your feet when you were playing cricket there. The following day the rain had cleared and playground cricket was in full swing. Clubby Nash, the art master, was supervising. Except – his idea of supervising was to join in the game. His clubfoot never seemed to bother him. He was a steady bat and a crafty bowler. The stumps were set in a block of wood and we were not allowed to use proper cricket balls, they were reserved for our house matches played on the cricket field. Here, on the asphalt, we had to use an RCC – a rubber covered compound – which was seamless. Even so, Clubby managed to bowl a half-decent off-spin and at the crease he could clout the ball clean into the Garden for a six. I was a bowler, but as a bat I usually went in at five in the house matches.

After that day of rain Clubby and I were drawn on the same side and we both unexpectedly and very annoyingly got out. I only scored six and was then clean bowled by Thomson to his hardly disguised delight. After that Clubby and I sat on the bench at the lower end of the Green. He said, 'Your artwork is a lot better than your batting. I see you've been doing some more drawing. The back court. Using Conté crayon.'

I nodded. I had made drawings of most of the school buildings and was getting stuck for subjects. 'Do you think – well, would I be allowed to draw some of the farm buildings, sir?'

'Don't know, Hartside. I'd have to check with the head, probably the farm manager too.'

'Would you, sir? While there's good weather, I mean.'

I was sucking up and he knew it, but he didn't mind. I was good at drawing and painting, so was one of his favourites.

Sunday dawned hot and dry and we were able to walk on the Green again. The number of sisters, brothers, cousins, half-cousins and second or even third cousins had increased. Walking with a friend was becoming dangerously successful.

'Saw you playing cricket,' Anne said. 'You got out.'

'I only scored six. It was Thomson bowling.' She nodded and a silence opened up between us. After a while we found ourselves talking families. I had no idea where Anne's home was. I told her we lived in the country about forty miles from the school. 'It's called Yearsby Hall, quite old. Georgian.'

'It must be a big house, then.'

I nodded and explained that it was in a long valley and that there were two other houses quite near called Sproxton, and The Grange. I asked about her home and she surprised me by saying that she grew up in the South but that her parents now lived in the West Indies. 'We had a farm…not a very large one and my dad didn't like it – he could never get enough help. He decided to sell up and then applied for a government job…a kind of agricultural advisor. He got posted to the colonies.'

I was astonished. 'So where do you live?'

She wrinkled her nose. 'It's not very nice. I'm a sort of lodger really.' In the holidays she said she went to an auntie in the Black Country. Burslem. Her aunt was a widow. Her husband had been the manager of a pottery firm there.

I stopped in my tracks. 'That's terrible! Do you ever see your mum and dad?'

'Well, I haven't, not since they went away. It's a government appointment…I mean he's responsible to the government, but I don't know much about it, except he likes it there.'

I asked her where 'there' was and she said it was an island in the Caribbean, in the Lesser Antilles.

I had no idea where the Lesser Antilles were, but did not want to show my ignorance. We had just reached the terrace when the bell rang, signalling the end of the walk. I released her hand and just had time to say, 'But…that's thousands of miles away!'

She nodded, and as she turned away she said, 'It's called Dominica.'

I was still coming to terms with what Anne had said, and wondered if she would have to leave school to stay with her mum and dad half a world away. When I told Walt about it I asked him if he knew where the Lesser Antilles were.

'Dunno, Johnny. We could look in the geog room…there are those big maps on the walls.'

In the geography room my question was quickly answered. On the large map showing Florida, the Panama Canal and the whole of the Caribbean Sea were the Lesser Antilles, a string of islands curving north and westwards to the Virgin Islands and Puerto Rico. They stretched all the way from Grenada to Antigua. Dominica was a small island in the middle between Martinique and St Kitts. I said to Walt, 'It's a devil of a way off. That's where Anne's mum and dad live.'

'Yeah? They probably have slaves, y' know, blackies for servants who wear no clothes and live on bananas and coconuts!'

I told him not to be so daft. It was no laughing matter.

Mum's letter said she and Dad were coming at half term to take Paddy and me out for the day. A Saturday treat. That cheered me up. In my next letter-writing, which was compulsory each week, I asked a special favour. 'Can we go somewhere, not just the school inn? And can I bring some chums? My new friend is Anne, I told you in my last letter. We walk up and down together on Sundays. Also Walter and his friend Liz. And Pop Wilkinson. He was a Barnardo's boy and never gets taken out, and Anne's mum and dad live in Dominica so she has no one to treat her either.'

It was asking a lot. In her reply Mum wrote: 'Johnny darling, with Paddy as well it would be an awful crush, we'd never all fit into the Star, it's only a four-seater. But seeing that you have chosen friends we'll have to see what we can do. I'll ask your father if he could get Belinda on the road again.'

Belinda was a yellow charabanc, an open-top affair. It had been put together by Dad with the help of Bill Glaister. He was an engineer and had a motor business with places all over the north of England. Belinda was kept in our garage and was rarely taken out. It had what Mr Glaister called a revolutionary gear-change system, but it was not good on hills. It must have been improved because the good news was that Dad promised Belinda would be okay and there would be room for us all. When I told the others Anne was the doubtful one.

'I don't think Ma Neatley will allow me and Liz out for the whole day, I mean it would be very unusual. Normally it's half a day and only with your own parents.'

Walt and I debated. We decided the best plan would be for my mum to write to Ma Neatley…just to set her mind at rest. Mum agreed. I don't know what she put, but it worked. Permission was granted as long as the girls were back in school no later than 6.30 p.m.

I jumped for joy. So did Walt. A day out with Anne and Liz! Pop was as pleased as Punch. 'Johnny boy! Where d' you reckon they'll take us?'

I told him probably we'd go home.

'Strawberries and cream,' Paddy added. 'We could have a knock of tennis as well!' But we didn't really know. It was to be a surprise.

Chapter Ten

On previous visits the Star car had never caused a stir. I used to watch for its arrival from Taffy Jenkins' tailor's shop with its two windows looking out to 'the area'. But when on this occasion, for the first time, Belinda purred through the gates, she was the star. There were faces looking down from every single washroom window and a medley of cheers and boos went up as Pop, Walter, Paddy and I climbed aboard. Mum and Dad turned in their seats and smiled a welcome. Dad started up, swerved round 'the area' and out to the main road. Then it was down Back Lane past the farm and the nursery and into the Girls' Small where Anne and Liz were waiting. They were like twins, standing side by side, one with blonde hair, the other with black, and both wearing their blue summer dresses with yellow cardigans tied around their waists. They put on their straw boaters with the school colours. A. J. stepped through an open French window, spoke a few words to them and then turned to Mum and Dad. 'Take good care of them,' I heard her say. 'They're my favourites and do please have them back no later than 6.30 or Ma Neatley will have *me* on the carpet! And you boys, behave yourselves!'

Dad said, 'Don't worry! Lovely day for a drive! You girls climb in and you'd better remove your hats before the breeze does it for you.'

We all took our places, Mum and Dad in front. Anne wedged herself between Paddy and me, and Liz did the same with Pop and Walt behind us. I heard Pop mutter, 'It's buggy marvellous!' Dad fired Belinda up again and we turned on to Back Lane and out to the main road. I was excited. I could feel Anne's warmth through her light summer dress and her knee gave me a friendly nudge. Dad put his foot down and we started to motor. We couldn't talk much as we swooshed along, it was too noisy. I held Anne's hand and sat back to watch trees and clouds and patches of blue fly past overhead.

Nearly an hour later we turned into a road I thought was familiar. I knew where we were going now. Down to the coast. The final route was through flat fields of golden corn with sudden glimpses of the sea. A floor of diamonds winking and blazing under a dome of blue. Then there were buildings. And more buildings as we swooped down into the town and on to a bumpy road that led to the castle. It was Scarborough. The famous holiday town.

Mum said, 'Turn back to the town centre, darling, I have to pop into you know where.'

We didn't know what she meant but Dad did. Back we went and turned into a lane beside a big department store. Dad called, 'Everybody out!' So we clambered down and Mum took Anne and Liz aside. 'You'll want to powder your noses, so you're to come with me. Darling, take the boys for an ice cream or something. There's that café just round the corner with a view of the harbour. Girls, come along, we're to go in here.' So saying she ushered them through the front door of the store.

Walt and I looked at each other. I wondered what Mum was up to. Dad called, 'Come on, you lads, we'll stretch our legs. Down to the café. I don't want to leave the car unattended for too long!'

Walt said, 'Super motor, Mr Hartside!'

'So far, so good,' replied Dad.

The café with a view of the sea was like an old-fashioned cottage with a small paved garden in front and a few tables and chairs, some of which were occupied by elderly couples. It was Walt who spoke up.

'Excuse me, sir, but why have the girls gone in the store, and we've come here?'

'Ah! You'd better ask my wife,' he smiled. 'Now, what's it to be…coffee, ice cream, ginger beer?'

A waitress appeared. Pop looked up and said, 'If there's sandwiches, sir, can I have sandwiches?'

'No. No sandwiches, just a drink. We're going to have some lunch, so don't spoil your appetite!' He plucked a cigarette from his silver case and fitted it into his tortoiseshell holder. Pop grinned and asked, 'Can we have a ciggy, sir?'

Walt said, 'Pop! Behave yourself!'

Dad laughed. 'Good day for golf,' he said. 'D' you lads play? I know Paddy would like to, but he hasn't got his clubs yet.'

Pop said, 'Yeah! I'd like to play an' all, but it's just a game for nobs, ain't it?'

We all laughed and felt more at ease. Paddy chose a knickerbocker glory, Pop had ginger beer and Walt and I had hot chocolate.

When we met Mum back at the car I noticed that the girls were each hugging a brightly wrapped parcel. Shopping of course. We all climbed back on board and drove down to park on the South Cliff where the big white hotels fairly dazzled in the sun. I remembered it because one summer we took a flat there next to the Crown Hotel. There were big swing doors and a doorman in a smart blue uniform. We disembarked again. This was where we were to have our lunch.

'Hell fire,' murmured Walt. 'This is very posh!'

The table was close to a big window looking out over the esplanade and the tops of the trees to the wide blue sea with brown cliffs just visible to the south. Walt was nodding and smiling, and I felt quite proud of Mum and Dad. Liz said, 'Mrs Hartside, can we open our parcels…the boys are dying to know what we've got!'

'Of course, dear, as long as you don't spill anything on them.' Anne smiled across the table at me. 'It's like Christmas!'

'Except there's no turkey,' said Pop.

'Just you wait a minute, my lad,' said Dad. 'We'll have a look.' He asked the waiter to bring a menu and studied it. An expectant silence. 'Well, you're in luck, young man. There's chicken, lamb, duck, fish…or turkey. How about that!'

Liz exclaimed, 'Goodness! It *is* Christmas!' We all laughed. I had a good look at Liz. I had never studied her before, but she was very pretty, quick to smile. I suspected she might be a bit wild, but I liked her and I thought come the time she'd give Walt a good run for his money.

Anne was solemnly opening her parcel. 'Look! It's pure silk!' She turned to Mum. 'Thank you again, very, very much, it's far too good!'

'Well, you chose it, my dear!' She tapped her nose with her forefinger and winked across at me. 'Very good taste, Johnny.'

I was pleased. Liz said, 'It's so kind of you, Mrs Hartside, but you really shouldn't buy us prezzies.'

'Well, I couldn't bear it any longer, darlings. In the car, I mean. Whizzing along, and your hair flying all over, so I decided you should both have scarves. Always wear a scarf in an open tourer, you see, knot it under your chin.'

Then we all tucked in and had different stuff. I had crab, then lamb and potatoes. Pop chose turkey breast in a sauce with lots of veg. Walt and Liz both went for chicken with green salad.

'Walt said, 'We never get anything like this at school. We do get soup but it's more like potato water, and often there's mince or fishcakes and sprouts, and rice pudding.'

'That's semolina,' added Liz, nodding.

'No,' interrupted Anne, 'it's tapioca or sago.'

We stuffed ourselves with strawberries and sweet biscuits, and Walt, Pop and I were allowed a glass of Bulmer's cider. Paddy said if he ate any more he would bust. Dad lit a cigar. He said there was some cricket being played at the county ground and we could go and watch. 'If you'd rather,' Mum said, 'you could go for a walk. If you haven't seen them before it's quite pretty in the Cliff Gardens through the trees and down to the spa. There's usually a band playing there.'

A short debate followed. Pop and Paddy wanted the cricket. Walt and I preferred a walk with the girls, so we went our different ways. Mum chose to go back to the shops and Dad said he would take Pop and Paddy in the car to the cricket. We were all to meet up back at the café. 'Five thirty sharp!' said Dad. 'And take care in the gardens, it's a bit of a jungle.'

Before we set off he gave Pop, Paddy, Walt and me a £1 note.

It was quite a step along the road past the cliff tram.

'It's really for old people,' I explained. 'They use it when they come back up from the spa.'

The girls chatted and thought Mum and Dad were wizard. Anne said I was very lucky to have parents like them. 'I'll write them a letter, shall I?'

A bit of a jungle, Dad had said. I'd been down before, but I'd forgotten how steep the paths were, winding in and out of the trees and shrubs. As we descended I could hear the band playing. I recognised a tune…'Button up Your Overcoat'. Liz and Walt stepped on ahead. Anne let me put my arm around her waist. She was very slim. The bandstand at the spa was bulging with musicians. We plumped down on deckchairs and sat among the old folk to listen for a while.

Seagulls swooped and mewed overhead. On the beach a group of workmen were busy hammering tall girders into the sand. We took a stroll along the promenade to where the concrete ended and two army trucks were parked. Then we retraced our steps and started back up to the paths through the trees. A steep climb. Walt and Liz went ahead, but we loitered, took our time. Halfway up we came across a small rose garden, a flat, paved area surrounded by a box hedge. We walked in beneath a pergola. Trees crowded round and through their branches thin wisps of mist appeared, a sea fret blowing in, cooling the air and wafting music up to us. I took Anne's hand.

She smiled. 'Such trees! You said trees liked me, why did you say that?'

I slipped my arm round her waist. The band was playing a waltz. '"Three O'Clock In The Morning",' I said. 'Shall we dance?' So we did. Solemn, slow steps, the trees attending above the roses, lavender and thyme. A whole family of trees circling as if we were on a carousel.

Anne softly recited their names in three-four time to the music. 'Sycamore and chestnut, rowan, japonica, hazel and larch.' We held each other so solemnly, so carefully and we did not speak, but we kissed and Anne's eyes smiled. Then – a cry from above. Walter calling:

'Come on, you two, you'll be late!'

'Anne! I care for you so much…I want to see you always, not just on Sundays…'

Then words ran out. Silence. The music ended. She turned up her face and kissed my lips and I thought I would burn. She said, 'I know, Johnny, me too.' Then she grinned. 'I don't see why not, we're cousins, aren't we?'

We turned back through the pergola and climbed uphill. The rest of the day floated past like the mist. Going back in the car we sat very close together, her head on my shoulder with the silk scarf faintly perfumed and soft against my cheek.

Chapter Eleven

*I*n the week following our day by the sea a letter from home arrived.

Johnny darling,

It was lovely to meet your friends and I can see why you like Anne. Is she a very serious girl? Your father thinks she has a clever look and could be brainy. It was such luck we went to the coast last Saturday. We have heard that the beach and the promenade are being closed. Sea defences, in case of war, are being built so we were just in time. Tell Paddy we have the Slazenger and we'll keep it for him until the hols. And he was right about the Davis Cup team, it will include knobbly knees Jones and Filby. Must fly! The workmen are coming to start digging some sort of air-raid shelter in the paddock, *and* – of all things – we're to have gasmask drill!

I told Walt and Pop about it. Walt said it would probably come to nothing. 'The League of Nations won't allow it.'

I did not feel so sure, and Pop said *The Bulletin* reported bad things. 'It's all about the Jews who really are in trouble. Hitler has taken away their rights…sounds buggy awful. They can't get jobs, no pensions, and they can't be teachers or anything.'

The rest of the news was no better. We tried not to think about these unsettling events. The summer sun and blue skies had returned and in any case there was equally bad news much closer to home; a lot of swotting had to be done for the end-of-term exams. I was determined to do well enough to get moved up to 5A or 5B in the autumn term.

I actually looked forward to the art exam. In class Clubby Nash told me he had obtained permission for me to do some studies of farm buildings, horses and carts, hay rakes – that sort of thing. I could go on a Wednesday afternoon or a Saturday. All I had to do was to inform the master on duty. I did not tell him that I had a plan in mind. I told Anne I would be at the farm on Saturday afternoon and if she could slip away we could meet there. She did not sound very sure but said there might be 'a possibility'. And there was.

Saturday could not come soon enough. During evening break, to quell my impatience, I went down to the canal and thought to make a drawing of a tree I liked. I loved the trees there in the winter with their tracery of bare boughs and branches, but in summer in full leaf they were less of a challenge. After staring at my tree long and hard I fancied I saw – as the leaves moved together – the face of an old man. I think it was a man. He nodded as the breeze stirred the leaves. It was an oddly shaped face like that of an ancient. Then his expression changed from a benign smile to a fractured, troubled look as the leaves responded to the wind. Then abruptly it disappeared, like the grin on the face of the cat in *Alice in Wonderland.*

As she walked towards me, a wicker basket over her arm, and framed in the archway of the barn, I thought that was what I should do, a drawing of her then and there. A true picture. It stained my mind, indelible like a transfer that would never fade. She looked over my shoulder and smiled down at my pad of cartridge paper.

'You haven't drawn very much!'

'No, I was trying to decide.'

'Decide what, Johnny?'

'The composition. I want to try it from here inside the barn and looking out to the byre.' In fact, seeing her so close, and smiling, I felt quite odd and began to wonder if, like the Cheshire cat, *her* smile might disappear.

She set down her basket and said, 'I've collected about twelve but there are more, I'll have to go and get them.'

In the basket were large, brown eggs with bits of straw stuck to them. 'New laid,' she said. 'Some are still warm. They're beautiful.'

I told her I had been drawing trees, and how I had seen the likeness of a face there.

'Oh, Johnny! You and your trees! You've got trees on your mind.'

I took her hand. 'No, it's you. You are on my mind...all the time.'

She coloured, studied her feet, then murmured, 'Yes, I know.'

I drew her to me, held her closely and sought her lips, and it wasn't difficult because she offered them, she wanted to be kissed. Then she pushed me away. 'Johnny, I'll have to go, we can't be seen here together...it's out of bounds.'

I told her I wanted to talk, that we never had time in school. I wanted it to be like that rose garden by the sea when we could be alone, quite alone, and not just walking and being watched, and being treated as if we were some kind of experiment.

'Well, I can't be long,' she said, 'someone might come looking, there'd be an awful row.'

'I know we mustn't be seen...and we won't be.' I had spotted the ladder leading up to the hayloft. A place to hide. We climbed up and lay back on the sweet-smelling hay, soft as a cushion, beneath the low beams, and listened. A still air. No one about. We were safe. The only sound was the light jingle of chains or a harness maybe, and the rustle and breathing of the cows in the byre.

We kissed and I tasted the sweetness of her lips, and she let me touch the soft rise of her breasts. She closed her eyes and began to breathe more rapidly.

'No, Johnny, we mustn't, we can't, I don't want to.'

'Anne, I love you...'

She clasped my hands, raised them to her lips. 'I know, Johnny, I know, but...just friends. We'll always be friends.'

Again, that serious, studied, almost concerned look as my cheeks burned and our eyes met. 'Promise,' I said.

'I promise. Best friends. Always.'

My heart jumped. The words sang in my head. I folded her in my arms but she pushed me away.

'Listen,' she whispered. 'Listen, I think there's someone down there!'

Sure enough, I heard footsteps, heavy steps and coming closer. I was about to peer over the edge of the loft when the top of the ladder suddenly rose up and was lifted away. Disaster. Unless the ladder returned very soon we were stuck. I lay motionless trying not to panic. Then I looked over the edge again. There was no one to be seen. It was a long way down.

'We'll have to jump. Can you do it?'

She nodded. 'And be quick, Johnny, I have to go, we've been too long already.'

I said, 'I'll go first.'

It wasn't difficult. I held on firmly to the edge, lowered myself then let go. I landed safely and rolled over. I got to my feet and called to her to be quick. 'Hold on to the edge, it's not so far. I'll catch you!'

She did as I said. She let go and fell into my arms. We both toppled to the ground. I pulled her to her feet and with a wildly beating heart I held her close. A kiss for a brave girl.

'No, Johnny, I really do have to go!' She paused then exclaimed: 'Oh no! Look!'

On landing I must have kicked her basket over. Half the eggs had rolled out and were broken. Anne quickly dusted herself down and gathered up her basket as I ran to the corner of the barn. 'All clear! Come on!'

I watched as she waved then scampered away down Back Lane. No use crying over broken eggs, I thought, and anyway she had some more to collect. I retrieved my pad and pencils but I no longer felt like drawing the barn.

Chapter Twelve

*A*s the end of term came into sight spirits were uplifted. The days to the long summer holiday were counted down. I was as keen as anyone to escape from school – except the thought of not seeing Anne for two months was awful and I became moody and upset. Squeak Whiting observed, 'You've got it bad, Johnny.'

He and Squirt Fountain, a fair-haired lad with freckles, always chalked the days to 'freedom' on the blackboard in our classroom. Seventeen white strokes remained.

For the very first time there was to be an end-of-term dance in the gym for senior boys and girls, after which I would go home with Paddy to Yearsby and Anne would leave for her aunt's home in the Potteries. The Black Country, it was called. Pop would go to Macclesfield and Walter to his stepfather somewhere in Northumberland.

The Bulletin did not cheer me, even though some of the items were probably weeks out of date. Mussolini's troops had invaded Ethiopia and the Emperor of Abyssinia, Haile Selassie and his troops had been defeated. Another fascist, General Franco, had left Morocco for Spain leading an army of rebels. There was unrest and violence everywhere. The only other person who shared my unease was Jack Emslie, the 'wise owl' of Penn house. He was far from cheerful when I met him studying the notice board.

'It looks to me,' he muttered, 'as if everything is going fascist. I talked with Jumbo and he said so.'

The only good news was that the *Queen Mary* had crossed the Atlantic to New York in just over four days – an amazing speed. It was a short letter from Mum that told me about it. 'We're all so excited,' she wrote. 'Just think, on her next crossing your father will be on board! He has to go with the works' chairman. It's to do with business in New

York. I'd have loved to go with him but of course I can't. It costs at least £37 10s, and in any case I want to be here for you and Paddy.'

When I told Walt and the others that my dad was going on the *Queen Mary* they were definitely impressed – especially Pop. 'Buggy me!' he exclaimed. 'But that don't surprise me, Johnny boy! I could tell your dad was rich, with that big car, and smokin' cigars an' all!'

I did not want to brag. 'Not rich,' I replied. 'But I think he's quite important in his work.' I was going to tell Anne, and it was Mum's letter that gave me an idea. It was worth a try. If Dad was going away perhaps I could have Anne to stay for a week or two – if she was allowed.

The band in the gym was a surprise. I expected it would be Voss with Gracie on the piano, but instead it was members of the Raskell and Dewthorpe Colliery Band. Trumpet, accordion, clarinet, sax, piano and drums. The gym was crowded with more than the learners at the dancing class, but as before A. J. was in charge. She made a short speech of welcome and added, 'Now we don't want all you girls in one corner and the boys in another. The idea is to mix you all up, practise your steps and really get to know the dances.' She then explained that in the entrance hall there would be lemonade when the band retired for their supper break. She said, 'Helen has deserted her kitchens tonight and will be here with the refreshments, assisted by Mr Bellerby.'

He was the science master and had probably just stepped down from the labs upstairs to keep order.

Pushing her way through the throng Anne came to my side. She looked a treat with her shiny hair taken back and tied in a bunch with a tortoiseshell clasp. No school uniforms this time but a smart black skirt and a pale blue jumper over a white blouse. She smiled and whispered, 'Just as well refreshments do not include eggs!'

Walter with Liz appeared. 'Hi there, hoofers!' he called. 'You in the mood?'

We were all in the mood. The band struck up and off we went, bumping our way through other couples enthusiastically showing off.

This time we did not have to hold each other at arms' length, and, hoping Bellerby would not see, we snuggled unashamedly as we tried our steps with Anne light and easy in my arms. We started with a slow foxtrot. I had the tune in my record collection. 'Do Do Do What You Did Did Did Before, Baby!' I knew the words.

'You love music, Johnny?'

'Course! I could play this one for you on my gram.'

Another one I liked was 'My Heart Stood Still!'

She snuggled closer. 'I like that. It's a nice song.'

It was just so good, so unexpected. A magical evening. There should have been nightingales. Instead there was that funny old band as if it was playing just for Anne and me.

I thought…when the interval comes I'll ask her about the holidays and if she might come to Yearsby. I would have asked her then and there if we had not all been suddenly distracted. A shout went up. Couples around us stopped dancing. High above our heads and swinging across from wall to wall was a loop of the climbing-rope. Clinging to it like a monkey and grinning and waving was Pop. He must have climbed the wall bars to grab the rope and launch himself like an acrobat. The band stopped playing and Bellerby strode forward.

'Wilkinson! Stop that! Come down immediately, and tie that rope back. *Now*!'

Amid the laughing and cheering I heard Walt shout, 'You joining a circus, Pop?'

'Down!' yelled Bellerby. 'This minute – you're in trouble, Wilkinson!'

Pop, still grinning, did as he was told. Anne whispered, 'I think your friend's mad! But…he's very funny!'

Bellerby called, 'Clive Marr, where are you? Take over, will you! The rest of you continue with the dancing!' So saying he seized Pop by the elbow and marched him away as the band resumed. Anne asked 'Who's Clive Marr?'

'Prefect. Head boy. He's in Fox house. A nice chap.'

We danced on. Bellerby had still not returned by the interval for the band. Pulling Anne with me I made a dash for the doors before the other dancers had disentangled themselves. Once into the entrance hall and past the table with the lemonade, I took her hand and ushered her up the stairs to the science labs.

'Johnny! What are you doing?'

I told her not to worry about the lemonade, I wanted to talk. We stumbled into the upstairs corridor. It was dark but I found our way into the biology lab and we plumped down onto a bench.

'Listen,' I said. 'We can't be long, but it's about the hols.' I took a deep breath. I said, 'D' you think, I mean, only if you'd like to…but, well d' you think your aunt would let you come to stay at Yearsby, even if just for a week? I mean – only if you want to.'

She turned towards me and I sensed her surprise.

'Please! It would be so…d' you think you could ask? Mum likes you and I'm sure she would agree.'

No reply. Silence. I could hear the band starting up, thumping away. Then she whispered, 'I don't know, Johnny. I could ask but, well, I don't suppose she would let me come on my own.'

'You mean your aunt would have to bring you?'

'I don't think she'd let me stay at Yearsby by myself. I mean – she hasn't met you, or your family, and she's rather old-fashioned…'

'Well, *we're* not. Mum's a modernist, and you've met her.'

I felt her lips against my cheek and she whispered, 'I'd love to come, Johnny.'

'So – you'll try?'

'Well, it won't harm to ask.'

The band thumped more loudly and my heart bumped faster. Then I froze. I put my finger to her lips. 'Shush! I heard something. There's someone there!'

I held my breath. There was someone moving about…someone in the next-door lab.

'Wait! I'll go and look.'

I tiptoed to the inner door behind which I knew there was a kind of anteroom where bell jars, tripods and spare Bunsen burners were stored. I pushed the door back very gently and a beam of light shot through. There was someone working in there for sure. I peered round the door.

'Gosh! What on earth…it's *you*!'

It was Jeff Plowright, and he appeared to be busy stirring something in a glass jar and heating it over a Bunsen burner.

'Jeff! What are you up to? You'd better look out, Bellerby's on duty downstairs and he's bound to come to lock up for the night!'

'Nay bother!' Jeff replied coolly. 'He'll not know.'

I remained just long enough to see him pouring yellowish liquid into a jar, and a cloud of something that smelled very sickly arose.

'I gotta recipe,' he said, concentrating over the flame. 'It's for jelly wi' nuts in.'

I closed the door firmly behind me and turned back to Anne. 'It's all right, it's only Jeff messing about with some concoction. We'd better get back.'

We trod carefully down the stairs and joined the crowd still milling around the table in the hall. Bellerby had returned and was busy decanting another supply of lemonade aided by Helen the cook. We had not been missed.

Chapter Thirteen

own on our knees. Praying position. That's how we were, Paddy and I, steadily kneeing our way forward up the grass court, each armed with a dinner fork. We were removing plantains. This was, after all, one of the best grass tennis courts in the north. We cut and rolled and marked out the white lines every summer. Our work was being closely scrutinised, with some amusement, by Anne who stood, arms folded, watching from the summerhouse close by. She had kept her promise and asked her Aunt Clare if she could come to Yearsby and, after some debate, the answer had been yes. Her aunt had seen her on to the train at Burslem, and I had gone along with Odd Job Harris, our gardener, in the Star car to meet her at the station.

As we were nearing the end of our plantain hunt, Mum called from the house to wash our hands for tea, and said that Amy, our housemaid, would bring it out to the summerhouse. Over chocolate buns and cream cake with home-grown strawberries, we made plans for the next day. Every one of our six days together was precious. Paddy had invited local chums to come for tennis, which left Anne and me free to go our own way. Mum said, 'Johnny darling, why don't you introduce Anne to our lovely countryside? I'm sure you would like that, dear.'

She said she would, and I said we could take a picnic – except that, while I could actually drive the Star, strictly speaking it was not allowed, and certainly not on the main roads. If we wanted to take a decent drive we would have to get Odd Job to take us. He was local and knew all the best spots, except the seaside.

'Niver go to t' sea,' he would say. 'It's that cold. Allus keep inland in yon valleys.'

And so it was arranged. While Paddy entertained his friends, we'd take an afternoon out, courtesy of Odd Job. Anne said, 'You could do some sketching, Johnny.'

'Remember to take something warm to wear,' Mum reminded us. She added that she would get Edna, our cook, to make something up…ham and tongue sandwiches with lettuce, some greengages and apples. A flask of tea, and a bottle of John Smith's for Odd Job.

Wensleydale was my choice. It would be a long drive but we had the whole afternoon. We put the picnic on the front seat of the Star and took our places on the seats behind, and we were off.

At Sutton-under-Whitestonecliffe Anne said, 'Your mother is lovely, very trusting.'

'Of course, because she really likes you.'

At Skipton-on-Swale I held her hand and she twined her fingers round mine and made them tingle.

At Sutton Conyers I slipped my arm through hers. I heard distant bells. Ripon Cathedral, perhaps. She rested her head on my shoulder. 'Can we go and see the town?'

Odd Job heard her request and shook his head. 'Fair bit to go yet, miss,' he called over his shoulder.

At West Tanfield I rested my hand on her lap and felt her warmth. At Masham she removed it. The brilliant sun following behind gazed brazenly into the car turning it into an oven. We dozed then awoke at Layburn.

Odd Job pulled up outside The Blue Lion Inn…or was it The Bull, or The Mucky Duck? He said he was in 'a fair sweat' and would get a pint in the pub. We were also parched. Anne said, 'A lemonade would be lovely.' I bought Odd Job his pint, ordered two glasses of cider and carried them through to a table in the cool, beamed recess. 'That's not lemonade,' observed Anne, and sounded quite put out.

'It's Woodpecker. Much better, you'll like it.' She did. Then it was back to the car and on up the dale where the corn in the lower fields burned gold awaiting the harvester.

At West Wilton I put my arms around her. We hugged and exchanged a cidery kiss and her lips tasted sweet. At Aysgarth we clambered out. I wanted to show Anne the waterfall where the water gushed over the limestone slabs but the hot weather had reduced the flow. It was disappointing. I told Odd Job we should drive a few miles further to

Hawes and we could then walk up to see Hardraw Force, which was supposed to be the highest unbroken waterfall in Britain. Anne carried the picnic and I gathered up my sketchpad and pens. Odd Job disappeared to find a pie and a pint in the village and would wait there for us with the car.

The air cooled as we clambered up to the waterfall and found the cascade, the sunlight slicing the downward spray to create a myriad droplets, all rainbow colours. At the foot of the Force there was a small pool, and lower down a larger pool so clear you could see the rocks and trailing fronds below. Anne stared. 'Magic!' she said. 'It's wonderful!'

I took her hand and we set up our picnic beside the pool and beneath the trees. Alder, willow, larch and miniature rowan with berries forming, which would be blood-red in a month or so. Many flowers surrounded the pool. We munched and Anne surprised me. A blue flower. '*Iris laevigata*,' she said. 'You see? Beside those spiky ferns…and that white one is a *Primula japonica*.'

'Imagine you knowing those names!'

'My garden. Don't say you've forgotten, you dunce!'

I would have kissed her but my mouth was full of ham and tongue and crispy lettuce. I watched as she set out the flask of tea and two cups. That head of hers…the big brow. If I could have seen into her head I fancied I would find it beautiful like a garden, brilliant with flowers.

※

'Johnny, whatever are you doing?'

'I am saying hullo to the trees!'

'But why do you put your arms around them? I've never seen anyone embrace a tree before. You'll fall into the water!'

'Trees are individuals. Like people, and all different. They should be loved. They deserve a cuddle.'

'You and your trees! Honestly!'

All I really wanted to do was to embrace her and hold her to me. But – she did not beckon. Perhaps she was waiting. She said, 'Do you think the water is very cold? I'm going to dip my toes in.'

'Cold as ice, I should think.'

She removed her white socks and shoes. Slim ankles and beautiful, slender feet. If I had been nearer I might have kissed her toes, but I was too late. She pulled her frock up to her waist and trailed her ankles in the water. 'Freezing!' she called. 'Not for swimming!'

My brain was turning in my head. I felt dizzy as I visualised her naked, her pale slim body and her breasts I longed to touch.

It would make an ideal composition – at least I hoped so. She untied her hair and let it fall to her shoulders as I arranged the pose, her back half-turned to the high cascading Force and beneath a heavily leafed tree teased by shafts of sunlight and disturbed by a downward draught from the falling water. I was learning to draw from life, recording as much detail as speed allowed, for I was attempting to work fast. Clubby Nash taught speed for hand and eye. 'Don't dwell,' he always said, 'work quickly…you're catching a bus.'

Time passed. The world passed. It had forgotten us. I concentrated very hard. The air became still. Anne was still. She made a good model and I worked in as much detail as I could, and time devoured itself and was lost. Even as I worked, I think I knew he would appear and he did, in the branches above her head, as if inviting me to include him in the composition. It was the face in the leaves I had seen before. The same face, with a stern and steady gaze until a breath of wind shifted the expression and the countenance became a menacing smile before abruptly vanishing.

Who was this fleeting stranger, denizen of deciduous trees, and why did he haunt me? I shivered. My hand froze and I put down my pen as the green smile melted.

Anne called: 'Have you finished?' She straightened up, stretched her back and walked over to me. 'You've taken a long time, Johnny.'

'I've only just begun.'

'Can I look?' She peered over my shoulder. Then she stepped back and I heard her gasp. 'Johnny! Goodness! I mean, you've drawn my top with no clothes on! How *could* you!'

'Anne, I so wanted to, but I did not think I could ask – or if I did you would only refuse, so…'

I turned to gaze up at her. She was blushing and confused.

I said, 'Are you angry?'

Silence. Then she said, softly, 'Do you think I really look like that…and those words you've written all over me!'

'Notes. I'm going to make a painting and I have to remember the colours for when I get back.'

'Johnny! You are wicked!'

It was the way she said it. She didn't sound angry. Or upset. She bent lower, brushed my cheek with her lips and said, 'But I think you're very clever.'

'Not as clever as you…and certainly not as beautiful!'

'Honestly, Johnny! *You!*' She laughed, so I stood up and put my arms around her, held her closely, then time returned, reminding me that we should go.

We snuggled together in the car all the way back to Yearsby, and she whispered: 'If you had asked…well, I think I would have let you.'

I felt stupidly happy and said nothing. Evening was approaching but the sky was still bright with the last of the sun and birds circling, swooping, diving. Harbingers of the autumn to come.

Chapter Fourteen

*T*hose six days of summer set my mind in a whirl. I thought I must be dreaming, but this was real and my hands and arm left hers only when we were summoned to Mum's table for food, and when goodnights had to be said. Anne clearly loved my home and I wanted to show her everything. We floated from the wide-windowed drawing room and the white-panelled recess with the big fireplace, and the chairs and settees in green and white, the grand piano in one corner and the new radiogram in the other beside the secretaire. Then on to the study with its wall of books and worktable by the high window, and the dining room with the oval table and glass-fronted case for the china Mum collected. Then, we explored upstairs…the nursery where a bed had been made up for Anne, Paddy's disaster-area of a room with posters of sporting heroes on the walls. My room was tidy, with a bookcase and green desk and a casement window above the bed. More rooms, including the empty granny flat, and through a glazed door the back stairs led to the servants' quarters and the 'top room', an L-shaped attic under the rafters. Anne said she had never seen such a lovely home.

One day Mum drove us down to Harrogate where Paddy was to have tennis coaching at the Majestic Hotel. We went with Mum to a store called Brown and Muffs and Mum made Anne choose a present of a pretty blouse and put it on her account.

Returning in the car Anne was quiet, then later said, 'Your mum is the kindest person I've ever met. My aunt is very kind but, well…she's a sad person compared with your mum. She still misses my Uncle Ted so much.'

Dad returned from his trip on the *Queen Mary* the day before Anne had to leave, so we had a welcome-home and a goodbye supper all in one and afterwards over coffee he showed us a collection of menus he had brought from the ship. They had been beautifully designed. Anne said, 'You could do that, Johnny…I mean you really could.' Then she blushed and I realised she was remembering the drawing I had made at the waterfall.

The morning Anne left we took a last stroll round the garden. Beside a bed of lupins and beneath a monkey tackle tree we held each other and kissed long kisses. I did not want her to go. Too soon it would be back to school. I told her I loved her, that I would always love her.

She said, 'I love you too, Johnny.'

For the first time in weeks the sky darkened to a cloudy grey. On the draughty platform at the station as we waited for the train a billboard proclaimed 'Britain ready to defend France. Official.'

The autumn term began with a surprise. Walt and I were made prefects and given charge of the dormitory for the juniors – a pretty badly behaved bunch. Discipline demanded that we punish the worst of the harum-scarums and we did so with six swings of a slipper on their bums. It didn't seem to make much difference.

We had been moved up to the fifth form and that meant extra class work for the exams. It did not prevent me from serenading Anne with my gram from the classroom windows. The hits of the day.

I was excused some of prep and allowed to work on art in the studio under the eye of Clubby Nash. I'd shown him the waterfall portrait of Anne and he liked it.

My anatomy, he said, left something to be desired, so he put up a small maquette of Rodin's *The Kiss* for me to study. It was terribly sexy. I planned to paint the portrait near life-size with a limited palette that Clubby chose for me. It included vermilion, Prussian blue, burnt sienna, raw sienna, crimson lake, ivory black, and white.

In the fifth we endured a heavy programme, which meant a lot of swotting. I did well with English, geography and history but made heavy weather of French, German, science, and I found maths quite impossible as my school report showed. Arithmetic – poor, not enough effort made. Algebra – is far below the standard. Geometry – he finds elementary work difficult. I heard from Liz, via Walter, that Anne was very hot on maths and that she had distinguished herself with a paper entitled 'A mathematical perspective on probabilities and certainties'. Her teachers were astonished, but I was not wholly surprised. It simply went to prove what I had always believed – that she possessed a kind of brilliance, a remarkable intellect.

On those Sundays when we walked the Green she tried to explain the difference between what she called pure maths and applied mathematics, but, try as I may, it was double Dutch to me. Not to be outdone I responded by reading poetry to her by those seventeenth-century blades who sang of their courtly love in wonderful words. To my chagrin Anne also seemed well up on her English studies as well. If I imagined I had a monopoly on John Donne I was mistaken. She could out-quote me:

I wonder by my troth, what thou, and I
Did, till we loved? Were we not wean'd till then?
But suck'd on country pleasures, childishly?
Or snorted we in the seven sleepers' den?
T' was so; But this, all pleasures fancies be.
If ever any beauty I did see,
Which I desired, and got, t' was but a dream of thee.

I think I said, 'Oh heck!'
'Heck nothing, Johnny! *You* should be reading it to *me*!'
All went well through the first half of term – too happily perhaps. It could not last. And it didn't. A fire in the science lab caused a scandal. Jeff Plowright had been careless with the Bunsen burners and the fire brigade from Ferniehill had to be called. Poor Jeff was instantly and rather unfairly dismissed. Then there were more alarms and excursions. Helen, the cook…Helen with the face that launched a thousand chips eloped with Bellerby. Schedules had to be seriously revised and the quality of our meals took a dive.

But not all was disaster. Autumn was the big term for music. Walt and I both played in the school orchestra. He developed highly individual skills on the double bass and I played timpani and had a full set of drums. We enjoyed playing *Tales From The Vienna Woods*, some rousing marches, and we were in the band for the annual G and

S – this time *The Pirates of Penzance*. Both Anne and Liz sang in the school choir and we all four contributed to the major offering, Handel's *Messiah*, with visiting soloists. The worst news from the outside world came via Owen Hardwick in the wireless room. Children in towns were being given gasmask drill; defence was to cost £100,000,000, while in Germany more Jewish people were being rounded up and imprisoned. Jumbo Liddington told us there was one hopeful sign. The government had made a deal with Germany over Czechoslovakia. Prime Minister Chamberlain confirmed it. He returned from a meeting with Hitler and declared there would be 'Peace in our time!'

Our time turned out to be very short. Later news bulletins announced that Hitler's hordes were pouring into Prague. Children were now being evacuated from cities and towns, including Paris and London. And then – it happened. The Germans invaded Poland. A very solemn-faced Whack announced from his breakfast pulpit that Britain was now at war with Germany.

The school term ended earlier than usual, several days before the Christmas break. Whack indicated that some of the parents had demanded the change. He declared, 'All Europe is in conflict and the war machine grows larger and more menacing by the day. At this school, and among many parents and, indeed, for some of you, peace is our aim and always will be. But while we feel the war will not last very long we deem it wise to take every precaution. Next term you will find our windows blacked out at night, and we are converting the cellars beneath this dining room into an air-raid shelter. We will do the same beneath the classrooms and also on the West Wing, where Miss Neatley is making similar arrangements.'

Back at Yearsby, because we were in open countryside and well away from towns and industry, we did not feel to be in any danger. Dad told us that we should stay 'steady and calm'. He said, 'We will not allow this present situation to disrupt our way of life and the standards we hold dear. There will of course be changes. Some of the older men at Sproxton and The Grange may carry arms, purely as a precaution, and will be formed into groups for tactical training. I am being asked to take charge of a small area…some fifteen square miles around Yearsby.'

Mum added, 'On a happier note, we are still going to have Christmas. We'll carry on and have our usual party on the twenty-fourth, and I've managed to get a turkey – a plump twelve pounds for Christmas Day. So, darlings, I want you both to make lists of who you would like to invite for our Christmas Eve party and I'll get the invitations out right away.'

There was only one person I wanted to invite and she was in Burslem. It wasn't difficult for Mum to guess my mind. 'Johnny darling, it would be lovely to have Anne, but it's Christmas, it's a special time, and she won't want to desert the family nest, will she?'

I plucked up courage and said that the Black Country was hardly a family nest, especially as her mum and dad were in Dominica and the only person Anne could be with was her Aunt Clara. I made what I hoped was an eloquent plea, reminding Mum that Burslem was in an industrial area and if there was to be bombing Anne would be much safer with us at Yearsby.

It was a good try, but the answer was no. Then, the following day, for reasons I never understood, Mum changed her mind. She said, 'I've had a word with your father and he has agreed that you can ask her. But I suppose we'd have to have her aunt as well.'

As a family we were not given to extravagant demonstrations of affection, but this time I did not hold back. I flung my arms around my wonderful, generous-hearted mum and gave her the biggest hug she had probably had since she married Dad.

I wasn't sure about the aunt, but she had allowed Anne to visit once before. I hung about until Mum made time to get to the telephone. The chill December day was closing down. Snow began to fall.

Chapter Fifteen

So. Aunt Clara came too, and I was pleased. Young Paddy was not.

'I suppose I'll have to buy her something,' he grumbled. 'And I don't see why. I don't even know her so she won't get me a present.'

I told him none of us knew her, except Anne. He did not have to buy her anything, it was just family presents. When Aunt Clara arrived, she probably surprised us all. She certainly surprised me. Because Anne was brainy and academic I expected her aunt to be the same. She wasn't. She was…homely. She was jumpers and pleated skirts. Tall. Bony, quiet, with a kindly face but sad grey eyes. She seemed shy and defensive but when I showed her to the granny flat I sensed that she was pleased.

'Goodness! This is very kind of you.'

I suppose it was more than she had expected – the large bedroom with a double bed, an adjacent bathroom, and a pretty living room all self-contained and with big windows overlooking the terrace to the fields beyond.

She and Anne had arrived in good time on the twenty-third. I carried Anne's case to the nursery where she had slept the first time she came to Yearsby. She gave me a hug.

'My aunt won't say very much but it doesn't mean she is unhappy. I think that she is quite pleased to be here.'

'And you are too?'

'Johnny! You are a chump! I wouldn't be anywhere else.'

'Your mum and dad…they must miss you, and they'd want you to be there for Christmas.'

'It's impossible. Anyway, I don't think it would feel much like Christmas in that place.'

She turned to her case in a resigned sort of way and seemed tired, as if reluctant to unpack. I was puzzled and could not guess what she was thinking. Perhaps she really did wish she was with her mum and dad. I turned away and left her to settle in. At the corner of the stairs I paused by the glass door to the balcony that overlooked the tennis lawn below. It had started to snow again quite heavily and I could barely see across to the orchard. In the hall it didn't feel much like Christmas. The lights were not on and there was a smell of floor polish. By late morning Mum announced that there was cocoa and biscuits in the kitchen, then we would all help with the decorations.

'Odd Job's bringing in the tree and the holly from the garden, and later we'll put up the paper chains and do the balloons.'

In the kitchen, Edna's was the only cheerful face as she fussed around like a mother hen and said she was making mince pies for the party tomorrow. The dance would be in the hall when the Mortons from Sproxton and the Glaisters from The Grange came over with their kids. The only one I liked was Jenny Glaister, a tall girl with blonde hair and a lisp. She reminded me of Walt's Liz. And she had ponies.

Duties were assigned. Anne and I were paper chains, Paddy was balloons, while Aunt Clara and Mum, with Amy helping, decided to do the dining room for Christmas Day lunch. Amy was skinny and sniffed a lot, and any sense of fun or expectation seemed to have deserted her. She informed us mournfully that the milk boy had told her that with the rationing we would all have to get tickets to buy food.

Crêpe paper. Yards of it – blue, pink, green, yellow. Scissors and glue. We did the cutting and pasting in the study. It took ages. Afterwards, we decided to go for a walk.

'I don't advise it, darlings,' said Mum. 'It's still snowing!'

'You'll catch your death!' added Amy. 'The milk boy says it's going to freeze.'

I began to wonder about the milk boy and Amy and suspected she fancied him. But the milk boy was right. Freezing had started and the snow was crisp beneath our feet as we turned out of the drive and crunched our way down Moat Lane. It was a white world, a silent world. The birds were hiding from the cold, and although the trees looked beautiful, white-branched against the sky, I was in a white mood, too. Something was changing. The world was still turning but the sense of joy I should have felt had got lost.

Anne wore woolly gloves but I could feel her hands were cold. I said, 'Inside I feel as cold as your hands, and I don't know why. I suppose it's the war...trying to cancel out Christmas.'

'Johnny, you great baby, that's not like you, it's your imagination. And I think you're tired.'

No, I said, it was not as simple as that. I'd heard Dad saying to Mum that the government was expecting 100,000 casualties in the next few weeks.

'Well,' she replied, 'it may not be as bad as you think – and there's no war here, so we should try to cheer up.'

She was right, of course. Christmas cheer, if only for two days, should not be submerged, it must be welcomed as all Christians welcomed the birth of Christ, and if we could not find a sense of joy in a silent, white and peaceful world, then we would find it nowhere.

'Peace be on you!' I cried, not really knowing what I meant.

'And on you, too!' she shouted, running ahead. Then she scooped up handfuls of snow and started pelting me.

Christmas Eve began with furniture removing. We positioned the refectory table on the window side of the hall, and with Anne's help I hung the paper chains in place and forgot my miseries. Then I went to the study. Place names for tomorrow's table had to be done. Anne cut up pieces of white card and on them I drew the symbols and names. Anne, I knew, was Libra and I was Pisces. But what was Aunt Clara's sign?

'I think she's Capricorn,' Anne said.

The others were easy. Paddy was Gemini, Dad was Taurus and Mum was Aquarius: it was the twins, the bull and the water carrier. I finished the task as suppertime was approaching and – as it turned out – something else was approaching. The bell that hung outside the front door clanged and there were voices. Very young voices. 'God rest you, merry gentlemen, let nothing you dismay...'

'Villagers,' I said. 'Or probably the kids from the farms around here, they turn up every year.'

Mum went to the front door. There were six of them, four girls and two boys, and in they blew on a gust and a flurry of snow to stand in a circle in the hall. Rosy-cheeked smiles and shy glances and snowflakes on their woolly hats. Mum then went to the grand in the drawing room and called, 'Come on, children, what's it to be? Let's have your favourite carol!'

A small voice piped up, 'Away in a manger, Mum, no crib for a bed.'

'That's a good one. Hold on till I find the music.'

Four chords on the Bechstein and, song sheets in hand, they began, the tallest girl leading the way to the manger. Then we harked the herald angels, watched the flocks with the shepherds by night, visited David's royal city, and came with all ye faithful. When they had finished the audience of four – Anne, her aunt, Amy from the kitchen, and me – applauded and they turned away to leave.

Mum called, 'Hold on! One more, then you shall have your reward!'

They shuffled, coughed and stood their ground. The snow from their coats had thawed out and made small pools at their feet on Amy's polished floor. Mum called, 'What about *Stille Nacht, Heilige Nacht*? D' you know that one?'

'No, not that one!' said a gruff voice by the door. It was Dad who had just returned from visiting in Sproxton. 'We don't really want that one. Nothing German here, thank you.'

'Does it matter?' responded Mum. 'It's a lovely carol!'

Dad was adamant. 'Thank you, children, you're very good, but that is all.'

'No it is not!' It was Edna who had bumped her way through the double baize door from the kitchen bearing a loaded tray. 'Mince pies!' she announced. 'They're just from the oven, mind you don't burn your pretty lips or you'll never sing again!'

Giggles. Shuffling and murmurs of anticipation as the songbirds obediently arranged themselves on the long window seat. Mum came through from the drawing room. 'There's a hot drink, children, or if you don't like it there's orange juice.'

The songbirds did us a good turn that evening, and we all started to thaw out ourselves as we lit candles and placed them around the hall. It began to feel like Christmas at last. We helped Mum to dress the tree, then got ready for the dance.

Numbers were down, probably because of the snow, and only fifteen came including the two lads from the carols.

The best part was the music that came from the drawing room, with the volume turned up. The new radiogram could take eight records, which dropped to the turntable automatically, so foxtrots and quicksteps played nose to tail. We had 'Nobody's Sweetheart', 'Dance, Little Lady', 'The Best Things In Life Are Free', and lots more including 'The Charleston', with Mum and Dad joining in and showing us how to do it. We even had a last waltz – 'Three O'clock In The Morning'. Anne and I were becoming quite expert but tried not to hold each other too close as I had spotted Aunt Clara keeping an eagle eye. Then – we all flopped. It wasn't three o' clock in the morning, it was barely 10.30 of a Christmas Eve with Edna doling out bowls of piping hot broth to speed our parting guests on their way.

Chapter Sixteen

*W*hen we were very young we used to wake up on Christmas morning to the excitement of a pillowcase of presents. Later, small net stockings hung at the foot of our beds. Pillowcases were deemed unsuitable.

On *this* Christmas morning when I awoke I did not expect to see a pillowcase or a stocking. But I did. A small stocking. On examination it offered me a rosy apple, an orange, a bar of choc, a bar of soap – and a tea towel. I heard Paddy laughing. He had probably made a similar discovery. There was another surprise. Amy appeared with a tray bearing mugs of steaming tea.

'You needn't give me one of your daft looks, Master John. There's tea because we've company...the lady and the young miss.'

She wrinkled her nose, attempted a curtsey and announced 'Merry Christmas!' before clattering along to the other rooms. I climbed out of bed then stumped across to the nursery and tapped softly on the door.

'Anne, are you awake?'

A muffled, sleepy yes.

'Merry Christmas! Can I come in?'

'No, I'm still in bed, I'm not dressed yet.'

' Santa has a present for you!'

'No you haven't! Your mother said the presents are under the tree.'

'I could make a drawing of you in bed...'

'Johnny! Go away!'

Breakfast was porridge with Lyle's golden syrup, toast and more tea. Then we had to change for church and the Christmas morning service. I explained to Anne that although Mum's parents had been Quakers and she had been brought up as a member of the Society of Friends, she seldom went to meeting for worship now.

Getting to church was more like a polar exploration as we trudged, slid, slipped, and slithered on the frozen snow, beckoned on by the tolling of the single bell. Around us, as far as you could see, the world was white. It was a relief to crowd into the honeyed warmth and smell the woody smell from the old pews. We squashed up together with Paddy, me, Anne and her aunt. Mum and Dad were at the end of the row saluting with smiles and nods and a flutter of hands the parishioners they recognised. When the minister appeared, Paddy whispered, 'Golly! It's old elephant again!'

The Reverend Ephraim Oliphant was an ample, rounded man, small, balding, ruddy-cheeked and, I thought, more like an owl with his black-rimmed spectacles. A word of welcome, then we all stood for the first hymn. The six young carol singers who had serenaded us sat with the three ladies in the choir and led us into an enthusiastic 'O Come All Ye Faithful'. Before the readings and the sermon four children stood up facing the minister, each of them clutching a present.

'Now, children,' boomed Oliphant, 'I wonder what time you woke up on this very special morning? Hands up, anyone at six o'clock!' No hands. 'Five o'clock?' Nothing. 'Four o'clock?' Not a flicker. 'Three o'clock?' The smallest girl raised a hesitant hand.

'Ah! Lucy! That was very, very early. What did Santa bring you?'

Lucy stepped forward, held up a book and said, 'There's pictures…animals and big fishes like sharks and whales and octo…' And there she got stuck.

'Octopus?' said Oliphant coming to the rescue. 'No ponies?'

Lucy shook her head.

She was followed by a boy who looked all of five years old. He stepped forward and held up a miniature of a red racing car. 'Dinky Toy,' he said. 'I got three and another one if I am a good boy and say my prayers.'

'Excellent!' beamed the Oliphant. 'Now, Jane is it? What did Santa bring you?'

A sweet lass with a pigtail presented a doll half the size of herself.

'Is that your baby?'

The toddler nodded, then lifted the doll's skirt. 'She got her knickers on.'

A ripple of mirth ebbed round the pews, and Jane said, 'It's her birthday!'

'Ah yes. And it's someone else's birthday today. Hands up who knows who it is!'

Silence. Then the eldest of the children, a boy, raised his hand and said, 'Hitler!'

Oliphant stood his ground. 'No, not Hitler, of course not! Give me another name.'

Silence again. Then Jane said, 'Baby Jesus.'

This time there was a ripple of applause from the pews as Oliphant beamed and said, 'Well done, Jane! Baby Jesus, born this day in Bethlehem.'

The tall boy suddenly declared, 'I gotta gun, see!' And he produced what looked like a toy Luger and pointed it at Oliphant. 'Hands up!'

The minister obediently raised his hands and the boy took aim and pulled the trigger. A jet of water shot from the gun, followed by another and another directly into Oliphant's face.

Hoots of laughter from the faithful. Then a woman in the front row stood up and declared, 'Jack Hargreaves! For shame on yourself! Put that away and come here this minute, d' you hear!'

Anne whispered, 'No Christmas pud for him!'

After the service, as was the custom back at Yearsby, there was sherry in the study. When no one was looking Anne tipped half of hers into my glass.

As usual Dad commented on Oliphant's sermon. 'I didn't think much of his observations on science and the telescope telling the story of God's creation. To explore the heavens is to do with science and discovery, and that's as maybe. But faith does not depend on telescopes. And I am not sure that he should have used this day of all days to commend young men who were joining the army to fight in the war. If we are to be true Christians the advice from the pulpit should be to follow Christ's teaching and go in the ways of peace.'

Mum said, 'Darling, don't be so critical. Oliphant is a good man, he means well, I'm sure.'

No one appeared interested in continuing the subject, but Mum added, 'Well I know he would approve of what Amy has to tell us.' She pressed the bell by the fireplace and Amy appeared.

'Now, Amy, what have you to say?'

'The turkey is ready, ma'am, and cook says we're to go to the table.'

'Yes, thank you, Amy. Is there anything else you'd like to tell us?'

'As you give me permission, I got the milk boy.'

'And?'

'And he says he'd like to come, so I made a place for him.'

Mum than explained that the milk boy was an orphan. She said, 'Thank you, Amy, but tell us his name, please, we can't just call him milk boy!'

'He's Alfred. Alfred Gladly Weatherston Jones.'

I confess I burst out laughing. Mum looked quite cross. 'Johnny, behave yourself! Thank you, Amy. Now, come along, everybody, I hope you've got good appetites!'

The sherry had gone to my head and I felt a bit dizzy, but not too dizzy to tuck in.

Dad carved and Amy passed round the mashed spuds, the peas, chestnuts and celery. The crackers Aunt Clara had brought were terrific with small gifts like whistles and paper hats. There was Christmas pudding with threepenny bits and a silver horseshoe, then crystallised fruits. It was a proper feast. My place names were admired and caused much amusement.

I said, 'On the back of each card you'll find appropriate words and you have to read them out.'

Everyone turned them over. Mum said, 'Johnny, you didn't tell me about this, I do hope it's fun.'

'It's your stars,' I replied, 'according to your birth sign. To demonstrate, I'll go first. I'm Pisces, the fishes.' I turned over my card and read: 'Imaginative, sensitive, compassionate, intuitive, secretive, vague.'

Hoots of laughter. Anne said, 'I think you made that up!'

She was next. Libra. She said, 'It's embarrassing!'

I said, 'Go on!' and thought it was exactly right. 'Diplomatic, romantic, charming, changeable, flirty. Johnny! It's nonsense!'

Paddy was next. He was Gemini. 'Versatile, witty, youthful, lively, cunning, intellectual.'

Mum cried, 'Intellectual? Pull the other one, darling!'

Dad was Taurus: 'Reliable, warm-hearted, persistent, determined, self-indulgent, greedy.' Everyone shouted, 'Hooray!'

Aunt Clara was Capricorn. She made a face. 'Oh dear, I'm the goat.' I assured her that goats were lovely creatures. 'Very placid and calm!'

Mum seemed quite pleased with her card. She read out, 'Humane, frank, humanitarian, honest, loyal and…goodness! I obey the Quaker advice to be open to the truth from whatever source it comes!'

We almost forgot Alfred Gladly Weatherston Jones, he had sat so quietly and spoken hardly a word. He certainly had a good appetite and I saw that he ate heartily. All eyes were fixed on him. He looked up uneasily. 'I ain't got one,' he mumbled.

'Ha!' shouted Paddy. 'Then you ain't been born, Alfie!'

Mum looked pained. 'Paddy, please! That is not kind.'

I said to Alfred, 'Just tell us when you were born. Which month?'

He hung his head. 'Don't know. No one told me.'

Of course. He was an orphan. Mum came to the rescue. 'Well, I think, Alfred, as you are with us at Christmastime you could be December.'

'Sagittarius,' I said. 'A happy sign. You'll be jolly, honest, truthful and…optimistic with lots of energy. You could become a schoolteacher.'

Alfred snorted. 'Nah! I don't want school and learnin'.'

'Well,' said Mum, 'I'm sure you will really like it when you are older.'

He shook his head. 'I like your puddin', missus!' And he held up his plate.

Dad said, 'Ah! I think you should be called Oliver!'

Amy came through to say she would give Alfred a hot drink in the kitchen to see him on his way home.

As promised the presents were beneath the Christmas tree in the sitting room, and after a short walk as the chill evening descended we lit candles and opened our parcels. I gave Anne a book – *The Lakeland Poets*. Dad was looking quite pleased with himself. He had bought Mum a magnificent silk garment. 'Darling, I love it! Anne dear, come and look, it's silk marocain with a lovely rainbow lining!'

'Saw it in the papers,' said Dad. 'Harvey Nichols – your kind of thing. Along the lines of Paris models for the smart occasion, that's what the advertisement said.'

'Pure heaven,' replied Mum. There were kisses all round as more presents were unwrapped and exchanged. Anne gave me a silver tiepin with a cornelian stone in it. She told me later that her aunt had given it to her – it had been left in her husband's will. It was hallmarked. I loved it and would treasure it forever. Mum gave Dad a table cigarette lighter and a box of fifty Havana cigars, and Aunt Clara came up with homemade chutney and a ceramic bon-bon dish. Mum and Dad gave me oil paints and a folding easel.

Later, Amy brought in some mulled wine and we got quite merry. Mum put on some records and said we should go into the hall and she would teach us the latest hits…the one step, the toddle and the tango. Dad gave Aunt Clara a turn round the floor and I held on to Anne very tightly. I loved her so very much, more than anyone could know. It was perfect. The best Christmas I'd ever had.

Chapter Seventeen

We did not feel up to much on Boxing Day, except for Amy who said there would be eggs for breakfast if we wanted them.

It was no warmer that morning as we crunched our way across the fields to The Grange for the Boxing Day meet. There was little chance that there would be the customary hunt, the ground was white and although the frost was beginning to give, fences, hedges and ditches would be lethal. On arriving at the paddock below the great house we saw the horses and hounds were mustering. It was a cheery sight, the master and several former masters in their pink with many of the ladies in green, with white breeches and shiny black boots, seated comfortably, smiling and chattering to each other. One of the gardeners from The Grange threaded his way through the throng with the stirrup cup. There was such a calling, joking and waving, with such a yelping and scuffling from the hounds who circled around, tails high – it was as if all was well with the world and any worries would disappear up into the cold, clear air like the breath from the riders and their mounts. One lady on a large bay trotted up and yelled, 'Top o' the mornin', master! Bloody bad luck, but I'm game to give it a go!'

The master tipped his hat. 'Morning, Val! No chance I'm afraid, but we'll try the long meadow down to Warton Bottom, the haystacks and over to Oliver's place and give him a blast, the lazy bugger! Won't be too bad down there and we could give 'em a mile or two!' One of the huntsmen raised a horn to his lips, sounded a fanfare fit to waken the dead, followed by three toots, then, jogging, snorting and with a jingle of harnesses, the Swale and Ancaster hunt moved off. We followed a little way down the field and waved them good luck. Anne asked, 'Will they get a fox?'

'Unlikely. I think it's just a run-out. Exercise.'

She looked glum. 'I don't like them killing things, the poor old fox doesn't have a chance, does he?'

'Oh yes he does. And remember, your poor old fox is a killer. He gets our hens, and he goes for the farmer's lambs as well.'

The word 'kill' seemed to unsettle her. 'We're into killing too, I suppose. The war I mean.'

She was right, of course, and the frosty air about us suddenly seemed chillier as we took our way via Sproxton back to Yearsby. For the first time in her stay Anne seemed troubled.

'Come on!' I cried. 'It's Boxing Day…it's still Christmas, we can't be sad!'

'It's tomorrow,' she replied. 'Back to beastly Burslem.'

'We won't think about it, darling. Let's go back and practise…what was it, the toddle? Or would madam prefer the tango?'

She paused, and frowned. 'We have to talk, Johnny.'

'Of course we do!'

'No, it's serious!'

We stood there, like muffled snowmen. Alone. The rest of the crowd of onlookers had melted away. I took her hands. 'Well, go on. What is it you want to say?'

'Can we go somewhere? Private, I mean.'

'Course we can! Come on, let's get back.'

I waited until the evening drew in. Then we trod the echoing back stairs to the top room, the old playroom. We perched on a couple of wooden painted thrones left over from a spectacular production of some years past. *Macbeth*. The memory came back…parents and friends who were invited to pay pocket money to witness our 'theatricals'. On this occasion there were no theatricals. Anne said, 'Please, you won't be angry, will you?'

'I won't, I promise.'

'I have to go away. No, I don't mean tomorrow, I'm not exactly sure when, but very soon I think.'

'Going away? But where?'

'Johnny, believe me, I don't want to but I have no choice.'

She explained that her mother had become seriously ill.

'When did this happen?'

'I don't know exactly. My aunt told me just before we came here, she had a cable from my father, and it could be urgent.'

With a shock I realised what she was trying to tell me. Dominica. That island half way across the world. 'You mean you have to go out there?'

'She is ill and I have to go. No, please, Johnny, please let me finish.'

She was trembling and covered her face with her hands. 'I thought they were due to come home next spring but my father has to stay. I don't know why or how long…I don't know anything, Johnny, except what my aunt said.'

I thought she might cry. I went to her and put my arms around her and tried to kiss away her tears. Darling Anne…a tenderness seized me. I could find no words. She had known since before Christmas and had kept it to herself like a terrible secret. She had not wanted to spoil our time together.

That night sleep would not come, there were too many questions. How would she get to Dominica, and how long would she have to stay, and what would she do? She had a whole year still to go before she ended school.

I could not bear to think of Whitworth without Anne. No Sunday walking together, no dancing in the gym and – even worse – no more visits to Yearsby. I was shocked and simply could not imagine her disappearing to an island, of all places, halfway across the world.

Chapter Eighteen

The single church bell floated its message down the midnight breeze and across the snowbound fields. At the hall window Mum counted the twelve strokes then tip-tapped her way into the study to give Paddy and me a kiss and each of us a pair of new gloves.

'Happy New Year, darlings!' She raised her glass. 'Here's to all of us, not forgetting the lads far away from their homes and their loved ones. Let's hope for happier news.' She put on a bright smile but was not her cheerful self. The war seemed to be spreading. The Russians had just ended a brutal attack on Finland, and there had been a huge loss of life on both sides.

Dad went over to Sproxton and The Grange to first-foot the families there and give them New Year wishes. He returned with Mr Glaister, who entered with a cheery wave, and bearing a lump of coal for luck. 'Blessings on this house!' he called. I think he was a bit unsteady on his feet as Dad ushered him through to the sitting room to drink a good luck glass and pile fresh logs on the fire. I should have joined them but I didn't feel up to it. Mum tried her best. 'Come on, Johnny darling, do pull yourself together. I know how you feel, but Anne will probably be back sooner than you think. Off you go to your bed and stop worrying. She will be perfectly safe. There is no war where she is going, and things are bound to get better now that Mr Churchill is to be in charge. We must all look on the bright side.'

A week later, shortly before Paddy and I had to return to Whitworth, Aunt Clara telephoned. She said a passage had been obtained for Anne on a cargo boat sailing out of Liverpool and bound for the Caribbean. It was a 'twelve ship' and could take passengers as well as its cargo. The Colonial Office were seeing to it as Anne was the daughter of a colonial civil servant. That was all very well, but it was terrible Anne was going all that way on her own. Under normal circumstances I might not have felt so bad, but times were far from normal. According to the wireless, German submarines had been ordered to attack even neutral shipping in the Channel and the North Sea. In a speech the War Minister said it had to be expected that the U-boats would also head for the North Atlantic and that convoys from America would be an obvious target. Dad said later not to worry. All convoys were protected by British naval vessels well equipped to deal with attacks.

When Aunt Clara telephoned she said that Anne was packing, she was being very plucky, and sent her love. She would write as soon as she could. If I wished to write I was to send my letter to her. She would pass it on to the Colonial Office and they would send it out in the government bag.

Back at Whitworth for the spring term, to concentrate on my books was difficult. My chums were sympathetic but they had their own interests and pursuits and were not going to give much time to my anxieties.

Pop was the best. He bullied me into the house matches and I found that being active lessened the miseries. I played harder, and faster on the field than ever before and, after one bruising encounter, had my shirt pulled and ripped. After the match I called in to the tailor's shop, which was in the narrow passage that led to 'the area'. Taffy Jenkins was there, as ever, seated cross-legged on his high bench by the window, head down and stitching. I liked to look in there from time to time, and I felt I could confide in him. I gave him my shirt to mend. Then I told him about Anne.

'Old news, boyo,' he said. 'The word gets around. Not much happens I don't hear about. You and that girl, got her in trouble, have you? You better see your housemaster about that, no good come crying to me!'

I told him that was not the problem.

'You mean you never?'

'Never, Taffy. Course not!'

'Bit of it about, Johnny. There's that Helen and your Mr Bellerby did the disappearing act, didn't they?' He put down his needle and touched his nose with his forefinger. 'I reckon he got her with child.'

I told him I didn't know. Nor did I know how Anne was or where she was, I'd had no news of her for weeks.

'Look, boy, you got to be patient. This shirt of yours? I can mend it but it will take a bit of time. You give yourself time, boy, and it will come right. Get your mind on other things. There's more than girls – we got a war on, see?'

I saw. And I tried. And I found that spending more time in the studio helped. I completed the painting I had made of Anne. It caused considerable interest and I was encouraged to tackle other subjects. I chose to draw, and, in some cases, to make coloured sketches of what I called 'Penn House Personalities'…Walter, Cumberland, Pop, Squirt Fountain, and Jack Emslie. I became absorbed, and was much encouraged by Clubby Nash and Jumbo Liddington, who was amused to see I had improved the looks of his charges.

As Easter and the end of term approached, there was the usual exhibition of schoolwork. There were a lot of other paintings and designs, including calligraphy and craftwork…coffee tables, pewter ashtrays, hand-thrown pots and much more.

Parents were invited to the open day, but Mum and Dad could not come as they were involved in Red Cross work. Those who did come to look round seemed to like my stuff, and Clubby Nash said he would make up a portfolio of some of my drawings and send them to Goldhawk College. He said he felt they were of sufficient merit to gain an entrance for me if I wished. I said I did.

Chapter Nineteen

*T*he holidays were late and looked bleak. The blackout and rationing would hardly make Easter the celebration it should have been. On my return to Yearsby I could see that I would be kept busy. Mum and Dad had formed a local group to send items to the Red Cross, which would supplement parcels despatched to the troops abroad. They collected the items from the district around and I helped with the packaging.

Dad was well placed to develop supplies. He had a second job, part-time, and was chairman of a group of manufacturers and distributors of groceries, which, normally, were sold in shops throughout the north of England. The government classed him as being in a reserved occupation, doing work of national importance. Any extra supplies were strictly controlled, and the only Easter eggs in our house came from the few hens that Odd Job looked after in the paddock. Mum said, however, that there would be Easter presents…'but only small ones'. She said I would have to hunt for mine in my bedroom, which I thought rather silly, especially when having made a thorough search I could find nothing. It was not until I climbed into bed that I discovered, under the pillow, a large brown unsealed envelope. In it was an Easter card signed by Aunt Clara, which sent greetings to 'all at Yearsby'. With it was a smaller white envelope, also unsealed, and inside I found a letter in Anne's hand.

My dear Johnny,

You must have thought I had disappeared forever, but here I am in Dominica. I hope this reaches you as it was put in the box that the diplomats send to the Colonial Office. I am sorry to tell you that my mother is very poorly. The problem is no proper medical help and only one very small hospital. It seems she ventured alone into the forest (the island is all trees). She fell and broke her hip and was not discovered for nearly two days. She lost a lot of blood, and was unconscious. The wound became infected and she is in a coma. It's awful, there is a shortage of everything, including medicines, and my father has sent requests via the cable office, but who knows whether supplies will get here?

The voyage out was three weeks, not as bad as I expected, except I was very sick until I got my sea legs. There were only six other passengers on the ship, the S. S. *Dalmeny*, government people and very kind. There were several empty cabins, and the cargo was mainly sheet metal, iron products and salt. I never guessed this would be such a primitive place. It used to be a slave colony. Basics like bread, salt, butter and petrol all have to be imported. My father has an estate house, quite a large bungalow with hurricane shutters. It's on a hill outside Roseau, the capital. I am missing you so much, Johnny. It's hot and humid and it rains every day.

She ended by sending 'lots of love to you, to your mum and dad and Liz as well when you see her'.

I was overjoyed to receive the letter and went through to Mum who was just getting ready for bed. 'It's from Anne!'

'I know, darling. I'm so pleased she is safe and well!'

She had obviously read the letter, but I didn't mind.

Back at Whitworth the summer term would be my last term and it should have been the happiest, but it wasn't. No Sunday walking with Anne, no gardening. In some ways it was just as well. I had to get my head down over my books in preparation for finals. Walt understood about Anne. He knew how I felt. 'Why not ask Sarki Stan for an extra class,' he suggested. 'See if he'd do South America, the Caribbean? Might fit in for the geog exam.'

It was a good idea. Walt added that he would be quite interested and, if we could persuade one of two others to join us, Sarki Stan might agree. When I told the others they quite liked the idea. I approached Sarki and gave him my 'roll call' of Walter, Jack Emslie, Cumberland, Mortimer A. V., Pop and Squirt Fountain. He expressed surprise and said if we wished he could manage a half-hour once a week. I think he was amazed that we volunteered to spend free time in class.

I had not expected such a ready answer – or such a performance, but that was what we got from our Sarki. The Lesser Antilles, he told us, were undergoing political change and Dominica, formally one of the Leeward group of islands, was now a colony of the Windward group. It had been British since 1770.

He liked to pace about a bit and on this first occasion made a great show of pulling down the large, shiny map.

'You seem to be interested in Dominica,' he said, and looked a bit puzzled, as well he might. 'It is generally considered to be a tropical paradise, a volcanic mountain of a place covered by a vast rainforest…a land of streams, 350 of them, one for each day of the year. Imagine a kind of Eden rich in fruits and flowers but little else. If there were an Adam and Eve there they would both be as black as night.'

That made my chums chuckle.

'Half a century ago,' he continued, 'their great, great grandparents would have been slaves working for English or French estate managers. They hated the white settlers and called them honkies because of their long noses. Imagine dense forests, towering peaks, wild pigeons, flocks of rainbow-coloured parrots, humming birds, butterflies, lizards, serpents, hanging gardens of wild orchids—' He paused dramatically, '—and also a flower, which, it is said, if you found it you could command anything you desired.'

I liked the sound of that. I was fascinated, but guessed he just made that last bit up to keep our attention. He told us the island had been an underwater volcano until it appeared, thrust up from the ocean floor some twelve million years ago. It had first been inhabited by a tribe called Arawaks, who had come from the River Orinoco in South America, and also by the Caribs. They were warlike tribes and many were cannibals.

'They ate each other until they learned better ways to survive. In the lower part of the forest they cultivated what we would call kitchen gardens and grew many crops including yams, bananas, citrus fruits, plantain, bread fruit, ginger, arrowroot, also coffee.' That, he said, was much more than the white settlers grew when they came along. They had cocoa and coffee estates, then changed to soft fruits of which the lime proved most prolific and profitable. 'When you drink your lime cordial today,' he said, 'that is where it comes from.'

He told us that if we wanted additional facts we could do no better than seek permission to visit the centre library. I took him at his word, and spent many hours in the big, book-lined room that smelled of dust and leather and also had great windows that gazed down the Green to the Japanese garden. It was the best way, the only way to get close to Anne, for turning pages and poring over chapters and sepia photographs I could at least picture her in that faraway place.

Towards the end of term finals hove into view and with most of my chums I had to endure the repeated rigmarole of exam papers dished out in the gym, which was set up with avenues of desks and folding chairs. I thought of Voss, of Pop performing like a monkey on the ropes overhead, and I dreamed of Anne and found it hard to work to the clock in the uncanny silence demanded by a succession of eagle-eyed invigilators. I felt I did quite well with the papers on English, French, geography, history and RS. In the French oral Tashy Watts said although my vocabulary was poor I would get by with 'a shrug and a wink'. Maths, as ever, left me bewildered, but art was different – it was a doddle. The exam offered lots of scope and for my essay I did Caravaggio. The tests were in the studio. I felt at home there.

As my final term came to an end I found, unexpectedly, that I was going to miss school and the chums I had made…my most chosen friends. I was even going to miss masters like Jumbo, Pisc Long, Rodgers and, especially, Clubby Nash.

When the entire school, the boys, the girls, the masters and mistresses, gathered on the last day in Fairclough Hall for a final address from Whack, I wobbled. It wasn't what he said, because he did little more than wish all leavers success in 'the world beyond these walls', it was that mixture of excitement and impending change, of not knowing what was to come. When we roared out 'Forty years on', like some of the others around me I was a bit choked and damp-eyed. I did not much like departures even though there would be many happy days to remember. I felt hollow as we filed from the hall for the last time to pack our trunks, shake hands and say our brave farewells.

Chapter Twenty

*M*um declared, 'The sooner Mr Churchill takes his coat off and gets this war over the better we'll be. It is all becoming too dreadful, and I can't bear thinking of what is happening to our poor lads.'

We were in the summerhouse, Mum, Dad, Paddy and I, and Amy had set out afternoon tea with scones, and cut-'n'-come-again, our favourite family fruitcake.

Dad said, 'I'm afraid we're up against it…in for a long haul. No easy answers.'

'Well,' replied Mum, 'you can all thank your lucky stars that you've got butter on your bread. We're now to have coupons for butter, sugar and ham, and other meats as well.'

Dad nodded agreement and added it was time to tighten our belts and prepare for worse to come. It seemed nothing could halt the blitz in Europe. France was in disarray and German tanks had reached the outskirts of Paris. Our soldiers, outnumbered and surrounded, had retreated to the beaches of Dunkirk. The attempt to rescue more than 300,000 of them was being disrupted by bombs and gunfire. There were mounting numbers of casualties, but the operation was being described as heroic. On the home front Britain's banks and businesses were being placed under the control of the government and all manpower was being mobilised under a Parliament Act. Churchill, on whom Mum pinned her faith, said all he could promise was blood, toil, tears and sweat.

As we sat in the warm sunshine looking down on Paddy's immaculate tennis lawn, smooth and green as a billiard table, it was unreal. The war seemed a world away.

It wasn't, of course. It was coming closer. Much closer.

Paddy, hands in pockets, had gone walkabout, mainly to inspect the tennis court, and as he was returning he said, 'It's really silly. I heard on the wireless we can only have five inches of water in the bath, and one bar of soap has to last a month.'

I thought – never mind the soap, there were more serious things we would have to think about. Not Paddy of course, he was still too young, but the call-up had begun.

Dad was looking at me and I think he guessed my thoughts. He said, 'Conscription is underway and all men between nineteen and twenty-seven are being called up. The reservists are in already and the navy has been on battle stations for some time…they'll be needing recruits. The air force, too.'

He opened his silver cigarette case, plucked out a Players and lit up. I was not going to say anything, but he did not sound like his old self. Not long ago he had spoken against the war and deplored the loss of life, and not least the bombing of civilians. Now, his tone was different. He said, 'You'll be getting your call-up papers, Johnny. Decision time ahead…army or air force?'

His words aroused Mum. She helped herself to a cigarette from his case, and snapped her lighter. 'Darling, don't be so alarmist! Johnny has plenty of time, there's months yet.'

Dad said, 'Every young man has to get to grips and do his bit. Before long the government will be calling on young women as well, I shouldn't wonder, and not just those land girls, all three services need them too.'

His words shut us up. He got to his feet. 'We'll have a chat about it later, Johnny. I'm going to take a stroll down to the paddock and inspect our air-raid shelter – are you coming?'

I replied that I had things to do, because in fact I had. I wanted to write a note in my diary, which I would then include in my next letter to Anne. My exam results had not been brilliant, but there were a few alphas, which had pleased Mum and Dad and certainly surprised some of the masters at school. Jumbo Liddington had even written a letter: 'In his final year his work improved in every way. Excellent progress.' Clubby Nash also sent a note to tell me he had been in touch with Goldhawk College and they would send me an application form and probably request my school record.

Several weeks later the letter from Goldhawk arrived. I sent back my exam results and filled in the application form. The reply from the principal of Goldhawk stated that I had been accepted as a student in the drawing and painting categories and that further details, including fees, materials and books would follow. Then another letter arrived. It was from Anne and had come to me direct, not via Aunt Clara, and it was good news. Her mother, she wrote, had emerged from that coma, but was still confined to bed in the island hospital.

She is under the care of an African doctor. He has been most attentive and we are so grateful to him. My father is more cheerful but there is nothing much we can do. He has his official duties around the island. I sit with mother in the mornings and read to her, though she is asleep half the time. I picked up a book on the island's customs. It is spooky.

It says the eighteenth-century Africans brought their spirits to the island, which was, and still is, mainly Roman Catholic. But – what about La Diablesse? She is a beautiful maiden but if you meet her on a mountain track and try to run away she will push you to the edge of the cliff. You can be saved only if you pluck out a few pubic hairs and put them between your lips! There is also Soucouyan, an old woman who sheds her skin, turns into a ball of fire and sucks your blood. Your only hope is to fill a bowl with peas and make her count them to get her skin back on. You would probably prefer Mama Glo, a mermaid who sits beside pools and makes you rub her back. If you refuse you have to collect 1,000 bamboo leaves.

I have seen a little of the island, it is very beautiful, but it is so hot and humid. The other night I had to take my mother's place and accompany my father to Government House. It was an official function in honour of a lady called Napier who has become the first woman ever to be elected to a Caribbean legislature. I don't like being so far away and I miss you so much, Johnny. I think of you all the time. I hope that when mother is quite recovered I will be able to return to the UK. Take care, dearest. We get very worrying reports on the war and can hardly believe the Germans have occupied all of France.

Chapter Twenty-one

*T*he professor was a small man, a little elf with a white goatee beard. He was an ancient with a surprisingly high-pitched voice. Making his way round the circle of students he came and perched on my donkey and with a sharp pencil he drew a thumbnail. I thought it was a joke. This was a life class and for lack of a live model that morning we were being made to draw the casts of naked Grecian ladies.

'Detail, Hartside! Detail!' he piped. 'Do not attempt to draw form so rapidly, because you cannot...who do you think you are, Leonardo?'

Silly old prick, he was more sarcastic than Sarki Stan. This was my first 'lesson' at Goldhawk and a bit unsettling. I had expected to be at the college in London but it had been evacuated to Oxford and granted temporary quarters in the Ashmolean.

I had to admit that the college was helpful in arranging personal accommodation. My lodgings were in a semi on the Woodstock Road, the home of a Mr and Mrs Angus McLeod, whose son Ruari was away; a lieutenant in the Royal Navy. They were a kindly couple but very Scottish and said things like 'Ye'll be takin' a wee dander after your tea?'

The only dander I took was on Ruari's bicycle down the summer lanes where, armed with pad and paints, I made watercolour sketches of farms, downland and stands of magnificent trees. I was happy out there, whizzing through the fresh air and the sweet-smelling grasses and flowers. At times I was aware of aeroplanes overhead, very high in the blue. Spitfires and Hurricanes, I was told.

The McLeods made a fuss of me, probably because they were missing their son and I was occupying the space he left behind. I knew no one in Oxford. They assumed I was lonely and went as far as to introduce me to their neighbours' daughter, Kirsteen. She was an attractive girl, about eighteen I supposed, and was waiting to start university. The McLeods meant well, but I soon realised that Kirsteen meant, or intended, something else. Occasionally she accompanied me on my forays into the countryside and was becoming a distraction. When I stopped to make a sketch and get out my paints she would pull up alongside me, dismount and flop down on the grass or against a wall to take 'a wee sunbath'. This entailed exposing her shapely legs and arms and sometimes hoisting her dress up a little too far.

Distracting as she was, and as absorbing as my studies became, I was more concerned about Anne, for I had received no further word from her until shortly before term ended. It was Mum who phoned. She had sad news from Aunt Clara. Anne's mother, having survived her awful accident and subsequent complications, had suddenly died. I was shocked. Mum said, 'I believe it was not wholly unexpected. She had been in hospital for some time. Did you realise that, Johnny?'

The news stunned me, for I thought she was recovering and felt sure she would have survived. My concern for Anne was mixed with sheer frustration. I longed to be with her. I knew I had to write, and I wanted to. But I simply could not find the right words. There would have to be a funeral and how terrible it would be to see your mother buried in a far country…no family or friends to support you, just you and your father. I prayed for them that night.

Aunt Clara kept in touch and when I returned to Yearsby for the holiday there was nothing that brought any comfort – in fact the news was worse. There had been a riot, or an upsurge of violence, then we heard no more. Silence. A news blackout. It lasted until I had to return to Oxford.

Two uneasy and troubled weeks passed before, at last, a letter was forwarded to me. It served only to give rise to further dismay. Anne hardly mentioned her mother's funeral, and I think I could understand that. But she was now troubled by other matters.

There is class prejudice here and we are warned to take the greatest care among the blacks and coloureds. It is not to do with colour really, just that they dislike being commanded to do almost anything. There is no use in telling the descendant of a former slave what he must do, you must not demand, you have to ask. Only then, in due time, will anyone do the task or errand.

With Government House people all may seem well. There are receptions, cocktail parties and Sunday picnics in Runaway Bay or inland on a river. The food is basic but there is plenty of fruit, and rum and ice is carried on every outing. Behind this I have to tell you, Johnny, that all is *not* well. Most people carry guns – and they are used. The other day the Rotary Club organised a donkey race, a very big affair. There was a lot of betting, and cheating as well. Two people were shot.

I was becoming alarmed at her news, and a second letter that arrived halfway through my term at the Ashmolean was even more worrying.

Dearest Johnny,

I really wish I had not come here. My father is glad I am with him but he is feeling the strain. The truth is, this is a very beautiful island but a dangerous place where violence can erupt at any time. A Canadian estate owner who was a friend to father, has been killed. And a European businessman has had his property in Roseau burned down, and on his land at Grand Bay in the south of the island all his crops have been destroyed. And that's not the end of it. Six visitors from America – tourists I think, three were staying with us – were bathing in a river when they were attacked and several injured. No one knows who did it. Some say it's the Dreads, a group of Rastafarians who are against privilege and class. I admit I am frightened, and my father is not just angry, I think he would give anything not to be here but says he can't bear to leave Mother, if you see what I mean.

It was a terrible letter. It was as if a part of the war through which we were living had crossed the ocean to invade what had been an island paradise.

War on the home front. That was what it felt like at Yearsby. It was Mum and Dad. Hostilities commenced. She became an ostrich, head in sand, determined to persuade Dad not to listen to the news on the wireless, which was so depressing. But he persisted. He listened daily and said the situation was very serious.

'London is still getting it. You have to realise the Blitz is killing thousands in those night raids. They're destroying the city.'

I realised the war was changing Dad. His attitude hardened. He'd been against the war, but now he said we had no choice. We could be invaded and we had to protect our shores. The entire country was rising to the challenge and there could be no argument about it – except Mum who seemed determined to argue. Every day. And she really was troubled. It all left me miserably undecided and I started to argue within myself. If we called ourselves Christians, as I had been taught, our duty was to renounce war. Killing did not bring peace, it served only to inflame hatred – and now the conflict was not confined to France and the Low Countries. That was bad enough but Yugoslavia and Greece had fallen to the Germans and in Africa the Wehrmacht were proving too strong for our troops. I did not have much faith in anything, though I did still try to believe in God. Instinct told us that Whack's morning readings at the lectern made sense. But now, I felt no comfort as the violence grew worse.

I took the phone. To my surprise it was Walt. He was ringing to ask a favour. Could he and Liz call by? 'We'd love to meet up again and if it was possible, Johnny, could you do with us for a night?'

I was delighted. Of course they could come.

It was great. Liz looked as lovely as ever, bright and bubbly, very grown up and smart, and Walt was his cheery, wicked self. They were like a ray of sunshine lighting the gloom at Yearsby. Walt explained that he was on his way to Catterick, the big army camp just off the A1.

'On His Majesty's service!' he proclaimed, snapping to attention and offering a pretended salute. 'Joining up! Got to do my bit for King and country, and Liz is too! Wants to be a Wren. She's off to Pompi, aren't you, Liz.'

I said I didn't believe it.

'It's true, Johnny,' she smiled. 'We've got to do something. There are women in the factories and on farms…you can't see me doing that, can you?'

Walt winked. 'It's the uniform. Probably the sailor boys, too!'

She put out her tongue at him.

Walt said he had news of our other chums. 'Pop's going for the RAF. Fancies himself as a bomber pilot, but he'll probably find he becomes a tail-end Charlie. Cumberland and Squirt? They're talking about the RNVR.'

'What about Jack Emslie?' I asked. 'Have you seen him?'

They had no news of him or of Mortimer A. V. or Squeak Whiting, but they'd heard Pee-Wee Smith fancied the Naval Reserve, and Plowright had been on a farm for some time, digging for victory.

Mum was as kind as ever and clearly found Walt and Liz a welcome distraction. She even stopped being argumentative. She said Liz could have the granny flat all to herself and Walt could bed down in the nursery. She told Amy to set lunch for us in the study so we could be together – 'and catch up on old times!'

I knew they were waiting their time to ask about Anne, and presently they did. I told them the latest. Liz was upset and Walt was not smiling. They knew better than anyone else what Anne and I felt for each other. Liz said, 'Don't take it wrong, Johnny, but Walt and I, we said from the start you were meant for each other.'

We fell silent. I didn't want to talk about it. Before nightfall we went for a walk across the fields to The Wagon Wheel, the one pub in the village. There were just the three of us, hand in hand, and I felt comforted and lucky to be with my best friends again. We ordered pints and perched by the fire that crackled with logs and sent the sparks flying. Walt spotted a squaddie at the bar and he went over to speak to him. Liz took my hand and said, softly, 'This is really chummy. We talk about you a lot. Walt thinks the world of you, Johnny.'

I was touched. I said, 'I think about you and Walt, too. And frankly, I wonder if you ever think of…you know, getting spliced?'

She shrieked: 'Married? Golly, to *him*?'

When Walt returned, they talked of Anne again, and Liz said how much she missed her. Then they wanted to know what I was going to do. Walt said he had the answer. 'You'll have to join up. What d' you fancy, Johnny? Why not sign on with me?'

I knew they'd ask. I told them I had not yet made up my mind, which was a lie really, because I felt I had. Well, almost. Walt decided that, on second thoughts, he could not see me in the PBI. 'You were always a bit of a high flyer, so why not the RAF?'

'Not too good at heights,' I replied, thinking of those chaps in their Hurricanes, up there.

As we paid up and donned our coats we were brought down to earth with a bump. The wireless on the bar counter crackled and announced that the Nazi mechanised war machine was pouring division after division across the Polish border into Russia.

Chapter Twenty-two

*T*hree weeks later – the most wonderful news. Mum forwarded a letter to me from Aunt Clara, in which she wrote that Anne and her father were planning to return to the UK. Whether or not it was compassionate leave was not clear, but the rest was great.

> It will be a hazardous undertaking. It seems there's a Canadian airman called Sandy who owns an island hopper, I think it's a seaplane. He is to fly them to Antigua via Guadeloupe and St Johns. From there they hope to board a boat for San Juan in Puerto Rico, which is American. Then from there they fly to La Guardia, New York. If they cannot get a flight they might get on a cargo steamer. I'm sure they should not do it. There are German submarines in the Caribbean Sea as well as the Atlantic. Anyway, I believe the Colonial Office has confirmed the attempt, and is helping.

It made my heart thump. Reports claimed that not only were German U-boats being launched from Atlantic harbours in France, they had armed merchant ships and they too were attacking our ships bringing supplies from America. Aunt Clara was right. Such a crossing would be fraught with danger, and while merchantmen from the West Indies were running the gauntlet to British ports they were taking a no-win gamble. That was what Dad said.

Back at Oxford I was finding it difficult to concentrate on my work. Prof made it clear he was not satisfied with my life drawing, and back at Woodstock Road the McLeods noticed and asked if I was unwell. I decided I had better explain about Anne. Mr McLeod surprised me by asking if I was a believer, and when I looked puzzled he said, 'Y' know, laddie, a belief in your maker. You're not church, then?'

When I told him I had been brought up as a Quaker from childhood he made a face and regarded me with a frown verging on suspicion.

'Oh, a Quaker is it? They're not believers, are they? Funny lot. Pardon me saying so, son, because I'm not well informed, but they are regarded hereabouts as miserable folk. They've got a place just outside Oxford, not like a church at all, but I suppose that's because they are not Christians. They don't have hymns, and no one really knows what they do.'

I was in no mood to explain and certainly had no wish to enter into an argument, but I did assure him that Quakers were certainly Christians who read their Bible and particularly the New Testament. He answered that was as maybe, and added, 'If you're worried about your girl over there, you should remember your prayers, my lad.'

Mrs McLeod had listened quietly to our conversation and I felt she might understand rather better than her husband. 'Father's right,' she said. 'About prayer. We worry a lot about our Ruari out on the sea, facing danger every day. But we say our prayers for him at night, yes, every night and at church, so we know he will be in God's keeping.'

At the term's end I arrived back at Yearsby on the very day the papers were delivered. 'It's your call-up,' said Mum. 'It seems so early, I don't expect you want them any more than I want to see them.'

Dad had obviously given some thought as to what I should do. 'If it was my choice, Johnny, I would say RAF. There are more aeroplanes coming off the line now, and it is said we have plenty of engineers, but more pilots are badly needed, and air crew, especially in Bomber Command.'

He took the view I knew he would take, now being wholly committed to what he called 'the struggle', and I understood his well-meant advice. But did I want to drop bombs on women and children? Did I want to shoot up young airmen, many of whom were probably my age? The truth was that in my heart I knew I did not...I had not been given life or leave to kill and take away the lives of others. To kill was wrong and I could not understand church people who supported war. It was not the Christian way.

Dad had another suggestion. 'With your talents, Johnny, you could probably be drafted into a camouflage unit. They're the boys who disguise guns and tanks and aeroplanes from the enemy. It's vital work. If you want I could have a word with Fladgate when I'm next down south. He's got influence...a group captain. He'd probably get a posting for you.'

I thought about it a lot. I tried to argue the case within myself and knew that I had to decide one way or another without delaying too long. I had been brought up a Quaker. I had a right to refuse to kill...there were others who took a stand on the grounds of conscience and I felt I should do the same.

Dad became quite angry. 'If everyone refused to take up arms we would no longer be a free country, we'd be like slaves under the Nazis!'

He stumped out of the study and shouted, 'And then see how you'd like it! Don't you know what they're doing to the Jews and the Polish people?'

The atmosphere was distinctly chilly and there was one other thing I dared not tell anyone, it was too personal, too strange. In Quaker meetings for worship there was something else. On occasion, in the deep silence, I sensed a presence that was no more than a shadow, a wraith that visited and paused in the very centre of our gathering, and it seemed to me that this was the presence of God, or maybe the barely discernible figure of Jesus. I could never tell anyone, they would think I had taken leave of my senses. But this experience occurred more than once, and never left me.

In the end it was an unexpected letter from Jack Emslie that sealed my decision. He was nearly a year older than I was, and much cleverer, and I was delighted to hear from him. He wrote that he had decided to register as a CO, a conscientious objector, and had to go before a tribunal. This he had done, and was now waiting to hear the outcome.

He told me, 'I applied to join the Quaker Relief Service. There are teams already overseas in several theatres of war – in Africa, Italy and Burma – and if I get the go-ahead I'll be free to join the training unit, it's near Birmingham I think.'

If Jack got permission I decided I would follow his example. There was a chance that I too might be able to join the QRS. My head and my heart were in conflict because I did not want to be branded a coward, and I so admired the courage of those who risked their lives in battle.

Chapter Twenty-three

*T*here was no point in going back to Oxford, so I remained at home to await notification from the tribunal. I had no idea where or when it would be held until a month later when the letter arrived. It had been an uncomfortable month with Dad expressing disappointment and Mum finding excuses for me.

'It's no surprise that Johnny takes the view that he does, it's what he was taught from the beginning *and* at Quaker school...and who sent him there in the first place?'

When it arrived the document was brief enough. It simply stated I had to report to an address in Marygate, York, which, Mum suggested, must be a sheriff's or a magistrate's lodging near the law courts. She drove me down and pulled up in the shadow of Clifford's Tower, a shell of a castle perched on a green mound and surrounded by prison buildings with bars at the windows. I did not like the look of that. I had heard of other 'objectors' who had been imprisoned for their refusal to obey the call-up.

I rang the bell of what looked like a small Georgian mansion house. Nothing happened. I rang again. Mum said, 'I'll wait for you in the car. And, good luck, darling.'

I had almost given up when the door swung open and an old chap in black knickerbockers and a casual shirt gestured me across the threshold.

'Mr Hartside?' he asked with a look of distaste as if I smelled of something bad. I nodded and he said, 'Upstairs, second door on the left. Knock.'

It was an elegant, panelled room, deeply carpeted and full of antique furniture. At the far end, near a window bright with the afternoon sun, was a table behind which three men were seated and before which was a single chair. The man in the middle shuffled some notes then looked up. 'You are Mr John Hartside?'

'Yes, sir.'

He motioned to the empty chair and said, 'Sit.' He then looked down at his papers again, recited my full name and age, the Yearsby address, my father's occupation and the fact that I was a student of painting and art history at Goldhawk College, evacuated to Oxford.

'Is that correct?'

I nodded.

'Speak up, man!'

The fellow on his right looked a good deal younger and, I thought, was probably army. He had a thin, blond moustache. He folded his arms and said, 'We understand, Hartside, that you are refusing to obey the call-up to join HM Forces. Is that the case?'

I answered that it was.

'You must understand that you are here to explain yourself. By what reason and what right do you have to refuse conscription? It is our duty to find out why you will not join the armed forces.'

The third man, a fat, balding fellow then uttered, 'You realise that people like you are a waste of time, government time. Have you not heard we are at war?'

I decided he was a fat, pompous oaf, probably a civil servant.

'Well, Hartside? What have you to say?'

'Yes, sir.'

His plummy face turned a darker shade of pink. 'Yes what, Hartside?'

I realised he was trying to intimidate me. I did not feel confident but I said I was a Quaker and thought I should explain further but he forestalled me by barking, 'We know about the Quakers...good works, eh, is that what you do because if it is...' He paused then leaned forward and growled, 'Why not do some good works for your King and country?'

I was about to inform him of the Quaker Peace Testimony when he straightened up and shouted, 'There was a time when cowards like you were put away...no better than traitors, Hartside!'

That really got to me. I stood up. I was not going to be bullied and I started to tell him how Quakers were advised to live 'in the virtue of that life and power which takes away the occasion of all wars', and that our conviction and belief was wholly and immovably a Christian belief. But I got no further. The man in the middle said, 'Sit down, Hartside!' I did so as the man on the right raised his head, studied the ceiling and asked, 'Suppose, Hartside, that you and your family found yourselves face to face with the Hun and that a trooper in the infamous Wehrmacht was about to shoot your mother…what good works would you do then? Would you not respond, would you not try to protect her and *fight?*'

'I don't know, sir.'

He exploded: '*Not know?*'

'I can't say, sir, because I have never been in that situation, I don't know what I would do!'

Eyes rolled. Glances were exchanged. The man in the middle sighed and said, 'Perhaps you would be good enough to leave us. Wait outside.' And he gestured towards the door.

On the landing, at the top of the stairs, the mysterious fellow in the black knickerbockers was waiting. He said nothing but simply stood there as if on guard. It was only five minutes but it felt like an hour before a voice shouted, 'Come back in, Hartside!' The knickerbockers nodded to the door.

I did as I was told, and sat in the chair and waited. The interrogators had risen and were standing together looking out of the window. I could not hear what they were saying. Finally, they turned and took their places at the table again. The middle man said, 'We have to accept what you have told us. But we do not accept that you can simply duck out when most other young men are prepared to do their duty, to fight for their country and for freedom. Indeed, at this very moment lads of your age are putting their lives on the line. We understand that your refusal to stand with them is a matter of conscience and you plead exemption. However, we have decided that you should at least do something for your country…a job, Hartside.'

I replied that I would be prepared to be employed as a non-combatant, and wished to be allowed to join the QRS. I would serve wherever I was needed.

The middle man said, 'It is not for you to choose, Hartside! We take it that you have a clean medical record and that you are healthy. Are you healthy?'

'I think so, sir. I played games at school. Soccer, cricket, tennis…'

'Never mind the games, Hartside. My colleagues see you as arty and effeminate. I do not necessarily agree with them but you could do with a bit of toughening up. We have therefore decided that there is a job you could do to help your country. You will be registered as from this month to do farm work. Work on the land. You will help in the vital task of food production.'

The apoplectic man piped up: 'That should suit you, Hartside, working with land girlies, eh?'

The middle man looked across to him and shook his head as if to say that was enough. Then he turned back to me: 'Farm work. That is our decision. It will be ratified with immediate effect. That is all.'

I tried to tell him that relief work with the QRS would be just as useful but he cut me short. '*Thank* you, Hartside. You may go.'

I turned and left the room and went quietly downstairs to where knickerbockers opened the door for me. Back in the car Mum asked, 'Was it hard? You look quite pale, darling.'

I did not feel pale. I felt disappointed. 'Futile!' I said. 'Futile!' I was very angry.

Chapter Twenty-four

The high hills. It was the names that charmed me, northern names like Wetherlam and Mickledore. I was to live among them as a farm lad and, oddly, it was Mum who found the place where I would work.

'I'll give Sara a ring. Sara Whitehead. We were at school together, but over the years we lost touch. I believe she married a farmer called William Borthwick. You never know but he might just be glad of an extra pair of hands.'

I did not think that my hands could be of much use to a farmer but I had no choice in the matter and in due course I found myself in a distant place not knowing what was to come. It felt miles from civilisation. I went there in a very poor mood, still cursing the tribunal for not allowing me to join the QRS.

William Borthwick's place was halfway up a long valley overshadowed by those hills. It was called Warnscale Farm and crouched low beneath the crags, an L-shaped grey stone building with blind-looking windows and a slate roof. Beside it stood a cluster of outbuildings…a long barn with a hay loft like the one at the Whitworth school farm, with several sheds or storehouses across a cobbled yard.

I was surprised to find a small hotel adjacent to the farm, which, I learned, also belonged to the Borthwicks. A badly painted notice board at the entrance to the drive announced 'Scarsdale House. Accommodation'.

To reach this outpost of civilisation from the rail halt miles away you took the Dalehead Traction, a once-a-day bus known locally as The DTs and which, in addition to transporting occasional hikers, carried supplies including groceries, coal and sometimes chickens or hens. It also served as the post bus, delivering parcels and letters. On arrival at the farm I was greeted by Borthwick's wife, Sara, and was immediately captivated. She was plump and roly-poly with dimples and a big friendly smile, and a neat head of brown hair plaited and curled to form a kind of crown. I guessed she would be in her forties. She wore an apron over her dress.

A handshake, a cheery wink and she said, 'Now then, let's see. You'll be Paddy, the eldest?'

'No, I'm John, but yes, I am the eldest. Paddy is still at school.'

'Did you ever!' she exclaimed, clasping her hands. 'My goodness – it's such a long time, know what I mean?' She paused, stared long and hard then said, 'Is that your case? Come in the kitchen, we'll have a chat. I expect you'd like a nice hot cuppa. My giddy aunt! Just think, all those years. I've only got one. Jamie. He's started agri college, then he's going to take over here when he's finished.'

Sometimes you meet someone you like and trust on sight. Someone sweet as honey and whom you feel could be a real friend. But when her husband walked in the feeling was hardly the same. He did not take my offered hand.

'You'll be the bloody artist,' he said, throwing himself into a chair by the kitchen range. 'Didn't want to go fight in the war then? Got a cup for me, Mother?'

Sara Borthwick frowned. 'That's no way to treat a guest, Bill, come to help us. Mind your manners!'

'He's no guest, are you, son? He's here to get down to work along with Zeke. I'll not object, long as he knows his arse from his elbow…you done any farming, son?'

'Take no heed,' Sara Borthwick said, quickly. 'He's not himself, just out of sorts. Lost a beast last night, didn't you, love?'

She filled a kettle. 'Set yourself down, John. I'll do us a cup then you can tell us all about your ma. Is she still a bonny little shrimp? She was pretty as a picture. We were like two peas in a pod. I was a strip of a lass as well, once upon a time, you know!'

A shadow passed across the window and a third person stepped into the kitchen. He was small but thick above the waist, strong and square built and, I guessed, about my age. He wore breeches, very muddy boots and brought a farm smell in with him. 'This,' said Sara, 'is young Zeke from over at Wetherlam Farm. Zeke, say hello to John, he's come to help us for the duration.'

He nodded, and took my hand with a grip that nearly cracked my bones.

'Tak' yer bloody cap off!' growled Borthwick. Then he turned to me and an evil grin spread across his face. 'You're his mucker. Ye'll muck out wi' him!' He gave a throaty laugh. 'Twa muckers better than one!'

The newcomer stood twirling his cap in his hands. He had a slightly slanting look, shy but not unfriendly.

'You can take his case, Zeke,' said Sara Borthwick. 'Show him his bed while I get supper on.'

Zeke picked up my case as if it was as light as a feather, which it wasn't, and said, 'This way, then,' and led me from the kitchen and across the yard to one of the small outhouses. We climbed a short flight of wooden steps. There was one door and one window. Inside were a narrow bed, a table and a chair. I guessed the place had not been used for some time.

'Bit freezy,' grinned Zeke. 'But tak' no bother. If they don't give you a stove I'll get one for you from my dad. Any road up, you'll be over to see us, and you'll be right welcome!'

A friendly grin. Another crunching handshake – and he was gone.

I sat down to supper at the kitchen table. There was just me and Mr and Mrs B. I imagined there would be food rationing here as there was everywhere else but it didn't seem to apply. Sara, as she said I must call her, served up a piping hot stew in thick brown gravy with piles of potatoes, beans and carrots followed by the sweetest and lightest bread and butter pudding I had ever tasted. And she explained about Zeke. 'He's a Millburn from over at Dalehead. They've a bigger spread than us, but mainly sheep. Herdwicks.'

I asked why Zeke didn't work on the Millburn Farm. Borthwick replied, 'They've plenty over yonder. There's old Zeke still active, but can't do the shepherding now, that's Isaac's job, with young Isaac and Lally and Ruth if needed.'

Sara added, 'There's Hetty too and Clemency, they're still teenage but we give them work here in the hotel, parlour maid, bit of cooking and bed-making.'

Borthwick surprised me when he said he had a small milk herd as well as arable and some grass. Sara explained that they used to run some sheep on the hills but it got too much for them in the winter.

We talked a little while longer, then she said, 'You'll want your bed, Johnny. I'll do a bottle for you, it will be a bit cold there across the yard.'

'No need to spoil him,' growled Borthwick. 'He's got to get to learn our ways…no place for softies here.'

It certainly was chilly in that shed. I did not sleep well. I think the mattress was stuffed with straw, and my head was stuffed with images as I tossed and turned half-asleep and half-waking. And, where had the war gone? I lay awake for hours listening to the silence.

They were too long in the leg, so Sara pinned them up – dungarees that she borrowed from her husband to spare my trousers. Spreading basic slag on the long meadow, she warned, would be a dirty job. Zeke was to be my instructor. He pronounced the stuff 'bassik', and arrived leading Neb, the carthorse, and showed me how to get him between the shafts of the wagon. We then shovelled masses of the slag into it. It was heavy work and took ages. Then, fastening the halter, Zeke said, 'Noo, me li'le creeket, get yourseln' up on the top and when we get through yon gate I'll lead Neb while you scale. Look, I'll show yer.'

He dug his shovel into a pile of the stuff, then swaying his body from left to right he turned his shovel so that he sprayed the slag in an even arc to one side. I thought – easy. But it wasn't. The slag was thick and heavy, like very small grey pebbles, and standing up on the cart full of it was tricky once Zeke started to lead Neb along. The ground was uneven and the cart swayed from side to side. Several times I lost my balance and fell over into the stuff, much to Zeke's amusement. After two lengths of the meadow he said, 'I'll tak' ower for a bit. Think ye could manage Neb? Tak' his halter and hold it light like, don't pull, and he'll go along wi' you. Never bother, he won't bite!'

He climbed up onto the wagon and I got down and took the halter as instructed. The moment I did so Neb snorted and took off. Sure enough, he didn't bite but such was his acceleration that Zeke yelled and fell off the back of the wagon as Neb made for the far end of the meadow. He nearly pulled my arm off, so I had to let him go and away he went hauling the wagon behind him. Zeke scrambled to his feet and gave chase, finally bringing both horse and wagon to a standstill. I ran to catch up with them and shouted that I couldn't hold Neb, he was far too strong. Zeke was laughing. 'No bother, me li'le creeket. It'll tak' him while he gets used to you. Get yourself back up on top!'

By this time I was aching from my legs to my arms and my back, but I did as instructed. I got into a rhythm scaling the slag and in due course we covered a third of the meadow. When we came to a standstill I was blowing harder than Neb. We rested a moment and I saw a small figure approaching. It was a girl. On top of her jersey and breeches she was wearing a maid's apron and had a basket over one arm. Zeke pointed and said, 'Yonder's Clemency, she'll be bringing our piece.' The piece turned out to be jam sandwiches and a flask of scalding tea.

Clemency had dark, sparkling eyes full of mischief. She looked up at me and said, 'Are you from the agri college?'

Zeke answered for me. 'No, you daft ha'porth, he's the one I told you, come to help us. Right, Johnny?'

'That's right. Zeke's showing me how to scale.'

She stared at me for a long time, then turned to Zeke and put her tongue out.

'Show yer? He couldn't teach a row a monkeys!'

Zeke set about her, tried to chase her away, but she returned and leaned against the wagon watching us eat. When we'd finished she gathered up the remains into the basket and started back across the meadow.

'Ye can come an' see us if ye like!' she called. 'I'm in the hotel now, y' know!'

Zeke shouted, 'Get off!' Then he turned to me. 'Cheeky little devil! Tak' no heed. She's allus flirting!'

We toiled on for a couple of hours then trundled back to the farm. Zeke took Neb out of the shafts and gave him some hay. Then he led him round the back of the hotel, gave him a slap and sent him off up a narrow valley. There was no road, just grass and a small swift-flowing stream.

'He likes it up there. Come to no harm. Ye can go get him in the morning. Now, we'll see t' cows for milking.'

The byre was behind the long barn and inside there were about seven beasts, some lying on the straw and one standing motionless with sleepy eyes and jaws chewing.

'Boss treats 'em like kids. They're right valuable. Ever milked a cow, Johnny?'

I shook my head.

'Never worry, I'll learn yer.' He fetched a milking stool and a pail, placed it under the beast and took the udders in his hands. 'Come on, Patsy,' he murmured, leaning his head against the cow's flanks and starting to squeeze and pull. Patsy swished her tail as Zeke began to hum a tune. 'Allus sing a bit,' he said, with a shy grin. 'Ye like a song, don't ye, Patsy!'

With a tinny sound the milk spurted into the pail...swish and spill, swish and spill, until the milk began to foam, rich and creamy in the bottom. He went round the rest of the herd, and gave me the stool and pail. 'Your turn, Johnny. Ye'll likely get the hang on it.'

Surprisingly, I did. It was easier than I thought. One of the beasts was dry, but for the rest we decanted the milk into two large cans standing at the door of the byre.

'See ye in the morning,' said Zeke, preparing to take his leave. 'We'll finish off that bassik.'

So ended my first day as a farm worker. It was nothing like I had expected, and I limped over to the back door of the farm, stiff and tired. When I pushed open the kitchen door I saw that Sara was busy ironing. Beyond her a tall girl was clattering pans on the cooking range.

'Now then,' said Sara looking up. 'You'll be tired, Johnny, that's heavy work with the bassik. You'd best get your overalls off and I'll give them a wash. It's dirty stuff.'

She turned to the tall girl and said, 'Hetty, this is Johnny who's come to help us.'

The girl looked up and nodded then went back to her pans. She was quite a striking figure, erect, blonde and with a pale complexion. Sara said she was Zeke's sister and older than Clemency. She put down her iron. 'You'll want a bath I daresay. You can't have one every day

115

because of the water. I'll be using ours here presently, so you can use one in the hotel. Hetty will show you. Here's a fresh towel.'

We went in the back way. Hetty took my hand and led me as if I were a child. She pointed to the stairs. 'It's up there, ye'll see the door's open.'

Before going up I peered into the lounge. It was deserted but for one solitary figure, an elderly man in an armchair before a fire of smouldering embers. He was reading a book and there was a little skullcap perched on his balding pate. I guessed he must be Jewish. On the table beside him was a half-bottle of whisky and a glass tumbler.

Chapter Twenty-five

*T*he hills fairly sang in that early light as I set off to get Neb. Their flanks and buttresses soared skywards out of a thin, low-lying mist. There were no trees, just bushes of juniper or thorn on the lower slopes. As I plodded along there was a tune in my head: 'And did those feet in ancient times…' 'Jerusalem'. That was the hymn and the only reason I supposed that it was in my head was Neb. The previous evening Sara had told me that Neb was short for Nebuchadnezzar who I vaguely recalled was the King of Babylon. 'It's Zeke's family you see,' Sara had explained. 'They've mostly got Bible names. Old Ezekiel, that's young Zeke's father, he's very religious. He'll quote pages of the Bible at you off the top of his head. You might think it a bit strange, but they're neighbourly folk over there by Wetherlam.'

I carried a small bowl of oats as well as Neb's halter in case he proved difficult to catch. It was a long trudge up that valley. Looking ahead to the far end I could see water like a silver streak falling from a forbidding buttress and splashing and dancing from rock to rock. It was beautiful. Eventually I spotted Neb and when he saw me approaching he lifted his head, and as I moved closer he backed away snorting. After several attempts he allowed me to come closer. Perhaps he could smell the oats. I placed the bowl on a rock and stepped back a few paces. He bowed his head and advanced, then his long brown nose was in the bowl. Breakfast time!

After that it was easy. He allowed me to slip his halter on and we paced gently back between the tufts and spikes of long grass.

Our first task was to complete scaling the bassik. Zeke did the shovelling while I led Neb. He seemed quite docile now and I felt a kinship with him. We were getting along just fine. 'Good old Neb!' I

117

shouted. 'Boss of Babylon!' Zeke paused, looked round then nodded and grinned.

If scaling that bassik was a dirty job our second task was worse. We had to muck out the byre. It was a squelchy, stinking chore. We sloshed the muck into the now emptied wagon then carted it round to the midden. It very quickly became clear to me that, for the most part, farming was dirty work, and it was even more clear that I lacked suitable clothing for the job. That was why, a few days later, after work Zeke said he would take me down to the village where I could purchase a pair of suitable trousers.

'Breeches, me li'le creeket,' he said. 'Summut the kind I've got. There's a place there will fit you up.'

Getting down to the village involved riding pillion on the motorbike that Zeke used each day to get from Wetherlam to Warnscale. It was an exhilarating, if death-defying ride, as Zeke leaned at speed into the corners of the narrow, winding lanes. Cottages, farmsteads and grazing cattle flew past and the hills dropped lower, criss-crossed by a network of boundary walls. On arriving at the village Zeke pointed out an ancient-looking haberdasher's store. It appeared to offer anything that could be worn, from lengths of tweed and coats, to caps, hats, ribbons and wool and – an odd addition – some second-hand books. The only thing lacking was breeches. The old chap who was probably the owner of the shop said he supplied breeches to order. They were made elsewhere. I decided to order a pair, bottle green and well buttoned, and accordingly he produced a tape measure and noted my 'dimensions'. He said the garment would be ready in about two weeks' time.

Frustrated, I was not going to return empty-handed so, at a shoe shop further down the street, I purchased a pair of really stout black boots.

Back at the farm Sara called out that DTs had brought the newspapers and the mail and there was a letter addressed to me. It had been delivered to the hotel so I went across immediately and found it on a table in the lounge. The Jewish gentleman I had noticed at the fireside was still there with a woman I supposed to be his wife. They were crouched over a small wireless set, listening attentively.

I recognised Mum's hand. She wrote:

> There is such a thing as the post, Johnny. We are still
> waiting to hear how you are getting on. I thought Sara
> might have written, but we've heard nothing. Perhaps you
> have sent a letter and it's gone astray. It wouldn't surprise
> me, they say the government's censorship is affecting letters
> everywhere. Anyway, do your best, we're anxious to hear. Is
> it a big farm? And tell Sara it would be lovely to hear from
> her as well. The war news is utterly depressing, but I have
> something to tell you that I am sure will cheer you up.
> We've heard from Aunt Clara that Anne and her father
> have just returned and are safely back in the UK. Isn't that
> wonderful! They are somewhere in the south. It seems they
> managed to get on a flight from America. We had no idea
> there was so much air traffic over the Atlantic, but it's
> mainly down to BOAC. They are flying American clippers
> on something called the Returning Ferry Run into Poole in
> Dorset of all places! It's amazing when you hear what goes
> on. Your father says BOAC are also doing the Ball Bearing
> Run to Sweden, and the Horseshoe to Durban, India and
> Australia! I don't know what it all means. How the airlines
> manage with the war it's difficult to imagine. Anyway,
> darling, I'm so pleased about Anne. If we get more news I'll
> let you know right away.

To say it was a relief would be the understatement of the year. I
just jumped for joy, it was so sudden, so unexpected, and I determined
to write to Mum that evening, and I would put in a letter for Anne
as well, which she might be able to send on to Aunt Clara.

I gave Sara the message from Mum but I didn't tell her about Anne.
She said she would drop a line to Yearsby. She sighed. 'This war! It's
all so upsetting. That couple, they're the only guests we've got, Polish
refugees. They fled from their home in Lodz and had to leave everything.
They've nowhere to go. We just ask them to pay a bit towards their

food but that's all. I'm so sorry for them, they've left family behind and have no idea what's happened to them. They listen to the wireless all day long.'

Sara added, 'If you ask me the war is spreading. The bombing in London must be terrible. They say people are weeping, those that aren't getting blown to pieces or burned to death with those fire bombs on the city. Twenty thousand killed and now other places are getting it – Portsmouth and even nearer. It's Belfast and Liverpool now.'

That night sleep would not come. I was too excited. Then I thought again of the Jewish couple, listening and waiting. Refugees with no home.

Chapter Twenty-six

*I*n the farming year, as I discovered, there are no official rest days, but Bill Borthwick allowed Zeke and me to take Saturdays and Sundays as half days. 'Far as I'm concerned you can bugger off, do as you like, chase the village tarts for all I care, long as the milking's done!'

Borthwick checked up on us but we did not see him every day. Sara said he spent a lot of time at the coast where he had other business interests and often had to stay overnight.

Our first available Saturday was not totally free. Zeke said Patsy was in season, she had to be serviced and the usual bull was down the valley at Crossgate Farm, home of a family called Durie. It was a good half-hour's walk for Zeke. He put me on Borthwick's rusty old pushbike so that I could act as flanker and 'head her off' if Patsy strayed.

At Crossgate Mr Durie – quite a young chap – took us round to a shed where the business was to be done. In the meantime I looked around and came upon a fenced pen with half a dozen bullocks grazing. I also came across a woman taking a photograph of the hillside behind the farm. When she spotted me she waved and walked across.

'Hello! You are bring the cow to the bull?' It was a foreign-sounding accent.

I nodded and said, 'Good afternoon, Mrs Durie!'

'No, it is not me. I am Catarina.'

A strange accent. She was certainly not English. She wore a short crimson coat buttoned to the neck, jodhpurs, and long boots. No hat, but she had a flock of hair as dark as Anne's, bright red lipstick and large questioning eyes in a square-boned face. I thought she might even be Spanish.

When we were ready to return I asked Zeke about her.

'I don't know nothing about her. My da says she might be a witch, but Mrs Borthwick knows her. I reckon they're friends like, you'd need to ask her.'

We took our way back down the lane, very slowly. Patsy seemed to be in a dream and inclined to wander. I could swear she was smiling to herself as if all was well with the world, and I daresay it was for her.

✳

'She's very interesting,' said Sara that evening when I asked about Catarina. 'She is Argentinean, from a rich family and there are relations in London. Government people I think.'

The valley, I felt, was becoming more intriguing by the day, and when Sara added that she was an artist…'a right clever painter', I wanted to know more.

'If you'd like to meet her, Johnny, I'll see if she'd like to visit, she comes around from time to time for a chat. I'll ask her, but not when Bill's here, he thinks she's a spy for the Germans. That's just nonsense!'

I admit that she seemed a bit strange when I met her at Durie's farm – and she was using a camera. But then – if she really was an artist she might simply have been taking reference pictures for a painting. As it turned out that was exactly what she had been doing. She told me herself when, a week later, she drove up in a battered farm trailer to have tea with Sara, and I was invited.

We sat round the big scrubbed table in the farm kitchen with mugs of scalding tea. In profile Catarina looked younger than I had first thought. She was probably about ten years older than I was and was certainly very slightly coloured. She was cheerful and smiled a lot.

'Tell me what is your name? You are too young to be in the war?'

Sara explained that I was helping on the farm. It was my war work as I had chosen not to join the army.

'That is most sensible. You are neutral – like my family. You have a name?'

'Johnny,' I replied. 'Johnny Hartside.'

'Hartside? Then you have a good heart I think. That I like. Sara tells me you are artist. It is true?'

'Student. I was a student until the war. Painting and drawing.'

'I am a student also. For all of my life. If you are a painter you are always student. There is no end!'

She said her name was Catarina d'Vascon Sallis. Her father was titled and her main family interests were several ranches – with beef cattle I supposed – on the pampas to the south of Buenos Aires. She explained that her time here in the hills was limited and that she would return to London in the autumn on her way back to Argentina. I left her at the table as I had to attend to the milking. Later, on her way out she looked into the byre.

'Perhaps you will come to see me in Crossgate? In my studio I show you some of my work.'

I told her I would be pleased to call by but it would have to be a Saturday or a Sunday afternoon.

'We will arrange. I also have my teaching work, it is in the big school by the lake but for only two days each week. Adios, artist!'

At last, a letter from Anne arrived, postmarked Burslem.

Dearest Johnny,

I could not believe it when I heard you are working on a farm! What *can* you be doing? I want so much to see you, but I am stuck in bed. Aunt Clara is bullying me, she says I have a fever but I do not feel too bad. I cannot tell you how much I am missing you. We have had a difficult time, not so much the flying but getting up here from the south. The trains are packed, mainly with soldiers, and you have to stand in the corridors. My father had to go to London and will be getting a new job. Please write, Johnny. I will wait for a letter. Will you get any holiday?

I had written a hundred letters to Anne. In my head. They were letters to tell her how much I longed to see her, to say how much I loved her, and that nothing would change in my head or my heart. We were now no more than about 120 miles apart but it might as well have been thousands, for we could not meet. The higher the sun the more urgent the work. It was not just milking or carting to and fro, there were ditches to be cleaned for the free flow of drainage water, fences and walls to be mended and the field beside the long meadow had to be ploughed and harrowed and made ready for sowing.

Zeke borrowed an extra horse from Wetherlam, a chestnut beauty called Moses with a blond mane and tail. He and Neb hauled the shining blade that Zeke called the coulter, while I led the team of two as Zeke expertly guided the shafts. We were working the land in much the same way as a yeoman farmer would have done centuries ago. One evening, washed and changed, I asked Sara if I could use the telephone. If Anne and I could not meet at least we would talk. 'Course you can, Johnny,' replied Sara. 'The best one is in the hotel. Our lines have been bad all winter. You can try but you might not get through.'

She was right. I tried the one in the hotel lounge but could not contact Burslem, or anywhere else. The lines must still have been down. The Jewish gentleman had been watching me from across the room. 'It's no good,' he said. 'We try but it must be the war because we can make no calls.' Then he pointed to the wireless.

'It is bad news, always bad. More bombing and many people killed. Also Germans in Yugoslavia, and now in Greece. In France a thousand of my people have been given into the Germans.'

He wrung his hands and his wife came across and put her arms around him. 'We must not give up, Leo darling. We can only be hopeful.'

I felt very sorry for them. I too wished to be hopeful, for my need to see Anne grew and grew. Frustration became the enemy of sleep and I was growing more and more bog-eyed at work. There were days when the sun broke through, dispersed the clouds and lit the hills, drawing from them a brilliance and a palette of colours that was almost blinding. Working on dry walls with Zeke I did indeed 'lift up mine eyes unto the hills'. Sara asked no questions but she knew I was becoming restless and depressed – and so I was until an unexpected lifeline was tossed my way. The Argentinean lady, Catarina, called in one day after work and declared, 'It is now time for painting, Johnny, the light is returning and I am going on the hills. You are an artist, you should come also. We make a little rendezvous with beauty, okay?'

A rendezvous with beauty sounded very okay by me, but I told her it would have to be a Saturday or a Sunday afternoon. 'That is my only time.'

'Any time is right time. First you can come to my studio and we make the preparations.'

When Catarina left Sara made another pot of tea and we talked for a while. I told her that I had been hoping to get out to do some sketching in the valley where Neb usually grazed.

'Then you should do it, Johnny. You can continue your art study, can't you? Farm work is not your life, it is just an interruption until the war is over.'

There was something temptingly peaceful about that narrow valley with its silver thread of a stream among the rocks. It made me think of those Italian masters who painted their Madonnas against a background of the hills and valleys they so clearly loved. And I also thought of my Madonna, and the day I started my study of her below the waterfall.

Chapter Twenty-seven

The studio at Crossgate was in a barn, one half of which had been separated from the store for farm implements and the remains of last year's hay. It had a small window but was dark. Small wonder that Catarina chose to paint out of doors in daylight. She had clearly made a start. I spotted four canvases in the far corner of her studio.

'They are sending to London for my show, and give the name to the exhibition. It is "Four Seasons".'

The subject matter of the paintings was identical – a range of hills seen from the margins of a lake bordered by a stand of trees. The colour change was striking for there was a season to each painting showing the hills as they would appear in spring, summer, autumn and winter. She asked me if I liked what she had done and I told her I thought it was a marvellous idea and very well executed.

As the day was warm with bright sunshine, Catarina declared that we should take advantage and make an expedition to one of the high hills. 'There are many fine subjects and if it is not clouds we will see great distance.'

I had brought my canvas bag in which I carried a pad of watercolour paper, pencils, pens and tubes of artists' colours. Before we set out it also contained a pack of sandwiches Catarina had prepared and a flask of tea. For the first hour we climbed steadily following the course of a stream.

The higher we climbed the steeper the way until finally, after one more scramble, we emerged on a broad plateau sprinkled with pools like miniature lakes that mirrored the cloudless sky.

'It is a noble landscape, you think?'

I told her I thought it was superb.

We settled beside a bulky rock formation close to one of the larger pools. Catarina spread a roll of canvas on which we sat and unpacked our materials.

There were no trees or bushes on this rocky plain but the view before us was wide and open to the sky with the arched spines of the hills stepping away below us into the blue distance. The day was kind to us and we set to work. But for the sun we would have been chilled, with hands too cold to draw or paint. We spoke few words as concentration took hold and I became aware only of the soughing of the breeze on the rocks that sheltered us. Catarina had said we should make a composition of figures in landscape, so we would draw each other against the magnificent background of rolling hills. After an hour or so she came to my side to inspect progress.

'That is good! I think you could make a big painting from this. You are a clever boy. You have drawn form of me but I must join more with the background. You know paintings of Poussin, master of landscape with figures? He should be your study.'

I knew exactly what she meant. Her composition was so much better, so assured and showed that she worked quickly with uninhibited tonal washes in ink and chalk. It was back to work, then another break for our sandwiches and the tea. We relaxed and she became easy with her conversation. Would I return to college to complete my studies, where was the college and what would I do afterwards? Where would I live and – most unexpectedly – did I have a girlfriend who was also studying art? I explained about Anne and how she had been away in Dominica. She said, 'Me also. My lover was in Argentina, very rich, but he is no more.'

It was some time later, and several more half-day excursions into other areas of 'landscape', before the message she wanted me to get came home to me. She was pleasant company and it became clear that she could teach me just as well as any professor of fine art. It came as a shock when finally I realised that she also had things to teach me other than composition, tonal values and colour. These values were different. She spoke of the art of love and the ways that Indian women practised it.

'They are expert,' she assured me, 'and for one person they will allow many lovers.'

We were putting our brushes and materials away in her studio when she made her thinly veiled proposition.

'You have a lover who is not here, you tell me, and I also. It is lonely for us, I think.'

What she said was true enough. She took my hand. 'It is like a wound when you can no longer be in bed with your lover.'

When I told her I had not been in bed with my lover she expressed genuine surprise.

'But Johnny…you are a strong boy, I think, and most handsome. Do you not want to do it? You do not sleep with your girl? I cannot believe it!'

I shook my head. 'We are not like your Indian ladies.'

She smiled. 'There is no need to be lonely any more, Johnny. I think we are good friends?' She then placed her arms on my shoulders and gazing up at me whispered, 'We could arrange…you would like it?'

I was embarrassed and could not find an adequate response. She said, 'If you are waiting till marriage maybe that is not good, it can be a disaster!'

I laughed. 'Not true! It is better to wait, then it will be…special!'

She shook her head as if she could not believe what she was hearing, then came close and pressed herself against me. 'Oh Johnny, Johnny, you are cruel to me!'

She put her lips to my ear and whispered, 'I think we can do it, it would be exciting for you also.'

I thought to push her away but she held me closely and I could feel her desire and her warmth beginning to steal into me.

'Sure,' she whispered. 'We will find a time. Like my paintings we can be together in summer and autumn and the winter too.'

Our first bed, and the one after that, was the sweet-smelling hay stored from the previous summer. From the beginning she showed great care and delicacy, aware of my inexperience, as with a firm resolve she appointed herself my tutor.

'No, no, Johnny!' she would whisper. 'It is not so quick. Like putting paint on the canvas. A little at a time, you see? No hurry now. Imagine it is a long, long time to cover all the canvas and you make something beautiful.'

Her lips and soft hands too easily defeated me. I burned, and I succumbed.

Chapter Twenty-eight

W ork on the farm increased and half-days were cancelled. With Zeke I helped to sow the big field. Panniers were strapped to our shoulders. We paced in line several yards apart and swinging rhythmically cast the seed to left and right. A cheerful Zeke chanted, 'And a sower went forth to sow…'

In the world beyond our sun-bleached hills more bombs were falling and more armies marching. In the evenings the wireless told how the seeds of war were being cast still wider. German divisions were storming into Russia, Nazi paratroopers had descended on Crete. I was restless, increasingly disturbed and anxious. I longed for Anne and prayed that she would be safe from the bombs. I stayed away from Catarina. I had not been fair to Anne. I had not been true to myself. My hunger for the valley and the hills that enclosed us faded and a sense of guilt began to grow as I heard of the dangers endured not only by the men and women in the services but by city dwellers, many of whom were being killed in their homes. What was I doing in the fields, so certain and so safe? More than half of me wanted to get away…to take a chance in a warring world.

It was now mid-summer and the time of haymaking. Our workforce grew from two to five, with help from the boss, young Isaac and Hetty. Borthwick feared that the weather would break and we were in a race against rain. Moses, as well as Neb, took his place between the shafts as we hauled load after load to the barn.

In the long, light evenings I took out my sketching materials, but not to Catarina. I chose to be alone and to draw a high rock formation behind the hotel. As I was doing this one evening Sara came out with a letter. All the mail had again been left in the hotel. I recognised Anne's hand.

Dearest Johnny,

I have been trying to determine a time and a place where we could meet. I realise you must be busy but I think there is a way. I have to make a short visit to Edinburgh next week (the 30th) and intend to take the Manchester-to-Glasgow train. For Edinburgh I have to change at a junction called Oxendale, which I think is somewhere near you. I will have a wait of at least two hours in the afternoon so is there a chance we could meet there? I have so much to tell you and long to see you. Can you phone through to Aunt Clara's? I may not be with her much longer…

It was wonderful to have her news. I decided nothing would stop us from meeting. When I asked Borthwick for the afternoon off he was not pleased.

'Bloody artist!' he growled. 'More trips with the Argentinean tart, eh?'

In the end he relented and said I could go provided he could get another pair of hands to take my place. Happily Ruth was released from her hotel work and co-opted. Better still, Zeke came to my rescue. He said he would lend me his motorbike, and told me of a short cut over to the next valley and on to Oxendale. He also enabled me to use the telephone at Wetherlam Farm. I hoped to speak with Anne but she was out. Aunt Clara was not, and I left my message with her.

I did not possess a licence to drive the bike, but this was a chance I was going to take, and nothing would prevent me – unless I fell off the thing. To make sure I would not come to grief I had an evening's lesson with Zeke.

❋

You could hardly call it a station, it was a junction, a halt, and a pretty poor one at that. Just one platform and a small waiting room. There was a tea bar inside with a steaming urn and a glass case containing a suspicion of sandwiches curling at the edges. Behind the urn was a young woman in a striped apron.

'Train's running behind,' she announced. 'Signals. Always the same. Supposed to be an express, there's a lark for you. They'll blame the war...or the unions.'

A wooden bench, a table and two chairs. I sat and waited. It was so quiet I could hear birds scuffing the roof, until the woman piped up. 'Tea's sixpence. D' you want a cup, young fellah? There's no sugar.'

I thanked her but declined. Ten minutes. It felt like ten hours as the afternoon wore on. Then, at last, the express arrived, snarling, hissing, gliding, then clattering to a halt in a cloud of steam, its brakes howling. A door slammed. A whistle blew. There must have been a stationmaster somewhere but I never saw him. A shadow clouded the glass panel in the door. It was cautiously opened. I got to my feet, my heart thumping. Then, there she stood. I hardly recognised her, but it had to be Anne. Smart hat, light tweed jacket. Lipstick. And a briefcase. I stared. She smiled that smile as she walked towards me. 'Hi Johnny! You made it!' She set her briefcase down. I opened my arms and she fell into them. 'Anne!' I held her fast and we kissed long, long kisses like drinking after a terrible thirst. Then I came up for air.

'Darling, I hardly recognised you! You've...changed!'

A shrug. 'No. I'm still me!'

She seemed older. Of course she *was* older but there was a difference. A professional woman. That was it.

'You two doing a runner for Gretna?' It was the woman at the tea urn. 'Never fear, I won't tell on you!'

We burst out laughing. I whispered, 'We can't talk here, there's a seat on the platform.' I called to the urn woman: 'We'll wait outside.'

A shaft of sunlight sliced across the platform and the air was very still. The famous express had puffed away leaving three coaches in the siding to be hooked to the Edinburgh train when it arrived. We sat. I took her hands.

'You first.'

'No, you, Johnny. I want to hear about this farm.'

I explained and she nodded. 'Yes, thought you might. I heard that conscientious objectors are being employed by the BBC. That would have suited you better than farming.'

'I had no choice.'

'At least they didn't put you in prison like some others. Is it awful on the farm?'

'Not really. I was lucky…nice people. Very peaceful. You wouldn't know there was a war.'

I told her about Sara and Borthwick and Zeke. I did not mention Catarina. Then words left me, I just wanted to look at her. Time, even a little time does strange things. Had we both changed? I knew I had not. Nothing had changed for me, unless it was surprise seeing her so smart, so serious and self-possessed. I was lost for words. Then I found my tongue.

'It must have been terrible for you. In Dominica I mean, and that journey, I don't know how you did it. I was so sorry to hear about your mum.'

She glanced away. 'Yes, but it was worse for my father, he was terribly hurt, and angry. Then he got depressed. I don't think he'll ever get over it. I'm hoping a new job might help. He may be going to the Forestry Commission. Northumberland.'

'You said you might not be staying with Aunt Clara, will you go with your father?'

She shook her head. 'Hold your breath, Johnny…then wish me luck.'

'You're not…surely you're not joining up?'

Calmly, and taking her time she explained that the reason for Edinburgh was an interview. 'The university. I think I've been accepted, but I've got to see a professor or a department head. I had to revise…at a crammer. Physics, chemy and biology. I passed to matric level. They said my English and Latin were very good. It's medicine. I've made up my mind. I want to be a doctor.'

That smile again. She squeezed my hand. 'Well? What d' you think?'

I did not know what to think. I said, 'A lot of study. Hard work. Five years' study, isn't it? You'll be twenty-three when you finish.'

She nodded. She looked excited, but I felt empty. I tried not to show my disappointment. Five years in Edinburgh…maybe more at another university. She might as well have remained in Dominica. We seemed destined to be apart. If I was going to finish my diploma in Oxford we would still be a world away.

'Do you really want to?' I asked. 'I mean, why medicine?'

'My father says it's a good choice. So does Aunt Clara, she was quite enthusiastic. They think I should do it. I want to try.'

That was very like Anne, but no more for me. Not now. Not here at a railway junction of all things, a place for the parting of the ways, with coaches going one way and the express going another. It hurt. I hated it. But I couldn't disappoint her. Instead I said, 'Anne darling, we'll have to decide how we're going to manage. After the war I mean.'

She moved closer and kissed me softly on my cheek. 'We'll take one hurdle at a time, Johnny. That's how we'll manage. If you still want to.'

Oh God, I wanted to. I loved her. I wanted her now. I needed to be with her for always. She knew that, and I knew, I'd always known. Nothing had changed.

'You'll let me know – about Edinburgh I mean.'

'Course I will! We can write. At least the war hasn't stopped letters.'

We fell into a strange silence. A void where thinking did not seem to happen. Then I said, 'Fancy a cup of tea? Is there time?'

She nodded. Then taking out a handkerchief she rubbed my cheek. 'Better not go back to that farm with lipstick on you. They'll think you've been up to no good!'

A quizzical glance. 'For a farm lad you look a bit pale. Is everything all right?'

I felt pale, sure enough. I felt my heart sink, but managed a smile. 'Come on then. A quick cuppa.'

We sat side by side in the waiting room, very close, listening, and I thought I heard the train. I could not take tea without sugar. It had gone cold anyway.

Chapter Twenty-nine

*T*rue to her word, some ten days later a letter from Anne arrived.

I can't think why they bothered, they did not want to grill me about results, they just wanted to find out how keen I was to go for medicine. I think I convinced them, and now I can hardly wait to get started. Have you ever been to Edinburgh – it's huge! I'll be going into digs, sharing with Kate Collinson. Do you remember her? She was a year ahead of me at school and a friend of Liz. She's doing languages. It's her mother's flat, or at least one of them, in a cul-de-sac, a crescent really in an area called Bruntsfield. I'll have a room to myself, which I think will be better than being in hall, where I'd probably have to double up with someone I don't know.

Anne's move, her initiative and single-mindedness spurred me to action. She was going to do something she really wanted to do. I decided I would follow her example. At least I could try. I did not feel very hopeful, but I applied to the tribunal again. I penned a very careful letter and, giving my reasons, asked if they would now allow me to join the QRS. To my surprise this time – and I'll never know why – their response was favourable. They agreed. I guessed my application must have been put to a different panel.

There was no time to lose. In due course I said my farewell to the hills that burned and to the streams that sang, to days dry-walling 1,000 feet up under the sky, to the milking, the ploughing and carting. And – I was sad. I said goodbye to Sara who had been so kind, to Zeke and his family and a horse called Neb who became a friend. When I told Catarina my news she was upset, and then very angry. 'You will go into danger!' she warned. 'The war will be for a long time I think. Here you are safe, Johnny, and we can be together. Why will you not stay?' And with a dark look she added, 'There can be more lessons…do you not want to be with me?'

I realised that she was trying to make me feel rotten…and I did. I was sad, too. Catarina was a fine artist, no doubt of that, and I wished her well. I hoped she would continue to make many more beautiful paintings.

It was strange to be back home at Yearsby with Mum and Dad. Just for a week. A hot bath every day. Clean clothes, and a chance to rest before leaving for QRS headquarters in London's Tavistock Square. Mum had very mixed feelings about my change of plan. She was pleased because she knew that QRS did good work, but worried because of the bombs on London, and if I was sent abroad I would be 'in the thick of it'. My dad was more upbeat. He said that if I was not going to take his advice and join an RAF unit I was doing the next best thing. There would be an increasing need, as he put it, for 'someone to help pick up the bits'.

It was only too clear there were 'bits' already. And plenty of them. Month by month reports were charting successes and defeats for the Allies. Malta had been almost bombed into oblivion by German and Italian raids. Allied bombers – 1,000 at a time – had devastated Cologne. In Poland the Nazis killed 700,000 Jews, with many others rounded up and sent to concentration camps. Battle lines in Europe were reducing towns and villages to rubble and vast numbers of people were rendered homeless. In the Quaker Meeting House at Oxford a touch of sanity prevailed. A famine relief committee had been formed. I learned about this when I arrived at QRS headquarters.

I found the atmosphere there informal, but businesslike with a lively management team consisting of women as well as men. Not all of them were Quakers, but they were COs and were sending fellow-objectors to hospitals throughout the capital from the docklands to the West End. There they became the responsibility of the hospital managements and worked as orderlies and trainee medics. I was sent to Hammersmith Hospital and told to report to the outpatients department.

On arrival I discovered that Jack Emslie had beaten me to it. He was already installed as a ward orderly, having been through a similar tribunal as mine.

Greeting me he said, 'I had a feeling we might be on the same track, Johnny. Welcome to doctors' headquarters!'

He was not joking. We were billeted in a small wing set aside for a number of the hospital's housemen. There were individual bedrooms and two bathrooms and it was clear I had got lucky. Jack said, 'You're not going to believe this but you'll get a knock in the mornings and a maid will bring you a cup of tea!'

I thought someone somewhere must like the Quakers, though I was not sure about Sister Thomson. She was in charge of outpatients and looked pretty formidable. She was a large, middle-aged battleaxe, I decided, from north of the borders. She smelled of surgical spirit and wore an immaculate white apron over her blue dress.

'Well now, Mr Hartside, d' you know anything about ward work, first aid or sterile procedures?'

I told her I had never been in a hospital before and knew nothing about medicine. With her hands on hips she regarded me with suspicion, then said, 'Well ye'll have it all tae learn if you're going to be any use here. You'll do as I say, but you'll also be under Dr Marlowe who is now a surgeon.'

It was obvious I was in for a hard apprenticeship but was more fortunate than Jack. He'd been put to a surgical ward and spent his days and half his nights coping with bottles and bed pans and elderly patients who kept trying to escape.

Not infrequently the air-raid sirens sent their wavering howls over the rooftops followed by the thud of bombs and intermittent gunfire, and we stood by to receive casualties. Although the bombing seemed to be further down river we got our share nightly. Patients with burns were sent to a special unit while we dealt with fractures – usually legs – cuts, bruises, and bruisers who were drunk and sometimes violent.

One of my worst moments early on was when a young woman was wheeled in and was, apparently, in the late stages of giving birth. Marlowe, a nurse and Sister Thomson were in charge but insisted that

I stand by and mop the poor girl's sweating brow. I just about passed out. I'd never seen a birth before.

As the weeks passed I became more hardened to the miseries of people in pain. And I also learned that hospitals did not go in for half-days or holidays. However, from time to time on a quiet morning I would step across the road with Jack if he was free and call at a kerbside van marked 'Hot Drinks'. It was pretty vile coffee and a bread roll, but we both needed a breath of fresh air. When I had a free evening I started to make sketches of outpatients' activities and also scribbled notes that I would send to Anne.

> Seriously, I hope your medical school is not like this place.
> I've got a doctor with carrot-coloured hair who swears like a
> trooper and who, according to Sister, is a clumsy idiot with
> a foul temper. He's a cockney and the other day had me
> coping with a little girl who'd been brought in with head
> wounds. The girl's mother held her while to the
> accompaniment of cries and howls I did my best to clean
> the cuts and staunch the bleeding on her scalp. Marlowe
> said she would need at least eight stitches and I'd better get
> on with it and use eyeless needle sutures. They're those
> little half-moon needles with the gut swathed in at the end.
> Well, it wasn't easy. I never knew skin could be so tough.
> Marlowe shouted 'Push, man! Push harder!' I said I would
> not, it was hurting the poor child so much. In the end,
> assisted by Sister, I managed. I assumed the cuts and
> abrasions had been caused by flying glass or a bit of fallen
> masonry. Marlowe shook his carroty head. 'No way, mate!
> Likely it's domestic. Her dad probably clouted her. We get a
> lot of that.'

It made me very sad, and I wondered how Anne, starting her studies, would have coped. I guess she would have managed better than I did.

Chapter Thirty

*W*ould you like to be a surgeon, Mr Hartside?'
It was Sister Thomson. I told her I would not! Over the months I had been shunted around the hospital, first to the wards – medical and surgical – then to the dental clinic and theatre. Mad Marlowe insisted that I should attend a heart-valve replacement operation. The artificial valve was a new product, he said. The patient was a fifty-year-old Greek woman. The procedure I witnessed was a revelation as the surgical team stitched the valve into place with the delicacy and the artistry of petit-point embroidery in the hands of a genius.

The reason for Sister Thomson's fatuous enquiry about being a surgeon was simply that she had supervised my making and applying gutter splints for the fingers of clumsy doctors who had cut themselves during post-mortems, and because I had become adept with splints and plaster casts. After one busy session she actually called me Johnny and no longer barked and bullied.

QRS in Bloomsbury kept in touch on a regular basis and the day came when Jack and I were summoned to the Tavistock HQ with a dozen or so others, and a few days later we were sent to a training camp in Edgbaston. There, our base was a large country house, which suggested that a touch of luxury might be in store. That turned out not to be the case. We were accommodated in draughty Nissen huts with bunk beds. We endured a rigorous regime. Up early every morning, a compulsory run round a large lake, a cold shower and potato-peeling sessions before breakfast. In the mansion we were given instruction on basic anatomy, first aid, and introduced to bandaging almost every portion of the body, plus a lesson on VD. We were also made to dismember and reassemble the working parts of engines belonging to fifteen-hundredweight trucks, followed by driving lessons on an ambulance and an ancient lorry.

All this was in preparation for situations that we would probably have to face when despatched abroad. For some time QRS mobile teams had been at work in Italy, the Western Desert (with the Desert Rats), Ethiopia, Scandinavia, Burma, China and the Far East. For North West Europe we were divided into four separate groups each consisting of eight men with two ambulances and two trucks to each team. Free time was strictly limited but twice weekly we were encouraged to attend meetings for worship in the hall of the big house.

In the evenings I made time to write to Anne with my news, and I was delighted to receive letters from her. One of them suggested that she, too, had little time to spare.

> It is more or less as I imagined, pretty intense with acres of physiology and biochemistry and anatomy, anatomy, anatomy. We have a lady anatomist and she is a terror, a tough old bird who went bananas on the arm...just one arm! She has drilled into us the origin and insertions of every single muscle, the bones, the notches, arteries and veins. We are also beginning dissections and our recommended reading is a small, thick book referred to as 'the wee Jimmy'! I have a fair bit to swot up back at the flat and Kate does her best to distract me by suggesting good places for drinks, and a bit of shopping. We have been to a place called The Aperitif in Frederick Street where Kate introduced me to gin and orange. It's a hike to get there so we take the tram. I love getting your letters. I do miss you so much and say a prayer each night to wish you safe and well.

I felt quite envious. Gin and orange sounded much more fun than our weak tea, and we didn't have even a half-pint of beer in sight because we were not allowed anywhere near a pub. 'Don't you know there's a war on?' our instructors kept saying, which was stupid because we were able to listen to news on night-time wireless. It was said things were turning the Allies' way, but the war was far from over. In the Far East the Japs were increasingly successful with Singapore gone, German factories were being heavily bombed, Montgomery had long since been victor at El Alamein, battered German divisions had surrendered in Russia, General Eisenhower had taken D-Day command and the Yanks, it was reported, were having success in Europe. Refugees and homeless DPs (displaced persons) swarmed everywhere.

It was bitterly cold when, eventually, the time came for us to move out of the Edgbaston camp and drive down in a convoy of sixteen trucks and ambulances to a transit camp near Tilbury Docks in the Thames estuary. I was put into Section 8, which would be attached to 12 Corps, British Army of the Rhine. We were kitted out in battledress and carried a certificate that described us as members of 'A voluntary relief unit authorised to follow the armed forces of the Crown'. In the event of capture by the enemy we were to be treated 'as prisoners of war under the provisions of article 81 of the International Convention Relative to the Treatment of Prisoners of War'. Our 'rank' was equivalent to that of a lieutenant in the British Army. We did not wear pips on our shoulders, just a Red Cross badge. I thought we looked a pretty smart bunch, eager to get into action, but as one bright spark reminded us, we were still civilians and if captured we could be shot as spies!

We were two to a vehicle. Our leader in Section 8 was Stan Haxby, an ironmonger in civvy street and older than the rest of us. I was teamed with Len Barker, a small, cheerful chap, a civil servant by trade, and we drove one of the two ambulances. Stan drove the other one with Ray Trentham (engineer), and the other pairings in the fifteen-hundredweight trucks were Jeff Watson (school teacher) with Basil 'Baz' Clifford (lawyer), while Jeremy Cooper, a tall and handsome architectural student, was partnered by Dave Butters (solicitor). Stan, Len and Baz were married. Our convoy leader and in charge of all teams in Europe was Viscount Forrester, a Member of the House of Lords. He was a tall, spare-boned man who rarely smiled and, we decided, probably smoked his pipe even when asleep! Not that there was much sleep for any of us. The huts in the transit camp were cold and damp and the only place to keep warm was the officers' mess, where we ate our meals. Snow fell and the tough weather continued and made life pretty miserable as we boarded the tank landing craft with our vehicles. We sailed at midnight and were told our destination would be Ostend. It was a long time coming. In mid-Channel a storm blew up and we had to lay off, rolling wildly in rough sea. Most of us were sick as dogs. Our mess tins and rations remained untouched.

Chapter Thirty-one

*C*obbles are not the best surface on roads that are frozen solid. We slithered, spun and crawled, driving in convoy with great caution from Ostend to Ghent. It was freezing by day and night and an ambulance with canvas sides was hardly the warmest place on earth. As we progressed, Belgian children clattered along beside us riding the bicycle tracks and they were followed by priests also cycling, and by shabbily clad women walking, their heads half-hidden in big black hats. They shouted and waved as we passed by, and Len, at the wheel, shouted back in French. He said only a few would understand as most of the people here spoke only Flemish. At frequent halts I made quick sketches, very rough as my hands were so cold, and scrawled notes that, I decided, I would make up into a diary.

In the villages we passed through, the houses were pockmarked with bullet holes and away to the left I spotted a column of black smoke rising from a town that had recently been shelled or bombed. Our destination was Antwerp, which, we were told, was still being bombed. Unmanned V1 rockets called flying bombs (*fligende bombe*) fell to earth when the engines cut out and caused considerable destruction. We were advised to listen out as well as to look out.

On the credit side we found excellent quarters – a flat in the city's Frankreiklei. Its previous residents had been the German Gestapo and local 'collaborators', some of whom had been killed. The place was in good order and now occupied by Belgian Red Cross nurses who spoke English and welcomed us. We slept on our ambulance stretchers, and later moved to the Bar Normandie and bedded down on the balcony surrounding the dance floor. The V1s and also V2s were closer now, but there was work to do. Our section remained in town to assist local air-raid precaution services. Wearing our helmets and carrying gasmasks we manned posts at the docks and in the city.

Baz Clifford amused us by reporting that he had come upon a café in a side street, which was still doing business as usual.

'You'll not believe this,' he said, 'but in the doorway and a big window there are women sitting there like painted dolls, smiling and beckoning.'

The girls were waiting for customers and, as we later learned, they certainly got them.

In the centre of the city it was rather different. The main square was a shambles with piles of debris half-cleared to make way for vehicles. There were also many people injured. Stan arranged for them to be driven back to hospital in Ghent. They were all military personnel or members of *l'armée secrète*. There were more V1s and Jeff Watson was at our base when one fell nearby and nearly blew him out of the shower he was taking. The so-called 'front line' was not many kilometres ahead of us and US armour was reported to be meeting stiff resistance as German Panzer divisions broke through from the Ardennes.

After about ten days we moved across to Hasselt and set up a camp in a bunch of wretched huts – damp and filthy – in which the Germans had housed Russian POWs who were then sent to work in the local coalmines. We set about cleaning and disinfecting the huts. The army group to which we were attached seemed to approve our efforts. There were five Civil Affairs officers – Major Samuels, Major Langton, Captain Gustavson, Captain Lowndes and Captain Ramage, who was a former Intelligence officer and spoke French, Italian and Russian.

We left the camp to be staffed by a group of Dutch nurses, and drove on to Sittard, which was in the front line and where for the first time I became anxious about our position. Len and I found a comfortable billet in the home of the deputy Burgomeister, his wife and three daughters. They seemed to accept danger as an everyday occurrence but I found it alarming. The Germans shelled the place day and night and either you were lucky or unlucky. Army gunners were parked literally in the front garden and made the house shake as they returned fire. By day we were kept busy clearing a school, which would serve as a refugee centre. We were none too soon. Refugees and 'displaced persons' poured through the lines. They all had to be registered, then medically checked and deloused with DDT powder. Many were women and children and in a very poor state…severely under-nourished.

Captain Ramage said the kids' diet had included rats, mice and cats, which were sold as rabbit. Bread was made from brown dough and sawdust. There was a good deal of confusion and our *modus operandi* was spectacularly erratic. Disaster was never far away. A Major Grayston was killed by a shell and a little later two majors and a captain were dismissed, it was said, for inefficiency. The story was that they had uncovered a cache of champagne and helped themselves, with disastrous after-effects. They were replaced by a new bunch of officers.

Several days later, and in the midst of delousing a patient queue of about 1,000 refugees, we received an emergency call. Ray, Jeremy, Baz, Len and myself were hastily despatched to Susteran and Echt, where our advancing troops had met with stiff resistance on the push north. The towns had been liberated only a couple of days earlier. The damage was unbelievable and very many people had been caught in the crossfire and killed. There had been house-to-house fighting and buildings were literally split open. Trees were down and roads were mined. A forward detachment led us through and I was scared stiff, waiting to be blown sky high because not all minefields had been marked. There were corpses everywhere, and a prevailing stench of burning and shit.

We were joined by Dutch Red Cross nurses, by nuns and surprisingly by an American officer who gave us a lecture on typhus, and then the magnificent RASC (Royal Army Service Corps) joined us with their three-ton lorries and helped to round up droves of refugees, their numbers varying from 300 to over 1,500 a day. We were struggling to cope. We treated and transported some 1,000 in one 'lift' alone, many from Echt, Roermond and Linne. They all had piles of luggage – their worldly possessions – and a huge number of bicycles.

In the middle of a busy day our 'boss', the admirable Viscount Forrester, drove in bringing mail from the UK. There were letters from home for most of us and one from Anne was among them.

Johnny dearest,

I am starved of news. Can you not write more? I have
received only one letter and am worried that you are in
trouble. We hear daily of the fighting in the Low Countries.
I rang your mother and she is worried stiff as she has not

heard from you since you left. You must try to write to her – and me, please?

My news is that Edinburgh has hardly had any bombs. I am having to work hard but I like the practical disciplines. Life is not all anatomy, physiology and dissecting, we also have time to relax. One of the consultants seems to like my year and we have had a party in his house in the south of the city – the Grange, I think. He is called Tom McAllister and has a most attractive wife, a part-time physio, but it doesn't stop him flirting like mad! He is generous and good fun and as well as students he asks sisters, nurses and office staff to his parties! He seems very young for his position, he is a surgeon so of course we call him Mac the Knife! Kate I told you about cannot come to the parties, but we get along well and she chums me to the Saturday-night hops in the university union.

It was a joy to have Anne's news and know that she was well. I was still scribbling in my diary in the evenings, and also making sketches. I had written more than one letter to her but pick-ups were spasmodic and it sounded as if my notes to Anne and to Yearsby were taking a long time to get there. Len seemed to hear regularly from his wife. He said she was a nurse. They had been married only a year and he missed her dreadfully. Every night as he prepared for bed – usually the inevitable stretcher – he would shout her name…'Chrissy!' He asked if I had a girl and I told him about Anne. He said I had to be patient. 'You never know,' he added. 'We may get a spot of leave when things ease up.'

He was a good chap to work with and to share the driving…he was tidy and precise and told me what I had not known…that after going through his tribunal he had been sent to prison. 'It was Wormwood Scrubs, I was in with a bloke called Michael Tippett whose interest was music. I had many a chat with him when we were sewing mailbags, because we had music in common. I play the piano a bit.'

I felt I was lucky with Len. We looked out for each other.

Our section, attached to Civil Affairs, was unexpectedly ordered back. I thought it signalled that our forces were in retreat, but 12 Corps had simply been moved for a rest so we had to do likewise. We left the camp at Susteran in reasonable order and another Civil Affairs detachment took over. We were moved to a billet at Achel, which turned out to be a Trappist monastery, and which had been occupied by the SS and suffered some damage. Most of it was habitable, but the location was exactly on the Dutch-Belgian border, so we messed in Holland and slept in Belgium.

The countryside around had been heavily mined and our rest period was short-lived, because the number of refugees and displaced persons was rising rapidly. Many were injured and we had to attend to them and, as if that was not enough, a medical mission in Brussels decided that we should do a survey on the condition of Dutch and Belgian children who had lived through the Occupation. Heaven alone knew how they had survived, but now, thanks to a help organisation their meagre diet was being supplemented by biscuits and sardines. Other relief agencies were in action, including the United Nations (UNNRA), also Salvation Army units, and we were helped by local civilian doctors, nurses and nuns. Army supplies of food, blankets and medicines were limited but were efficiently distributed by the RAMC (Royal Army Medical Corps), who were doing excellent work backed up by the RASC. We co-operated well with the army and yet had the freedom to make many of our own decisions. We ferried wounded to a hospital in Eindhoven, and set up a storage depot in the Phillips factory with supplies from the British, American and Dutch Red Cross.

Len and I also rounded up some supplies of food and clothing and drove over to Venlo, which had been liberated only the day before. It was heart-rending to see the state of many of the refugees, and the locals who had lost everything. On returning to the monastery I was informed that I was next on the list for forty-eight hours' leave with Baz. We did not enjoy the long, exhausting drive back to Brussels in our fifteen-hundredweight truck. We were set down at the Officers' Club with half a dozen QRS men from other sections. I scribbled notes.

Incredible! Wonderful! Total luxury, dining in a great hall. Chandeliers, carpets, curtains, with wine and coffee served at lunch by waiters in clean white jackets. There are shops filled with a glittering array of merchandise, much of it probably black market. Bought some hand-embroidered lace handkerchiefs to take home to Anne and Mum. Also went to a performance of *La Flute Enchanté* in a fancy theatre. Back at the club – hot showers, absolute bliss. But the place was so crowded I had to sleep in a bath, with blankets and a pillow.

Returning to Achel the roads choked with vehicles, including tanks. General Montgomery's armour is being moved forward for what we are told will be an assault over the Rhine into Germany.

My notes were brief, but I was being allowed time to make sketches, hurried scribbles to prompt memory when I returned home. I had to select subjects carefully as paper was limited. I ended up stealing supplies held by other ranks. Exercise books mainly, with ruled lines.

Our efforts were now reinforced by two other QRS sections. At Goch and Kevelaer there was much to do as both places had been severely damaged, with more house-to-house fighting. Fortunately there was one hospital still standing and occupied by the RAMC and nuns. We raided other buildings for bedding, clothing and surgical equipment and we co-opted the local population to help. Our quarters were in a hotel called the Gold and Silver Keys. After several weeks it was time to move forward again. I was very tired – and nervous now. I did not relish the next operation. It was over the Rhine and into enemy territory.

A Military Government major led our convoy to a few kilometres from the river. It was evening. As we paused, an incredible number of bombers towing gliders flew low to fields and woodland that lay ahead. We moved closer to the river, but then held back behind a stand of trees as there was a local action. Very noisy. Shelling. Machine guns. Tracers. Then at four a.m. in pitch darkness we followed tanks to the river. A pontoon bridge. Two runways for wheels. Miniature blue lights. Eighty yards spacing and over we went, very slowly. Len was driving – doing well. I chattered beside him to keep our spirits up. Below us the great, dark river swirled on, swollen by the rains. It seemed an age before we gained the far bank and turned onto a track running parallel to the water. Suddenly more firing broke out. Tracers, stinging our way. Then heavier gunfire. I did not wait. With Len I jumped down into a ditch.

'Damn fools!' he exclaimed. 'It's our own lot, they're firing at us.'

We kept our heads down. The firing did not stop until a beam from a searchlight swung across and picked out the big red cross on the side of our ambulance. As dawn came we camped in a damp field. A nearby inn was acting as a collecting post. Poles, Dutch, French, Russian, Italian, Belgian. Many injured. We set up a treatment centre, dressed wounds and got busy with the DDT.

Chapter Thirty-two

*T*he air warmed. It was spring – or something like it, and our hearts were lifted. A big corner had been turned and there was surely now no way the Wehrmacht, a depleted force, could stem the Allied advance. We too moved on and as we journeyed forward to Rheine and then Diepholz and Sulingen our regime continued, week by week. There were leaves on the trees…first leaves, very green, very young. All was well, and on one or two evenings we even made time, just the eight of us, to have a poetry reading and a short meeting for worship. Baz ministered and encouraged us to pray for the hundreds of thousands of many nationalities…civilians ripped from their homelands and set to work like slaves by their Nazi masters. There were even Greeks and Romanians among the refugees. In Sulingen I found a cattle shed large enough to shelter 300. Then we made the Burgomeister hand over supplies –- sacks of sugar, and potatoes. He had no choice. He was one of the defeated race. Perhaps we should have prayed for him as well.

At Nienburg we crossed the River Weser ('deep and wide') and continued to Soltau on the Luneburg Heide – a vast, aptly named heathland, and set up another centre in a wooden barracks. There we received 2,000 DPs a day, while the RASC trucked thousands of Westerners away. We had excellent quarters, with good food and even electricity so we could take a shower in hot water. The work was intense, and Baz was as peripatetic as ever. One morning, after completing the recce that he frequently made, he returned in haste, deeply disturbed. Len and I were checking a list with the quartermaster. Baz would hardly speak. He said, 'It's terrible! Terrible! You must get down there!' And he gave Len the name of some place an hour away.

We jumped into our ambulance and drove south across the flat land.

No sign of battle. Small bushes. A stony road, farms, but no villages. Len said the place was on the map. I checked. Bergen, that was it. Later I described the place in my diary.

> We parked and made our way to what was, or had been, a railway siding, and found a long row of cattle wagons. The doors stood wide. There were no cattle, the place seemed deserted. Then we saw it. About fifty yards away there was a long, muddy pit and beside it a large number of wooden coffins. We walked over. In the open coffins there were naked figures thin as sticks…just bones over which yellowing skin was stretched. Many had bullet wounds in head or chest and patches of blood. Village women were lifting out the corpses and tossing them into the pit. An army cameraman was filming. He turned aside to tell us the train had been there with its barely living cargo when the Allied troops arrived thirteen days earlier.

It was Belsen. One of the Nazi death camps. The pit was not the worst of it. There were heaps of rotting corpses piled high. One was vast…about eighty yards long. It consisted entirely of unclothed women. An RAMC major appeared. He said hundreds were being buried daily. He added grimly, 'Probably 600 every day. It is reckoned that 30,000 died here in the past few months, and there were 40,000 more found dying, beyond help.'

I moved away, my stomach turning. The stench was unbelievable and I spewed up…everything in my gut. I could no longer look, and with Len I walked back to the empty wagons. He said the majority of those slaughtered were probably older men and women too ill or too weak to work. Almost all would be Jewish, Polish, German, Russian, Hungarian. The major came over and asked who we were and we explained. He confirmed that the dead would be from many countries and they would have been starved, beaten, shot, gassed, left to perish with no help until the Allied soldiers arrived. They came. But it was too late. All they could do was to put the local village women to work, to help to bury the dead.

For me, it made the routine killing in hand-to-hand fighting seem almost decent. We were so shocked we could not speak. The ghastly images printed themselves on my mind. They would not fade. I would make drawings of what I saw…if I could. It was at that point that I began to wonder what kind of people the Germans were to allow slaughter on such an horrific scale. And in God's name – why?

My Quaker beliefs, my faith, was failing me. God – if God there was – could have had no acquaintance of this place. I was stunned. I could not even weep.

It was when I was driving the next long stretch that Len, sitting alongside me, said, 'No good arguing about it, Johnny. You can think what you like, but you knew about the Nazi camps before we left the UK…and those were not just rumours about Buchenwald and Auschwitz. Now they are saying the numbers there could be astronomic.'

We had talked half the night and in the back of our minds we knew there was a problem that affected us directly. We were now working with Military Government, no longer Civil Affairs, and our contact with German civilians – doctors, nurses, nuns – even with captured German soldiers, was increasing. The difficult part was that at home the government had issued an edict that was sent out to all troops and groups like ourselves. There was to be no fraternisation with Germans. This was difficult because our policy was to gain their trust and co-operation. Crudely put, we needed their assistance if we were to do our job effectively.

I felt I had reached a crossroads. After Belsen I was not so eager to accept the 'master race', but Len would have no sophistry from me. 'Grow up!' he said. 'And just remind yourself why you are out here!'

I was not going to fall out with Len – and I didn't. He was a good man, cheerier than I was. An optimist, and on occasions in the most unexpected places he sought to entertain us. He had the knack of unearthing the odd battered piano from buildings half-destroyed, and from it he would extract broken but recognisable melodies. The notes rose from the ashes like an injured phoenix…often a Vera Lynn number would float high above the smoke of destruction.

On 29 April an armoured division ahead of us crossed the River Elbe and pressed on towards the Baltic. Two days later, after many months of our stop-and-start journey all the way from Ostend we also crossed the Elbe, and drove into Hamburg – or what was left of it – then drove out of it to a nearby village called Ventorf. Hamburg was declared an open city three days later. 'Open' seemed to be a most appropriate word, for we found Germany's second city open to the sky. Most of its buildings were burned out, reduced to empty skeletons or piles of rubble. Great areas had been firebombed and we were to hear terrible tales of suffering, of families burned alive as they sat at their tables in cellars. Touch them and those grotesque tableaux crumbled to white ash.

In Ventorf we found quarters in a massive Wehrmacht barracks that had been cleared of troops that were captured and sent west to prison camps. In their place the barracks was already occupied by refugees and forced workers. Our billet was a handsome, half-timbered mansion, formerly Prince Bismark's private residence. Here, once settled, we were able to rest comfortably and, with our Military Government officers, mess on better rations. Many Italian POWs remained in the barracks and had established a well ordered community. Soon after our arrival Baz and Captain Ramage were invited to take supper with them. Baz reported: 'Some were ex-chefs or had been hotel staff and the food was brilliant. We had a feast! Their private quarters were stacked with provisions of all kinds!'

The barracks' population increased daily as vast numbers of refugees were trucked in until the volumes to feed topped 30,000. Five members of QRS Section 2 joined us. They had been captured in woods somewhere to the east but managed to escape. To my delight I found that Jack Emslie was among them. He was injured, with a broken wrist, but was otherwise cheerful. 'They were never going to shoot us,' he said. 'In fact they treated us quite well and made sure we got food.'

Most of the refugees were in a very poor condition, and one of our first tasks was to establish a medical centre, which was staffed by two German doctors and two nurses. We assisted them. VD was the most common disease and some of the patients had undoubtedly come from the camp's brothel. Our supply of appropriate drugs was limited and we had to inject many of them with sterile water. They were grateful, and assumed they were receiving proper treatment, poor devils.

✳

Our boss and mentor, Forrester, looked in with mail, but there was no letter from Anne or from Yearsby. We were kept busy driving the more serious medical cases to the least damaged hospital still standing in Hamburg. Advanced pregnancies were common and more than once I found myself driving the patient very carefully over the potholed and rutted roads and rubble in case I would have to stop and become a midwife on the spot.

An even sterner task was attempting to keep order in the barracks. There was a Polish community of about 10,000. Many of the men still carried arms – and they used them. There were shootings in the night and open violence by day. The RASC also brought in poor wretches from a nearby Nazi concentration camp. I lifted emaciated men and women from the trucks. Clad in their filthy, striped prison clothes, they were near to death and weighed almost nothing.

We had no hope of turning the barracks' population into a haven of peace and rejuvenation. There was little sense of order and no rest and rehabilitation for the forced workers before being trucked away to their own countries. After being registered and deloused, many Poles and Russians refused to report for repatriation. Matters came to a head when word went round that Colonel Zukov and his fellow-officers were to pay us a visit to ensure that the Russians were preparing to return. Suddenly, and unbelievably, half our population became invisible. They were terrified to return to Russia, fearing retribution. Most of them simply fled to the woodlands around the Elbe until Zukov and his men withdrew. Captain Ramage was detailed to parley with Zukov's officers. They observed protocol and invited him to mess with them. Hours later Ramage was returned to us virtually unconscious but attempting a song. He had been compelled to sink rather too much vodka in victory toasts. Poor Arthur. Among all our officers he was the one regarded as being almost teetotal!

The Zukov brigade were not giving up lightly, and when they returned more fighting broke out. I wrote in my diary:

> We may be part of a Military Government detachment, but
> government and good order is impossible. It is hard to

154

believe, but there is internal warfare. Nationals fight nationals. The Poles terrify everyone as they hunt down those they suppose to be German SS or others who had worked with the Wehrmacht or in the Nazi concentration camps. Tolerance and mercy there is none.

Chapter Thirty-three

*B*elsen had knocked me off balance and I tried not to think about it but the hideous scenes that Len and I had witnessed were like a vile vapour that hung about me and which caused a nightmare, repeated and repeated. I made drawings in the hope of exorcising the visions, and also wrote in my diary.

> Our mission in Europe is to provide succour and assistance to all who need it…the homeless, the dispossessed, the injured, the tortured, the sick, the ill and hungry and even the dying. At the outset I felt our duty was an act of compassion and care demonstrated in the most practical way. I carried in my mind the Quaker injunction 'to walk cheerfully over the face of the Earth answering that which is of God in everyone'. But now I feel I am failing…my faith is deserting me. How can I answer to a God who appears to be as lost as the hapless refugees themselves? How can I willingly assist former SS men, the Wehrmacht, or even other Germans who have allowed such acts of inhumanity in the Nazi death camps to continue?

The only thing that prevented me from falling into the deepest gloom was the clear indication that the war in Europe was at last coming to an end. We knew this at first hand through a chance encounter. Stan Haxby, Jeremy and Ray Trentham were halted on Luneburg Heath to allow a small German military convoy to pass by en route to Montgomery and his tent of staff officers. That was on 3 May. Four days later there was proof positive with the news that top-ranking German generals had signed an 'unconditional surrender' at General Eisenhower's HQ in Rheims. Thankfully it was beyond doubt. VE Day would be declared. The war in Europe was ended.

For our thousands of refugees and, I suppose, the millions of homeless Germans, the long awaited day had dawned. Peace was greeted with volleys of gunshot, gallons of vodka, dancing and whoring, a bellowing madness that lasted several days and nights. Joy was not so much unconfined, it was wild and dangerous. We were counselled to keep our heads down and remain in the safety of our billet until the worst of it was over. Even then, spasms of violence erupted. Reprisals. More horror. Captain Ramage reported that a bunch of Russians had set about a German district supervisor who had ill-treated them. They made short work of it. They killed him and buried him. There were several more such incidents. Another Military Government officer intervened in a scrap and prevented a German civilian being killed. When yet another such episode came to light I should have learned the lesson that hatred nursed over a long period cannot be defused. Alas, I did not.

In our medical centre Gisela, one of the nurses, was assisting Dr Hanitz and I was assisting her. The one narrow treatment room was in a block not far from our quarters. As I was returning to take an early supper before going back I spotted a small circle of men singing loudly. One of them was playing an accordion. Russians, I supposed. Or Poles maybe. As I drew near I realised this was not an impromptu concert. Voices were raised. There were shouts of 'Collaborateur! Collaborateur!' In the middle of the circle a man lay on the ground in terrible distress, waving his arms and crying out. He was being kicked violently by several of the onlookers. The singing rose to a crescendo of chanting. 'Collaborateur!'

I thrust my way into the circle and confronted the man who was leading the kicking and shouted to him to stop it. He was Polish, I think, so all I could cry was 'Halt! Halt!' and yell at him to hold off, but my intervention served only to make him redouble his efforts as the others cheered him on.

The victim was now bleeding badly from the head and I realised I would have to try to get him to Hanitz in the treatment room I had just left. But, as I stepped forward to hold off his assailant, I received thanks in the form of a vicious blow to my face and a second to my groin. I did not hesitate, I flung myself at him – and even as I did so I knew it was a mistake. We fell struggling to the ground and I tried to pin him down but he was bigger and much stronger than I was and I could not hold him. We rolled to the middle of the ring and up against the injured victim. With a malevolent grin my assailant suddenly produced a knife and tried to close his fingers about my throat. I found an extra pulse of strength and fell upon him as he raised the knife. I was in awful pain and after that there was little I could recall, except seeing the long blade of the knife as it sank not into my throat but into his.

When I raised my head I was lying on the table in the treatment room in bad pain hurting from head to foot. I could not open my right eye. I heard a gruff, thin-lipped voice. It was Stan.

'Take it easy, Johnny, we'll see you right, you poor bugger!'

Gisela was holding my hand. She said, 'You were losing your consciousness I think. Dr Hanitz is helping you for the pain.'

'Bruises,' I heard Stan say. 'Lucky we found you in time or you'd have got more of the same from the others that the poor devil got. This is serious. I've contacted Forrester. He's somewhere near Essen but he's coming over.'

My lips felt twice their size and it hurt to speak.

'They were killing him…kicking him to death!'

Stan said, 'They've taken him away. The other guy as well. He was a Polish lieutenant. For God's sakes, Johnny, why did you get into that?'

Hanitz interrupted. 'Important you rest. I have given you a sedative. Your eye is very bad. You must keep it covered and later we examine.'

The other guy. I remembered now. That knife. Then I heard Len's voice. 'What are you doing with my buddy?' He sounded concerned. 'You okay, Johnny?'

Stan said, 'No, he's not okay. We'll take him back to the house. Get him bunked up, out of harm's way.'

My head was swimming. I was very scared.

✳

Jack Emslie was sitting beside my bunk. I saw his arm was still in a sling, but as ever he was smoking his pipe and looking as wise as Solomon. He wanted to cheer me up.

'Couple of nuts, Johnny, that's what we are. Casualties of war!'

'Casualties of nothing. I killed a man.'

Jack puffed for a bit in silence, then he said, 'He's dead all right, but he deserved it. Self-defence from what I heard, Johnny.'

'They won't let me get up, I'm stuck here!'

'Don't try. Doc says it's a miracle your ribs weren't kicked in.'

They were all concerned, very understanding, and you couldn't call it an inquisition when Forrester appeared a day later. He said he wanted to see me but only with Stan and Len, and in the kitchen. The others were to be kept out. Len was the worst, he was very upset but tried to make light of it. They had found a black patch for my eye and he said, 'Okay, Captain, where's your parrot then?'

'That's enough,' said, Stan. 'Coffee. Tell the *hausfrau*.'

Forrester spoke calmly, almost coldly. He asked me what I could remember and I told him how the victim was grievously hurt and was being kicked by a very angry mob.

'Kicked to death,' said Len. 'To music. Grotesque. Terrible…I suppose it was to drown out the man's screams.'

Forrester nodded. 'These reprisals are all too common and they are likely to continue. There is animosity between many Poles and the German Nazis who declared openly their intention to eliminate every German Jew on Earth as well as those from the Polish and Hungarian ghettos. The tragedy is that many Polish people hate and fear the Russians as much as the Germans do. Reason disappears.'

How, I wondered, could he be so cool? Racial hatred is one thing, but mass killing in cold blood is another. I did not catch all that was being said, but Forrester made one thing very clear.

'These incidents should be dealt with only by military personnel, not by us or any other non-military group…the Red Cross or UN volunteers.' He paused, then said, 'As I understand it, you say the Polish lieutenant was the ringleader and that in the struggle with you he pulled a knife and you acted in self-defence. It could be interpreted as an accident, which resulted in his death. The difficulty here is that there were no witnesses, or rather the accordion player and the others who witnessed or compounded the incident were Polish. It would be most unlikely that they would blame their lieutenant, they will inevitably point the finger at you.'

That, I knew, was obvious. What I did not know was how the law stood. Would I be convicted, and who would make a case, and to whom? Section 8 QRS was attached to, and worked with, Military Government. But, as civilians, we could hardly be put before a military court.

Forrester said, 'I do not foresee any action being taken in law. My prime concern is how the Polish community here will react.'

He turned to Stan. 'You told me the Poles are the largest ethnic group in the camp, is that correct?'

'There are, or were, 10,000 of them,' Stan replied.

'Passions run high, as you have discovered,' said Forrester. 'There is considerable instability. My guess is that now there are those who will want blood, your blood, Hartside. They will seek what they would call justice in their own way. I have spoken at some length with Tavistock Square and they are in full agreement with me. It will not be safe for you, and possibly for Section 8 as well, to remain here.'

I was shocked. Surely our military detachment could take care of individuals with revenge in mind? Officers like Captain Ramage would understand, otherwise what was Military Government doing?

Forrester said the rest of the section would be informed. Repatriation. That was the decision. I would have to go, and I was dismayed. The thought of leaving a group of very decent men knocking their hearts out in the name of humanity…chaps I respected and with whom I had shared so much, it just seemed terribly unjust. But I could do nothing about it. I had no choice.

As it turned out, the intention to move me away from 'the field of conflict' was the right decision. That same evening a hostile crowd gathered outside our quarters and their anger was all too evident. They started shouting. We could not understand what they were saying, but we could guess. And they meant business. Shots were fired into the air and before the crowd dispersed bricks and rubble were hurled at our windows.

It was before dawn that I was bundled into Ray's fifteen-hundredweight with my kitbag and a Red Cross parcel of rations. By first light I was driven away from the barracks and hardly had the time or the opportunity to say my farewell. Ray took the wheel and Len, my good companion and guardian angel, insisted on accompanying me on the long drive south. Destination – the Officers' Club in Brussels. Once there arrangements were to be made to transport me back to the UK where I was to report to QRS in Tavistock Square. Heaven alone knew how they would react, or what I would do.

Len said not to worry. 'If they have any sense they'll give you a spot of leave, get your eye seen to, then maybe they'll find a job for you at HQ until demob.'

The drive back was one of the worst journeys I ever wanted to take. It was not uncomfortable – it was hell. My bruises were extremely painful but were nothing compared to my state of mind. Len was a rock. I know he spoke sense but I was sick at heart. I was a Quaker, with a message of peace who refused to kill, and then did exactly that.

Len said, 'Look, old chum, we all think what you did, or tried to do, was foolhardy but you meant it for the best. For what it's worth I think you showed real courage, I don't think I could have done it.'

I was in no mood for sympathy. I tried to focus on Anne. Dear God, what would she think? How could I confess my stupidity? How could I pray to a God who was not there?

The Hook of Holland to Harwich. That was the route. Then by train to Liverpool Street. I expected it to be crowded but it wasn't. I found a seat in a compartment occupied by two middle-aged biddies who rattled on interminably. One said, 'We tried the Army and Navy at Victoria but not with any luck. Molly wanted something really smart, but not costly…well, you could understand, he left her with those two kids. She come over something strange and said a new hat would help, make her feel better, back to normality.'

That really roused me. It astonished me. Two old dears going on about hats? Had they no conception of what was going on over there, across the water? It was all I could do to hold my tongue. I wanted them to know…about the homeless, the destruction, the obscenity of it all. And then, through the carriage window a fleeting glimpse. The suburbs slipping by, and it reminded me of the bombing, the blitz, and the Londoners with families killed and houses reduced to rubble.

Chapter Thirty-four

*T*he letter was waiting for me at Yearsby.

> Johnny, where are you? Have you written because if you
> have I've received nothing and I'm worried. I wrote c/o
> BAOR as usual but did you get it? If I have no word from
> you tomorrow I am going to ring your mother.

It was a worrying note. There was nothing about her lectures or
how she was managing. I had been granted a week's leave at home
but it looked like being longer because of my eye. Mum was terribly
concerned when she saw me with that black patch. She called Gaynor,
our family doctor, and he said there was nothing he could do, I would
have to see a specialist. I mentioned nothing about the Polish lieutenant
and invented a story. I told them a pole in one of our canvas stretchers
had caused the injury. 'Not really surprising,' I said. 'It's easily done
when you consider manhandling those things and lifting patients into
the back of an ambulance day after day.'

Anne had telephoned but left no number, so I sat down and wrote.

> Anne darling,
>
> Apologies, I'm sorry but it's been a bit difficult. I'm back at
> Yearsby for a few days' leave. A problem with my right eye.
> An accident. I was bundled off to a specialist at the County,
> and he said I would have to have an operation, but don't
> worry. Nothing serious. Please ring again, I long for your news.
> Is there a chance you could get down here for the weekend?'

The 'nothing serious' was, I hoped, true. The specialist had expressed a note of caution. He suspected a slight tear of the iris or a possible partial rupture of the sclera. A small foreign body, probably a tiny chip of stone, had entered the eye, but he was confident he could deal with it.

I had broken my journey home to call at HQ in Tavistock Square and learned that Forrester had contacted them again. They said they did not wish to see me until I could see them 'properly with both eyes'. Not very funny. They confirmed that Section 8 was being withdrawn from Ventorf to help organise a repatriation centre at Essen.

The County Hospital was not much fun, but I was only in for five days and doped down for the pain. The surgeon turned out to be a woman, tall and quite young, but she was very attentive and looked in to see me twice after the op. She seemed to be satisfied with her work but said I would have to keep the eye covered for two weeks then check with a doctor again.

To my delight Anne appeared the day after I got home. 'I'm cheating,' she said. 'The rule is no break until after the semester as in America, but I told my prof it was an emergency.' She regarded me with what I thought was the beginning of a very professional look. 'Can I see?' I said no, the consultant had said it was to be kept covered.

'Johnny! Just a little peep?'

'All right,' I replied, 'seeing it's you, doc!'

She lifted the patch very delicately, stared and said, 'Ouch! Not very pretty!'

I just thanked heaven for Anne. She and Mum wanted to cheer me up. They organised a VE Day supper party and our neighbours from the Grange and Sproxton came over. Anne and I made time to be alone together and I plucked up courage to tell her exactly how the injury had happened. She was shocked.

'I killed him! It was an accident but he was going to kill me!'

I needed to talk, to tell her, and to explain. She refused to criticise or reprove me for my stupidity and instead did her best to lead me into her very different world, her days and nights and the new friends that she had made. She did this, refusing to allow me to feel sorry for myself. I could picture her at those Saturday-night hops in the union, and her eyes sparkled as she spoke of a young doctor who had taken her under his wing. He and another house officer had invited her and Kate to drinks at a pub called The Cramond Inn.

'You would love it, Johnny, it's right on the riverside and it's quite famous. Alex, that's his name, Alex Gordon. He takes life very seriously, almost as seriously as his golf, which he plays at an Edinburgh club. He says we should go to St Andrews over in Fife. He drives a very smart little number – just room for four.'

I was not going to worry. At least, I tried not to worry – it would be unfair. She needed her friends no less than I needed mine…Jack Embury, Walt, Liz, Len and that devoted team in Germany who, in spite of everything, I was beginning to miss.

When I checked in at Tavistock Square they said there was no question of my returning to join Section 8. Instead I would be sent over to France. A Quaker post-war service had been formed. In France there were plans for an international school to be built in the Cevennes and a group of young Quakers from America were already on site and linking up with some French students. I was to go out to assess whether a team of volunteers from England might usefully participate in the scheme. If so I was to report back. It would be manual work involving the preparation of foundations.

Chapter Thirty-five

*T*wo days before the train down to Dover and the Channel ferry, Liz rang me and asked if we could meet. She had been posted back to London. I was really pleased and explained that I was holed up in Tavistock Square, but had time. I suggested lunch. 'Lyons Corner House, Marble Arch. Twelve noon?'

She agreed but her voice sounded strange. I waited nearly half an hour outside the Corner House before I spotted her paying off a taxi. Lovely Liz, very smart in her Wren's uniform, slim legs and a strappy, regulation handbag over her shoulder. A kiss. A big hug. The immaculate Liz, but now with a ring round her sleeves.

'Welcome, HM Navy!' I said. 'Promotion?'

She nodded. We found a table and ordered. Then she took my hands in hers. Our eyes met but they were not the eyes I remembered.

'Bad times, Johnny. You heard about Pop?'

I knew he had joined Bomber Command, but that was all. Liz said, 'Remember that little lad, Fountain?'

'Squirt? Sure. Course I do!'

'I bumped into him the other night in a NAAFI (Navy, Army and Airforce Institute). He said Pop bought it. Shot down over the Ruhr. Not captured. Missing, believed killed.'

Killed? It was a shock, like a blow below the belt. I could not believe it. Pop, the Barnardo's boy, the lad with a big mouth and an even bigger heart. I'd never worried about Pop, we all thought he was indestructible.

Liz was shaking her head. I said, 'And no one to grieve for him. No mum or dad. That's awful.'

She shrugged. 'That's war. We lost too many. Cumberland. He was Arctic convoys. They got a really raw deal, one disaster after another. He's gone as well.'

I did not want to hear any more. I'd known nothing, shut away in those hills. Even in Germany word had never reached me. Liz turned away, then she choked.

'I don't know how to tell you, but, it's Walter. He transferred to the Airborne Div and was doing well. Until Arnhem. You know what happened, the Guards got through to Nijmegen but couldn't make Arnhem. That bloody bridge, a fiasco. According to the WO, seven thousand of ours never made it back. Walt was one of the lucky ones, if you could call it lucky. He's in a burns unit. I haven't seen him.'

She gave in, dabbing at her eyes. I was stunned. Nothing I could say. That bridge over the Rhine. It must have happened about the time 220 Military Government and our section was crossing further up river, near Wesel. But Walt? It was terrible and I began to wonder about the others...Mortimer A. V., Squeak Whitely, Bamford and the rest.

I cancelled the order, we didn't want food. Neither of us could eat. I took her arm and we walked across into the park and found a bench. All I could think of was the man we both loved lying in hospital, burned, injured.

A breath of wind stirred and the first leaves, golden and brown, fluttered down to swirl in eddies at our feet. I looked up to the lower branches, to the darker leaves, and suddenly the face, that ancient I had seen before, emerged again. I was astounded. It seemed to be smiling, then faded, but not until, as the leaves stirred, it had flashed a triumphant scowl.

'Are you all right, Johnny?'

'No, I'm not. It's too awful.'

She took my hand. 'No need to be scared, the worst is over now...'

'I don't mean the war. It's up there. The trees.' And I told her about the face. It sent shivers down my spine.

She mustered a smile. 'You and your imagination. Anne always said you had a thing about trees.'

Thank goodness for Liz. We comforted each other. I told her I would go and visit Walt but not right away as I was being shunted off to France. I said, 'Keep me in touch, won't you?'

She took a scrap of paper from her handbag and scribbled an address. 'You could write to him. He can't use his hands, but I've heard they're wonderful there. They'll read it to him.'

I gave her the QRS address in Tavistock Square and told her she could write to me there, and they would forward the letter. I wanted her to keep in contact, and also to be in touch with Anne, so gave her the address of the Edinburgh flat. She tucked it into her handbag. I gave her a hug before we parted. She was so upset she had not even noticed the bruises around my eye.

✳

It felt like a long, long way. I had too much time to think of those friends I would never see again, and their voices, silenced forever. They say that when one door closes another door opens, and, of course, it did. But on a very different landscape. To reach it – another unfamiliar place – involved a journey that was lonely and exhausting. Train after train. London to Dover, Dover to Calais, Calais to Paris, where I had to change. Then Paris to St Etienne in the Rhone Valley. An interminable wait for a slow three-coach train to the little town of Chambon perched on the eastern edge of the high Cevennes.

My instructions were to rendezvous with a Pasteur Trocme or Pasteur Theiss who were Huguenot priests. It was midnight when I knocked on the door at the house of Pasteur Theiss. I waited, exhausted but impatient, my case at my feet. When, eventually, the door opened, I saw in a shaft of light an attractive young woman clad in nothing more than a knee-length jersey with two words printed across it: 'North Western'.

She smiled. 'You'll be the gentleman from London?'

I nodded, surprised that she spoke English –- and with a pronounced American accent. 'Come right in, we were expecting you.'

She took my case. 'You'll be tired. Your room's up here, okay?'

She picked up a lighted candle in a tall holder. I followed her up a staircase and into a small room containing a single bed. 'Make yourself at home won't you? We take breakfast early, but you can sleep as long as you please.' She turned away. 'Will you excuse me one minute.' She left the room then returned with a large jug of water, which she placed on a marble washstand in the corner. Then she extended a hand and said, 'I'm Jaqueline. Bienvenue! Welcome to our home!'

I shook her hand. 'Hartside. Johnny Hartside.'

She nodded, then turned away and shut the door softly behind her. I flopped onto the bed, too weary to undress.

My alarm clock was a bird, a persistent bird tip-tapping at the window. It dragged me from my sleep and sitting up I heard voices and laughter below. The water on the washstand was ice-cold and it shocked me wide awake, but I was not prepared for the sight that met my eyes when I pushed open the door at the foot of the stairs. Seated at a long table were six young women – I think I counted six – and at the head of the table a man in a black smock or robe got to his feet. He was very tall – probably seven feet, and he was smiling. The girls all wore identical jerseys bearing the words 'North Western' in bold black letters. What followed I explained to Anne in my letter dated Le Chambon, 11 September:

> Imagine my surprise. The girls, or young women, were all sisters, daughters of Pasteur Theiss. Each one solemnly shook my hand as the Pasteur introduced them…Jaqueline, Louise, Amy, Anna, Monique and Mado. The prettiest, noisiest nest of singing birds you ever saw! It was later explained they had all been wartime evacuees, sent to New England, USA, to attend a college called North Western. Pasteur Theiss welcomed me with a penetrating look and a crunching handshake, then set the girls scrambling to serve me breakfast. Never before have I been waited upon by six pairs of hands. Porridge sprinkled with crushed walnuts and delicious honey, coarse brown bread with real butter and quince jelly, and piping hot black coffee. Can you blame me if I seem confused? I am exhausted and dizzy, so much has happened over the past two months. Have you received the shocking news from Liz?

I added briefly what Liz had told me about Walter, Pop and Cumberland. In her reply she wrote that she had just heard.

Dearest Johnny,

The letter from Liz was an awful shock. I can't believe it,
except I suppose we should not be surprised. In wartime
people get killed but somehow it does not seem quite real
until it happens to someone close to you. Thank God
Walter is surviving, but if those are third-degree burns he
will be in awful pain. I'm not into burns yet, it's all
histology now and the structure of organic tissues (e.g.
kidneys and liver), more dissecting and 'abnormal
conditions'.

    Here at uni we are so removed from it all. Did I tell you
about Alex Gordon, the house officer? He does his best to
distract me! He introduced me to the Café Royal, it's just
fabulous with stained-glass windows and murals, Victorian I
think. The first time we went I had Dover sole, and the
second time turbot. Am I making your mouth water?! Do
please write soon and tell me all about la belle France.

La belle France felt to be a long way from home, and in the mountains
above the Rhone Valley it was a hidden place. I turned my mind to
work in hand and my first duty was to contact QRS in Tavistock Square.
I cabled them as requested. My signal was short and to the point: 'Send
six men good and true. Pasteur Theiss advises tents and sleeping bags.
No accommodation in the village.'

Dearest Anne,

Yours of the 17th just arrived. The postal service here is
pretty chaotic. This as you know is a big country and
struggling to recover. I have cabled for a QRS team to come
over without delay. There will be plenty to do, but I don't

know what they will make of the terrain, or of the French garçon. They seem very young and come onto the site with the American kids who are billeted in Feugerolles. We have a pitched camp about one kilometre from Le Chambon and have made a start. Hard work. Pickaxes, shovels, and two very pre-war lorries. We are supervised by the two Huguenot pasteurs. They are giants and hugely respected. During the Occupation they worked with the resistance, the masquisards, and managed to smuggle numbers of Allied airmen, and others, down to Marseilles and out of the country.

Longing to see you. All my love, Johnny.

Anne's reply of 2 October arrived on the 10th with news I did not wish to hear. She had heard from Liz. It was Walt. He had been transferred from the burns unit to another hospital in Surrey.

Liz said he was doing well until they moved him. He was undoubtedly suffering shock and required more than one operation – probably skin grafts. Airborne infection is always a danger with burns, and sterile procedures are vitally important. I believe they may have moved him too soon. His wounds became infected. Fatal. And so it proved. I am devastated. Faulty or careless nursing, lack of proper medication, which is…well, it's beyond belief, and so awful for Liz. I have written and told her to come and stay, there's room enough in the flat and Kate is in full agreement. Johnny, I don't know what to say. When war and killing ends it doesn't really end.

That was only too true. The fighting in Europe had ceased and Japan had conceded defeat after the unbelievable obliteration of Hiroshima and then Nagasaki. It was too much for me, and it hurt because the whole ghastly business hit home. I had lost chums I truly loved – especially Walter. A bright light had been cruelly extinguished, a good companion, a most special friend. And Liz was left desolate.

Chapter Thirty-six

There were spaces in my brain that I wished were not there. Too easily they filled with images as in a bad dream. Bodies at Belsen. Families – very old men and women. And children half-starved. Gunfire and a knife. Half-remembered voices. Liz shielding her face with her hands. For many the war would never be over.

Working on the site where the new school was to be built helped to disperse those images, with the young French and American volunteers swinging pick and shovel and chattering like birds as they perched on the tailboards of the lorries. One of them caught fire. I was in the driver's seat and as I struggled to get free I scraped the skin down to the bone of my left shin. Blood. Gallic consternation followed by a doctor's visit and one week's enforced and uncomfortable idleness. My world shrank to the small garden behind Pasteur Theiss's house. Jaqueline was no nurse but she was a willing companion and told me how she had loved her college in America. We talked down the last blaze of summer beside a mulberry tree and surrounded by flowers and shrubs. Anne would have been able to name them. There were also apple and pear trees, figs and walnuts. It was a hollow beauty in this no-man's land and to my shame I found no God, not even here in the shadow of a Resistance hero, a man of towering faith.

Dusk fell as I listened to the cries of the tireless volunteers. The day's work done, they played softball beside the campsite and answered each other with their songs. 'Frère Jacques, Frère Jacques, Dormez-vous?' And 'Sur le pont, d'Avignon'. From the Americans: 'I've been working on the railroad, all the live-long day'. Then the voices melted and there was only the incessant clicking of cicadas and the hedgerows blinking with the emerald spark of families of glow-worms switching themselves on and off. Occasionally Pasteur Theiss would appear, a gaunt, dark giant gazing down the garden towards me and nodding as if he knew something I did not.

The journey home from his parish and through the mists of northern France seemed shorter than the journey out. At Tavistock Square I learned that my group would presently be replaced by another team, and at HQ I was delighted to find Len and Jack Emslie sharing a desk. They said Section 8 QRS in Germany was being dismantled two by two.

Len said, 'We're not all out yet. The Red Cross and 220 Mil Gov are staying on at Ventorf. I volunteered to help out here. Bit of admin for post-war service until demob.'

'And Chrissy?' I asked.

'Of course, Johnny! Next weekend…haven't seen her for months. How about you? Does your Anne know about, y' know, the Polish officer?'

He shouldn't have asked, I was trying to put it all behind me. I buttonholed Jack Emslie. His plans were different. Between puffs on his pipe he told me he fancied a crack at politics. 'Always been Labour, y' see, and now they're in with a massive majority could be a few fireworks…Attlee, Morrison and Bevan. Big boys. I fancy local government. I'd like to get onto a council back home.'

'Then Westminster?' cracked Len.

Jack tapped out his pipe and grinned. 'Ah well, maybe. That's for later.'

We filled in the gaps and weighed up ambitions that evening over a few pints at The Coach and Horses round the corner. Len said he hoped to get his old job back with the civil service in Oldham where Chrissy was nursing. I told them about Anne up in Scotland but I did not speak about Walter, and Pop. I said I had no immediate plans, and that was true. The way ahead rolled out before me as empty as a snowfield. Too much had happened and I was not clear in my head. I would not be demobbed for a couple of months but I took no heed of that and decided to return to Yearsby without delay.

Mum was as perceptive as she was loving. She realised I was 'not myself' and had questions.

'We want to hear all about Germany, darling, such an adventure. And France too. I can't imagine you with a Huguenot family, did they know you are a Quaker? And all those poor refugees, ever so many, whatever will become of them?'

I did my best to tell her how it was, and I did try to tell her about Walt and Pop. Dad was sympathetic and said he was much saddened. 'I liked those lads. They did their best for King and country. Heroes in their way. Gave all that they had to give. We will remember them.'

It was months later that I learned just how many would be remembered. The final roll of those killed world-wide was estimated to be more than 55,000,000. Half that number were civilians.

I rang Anne and said I was coming up to Edinburgh. More than ever I needed to be with her to make plans as to how we would manage just as we had promised. It was then that she landed a bombshell. I couldn't believe it. She told me we should not meet, at least not immediately, it would not be a good idea.

'Course I want to see you, Johnny! But just now I don't think I should. Not now.'

What on earth was she thinking? I couldn't believe what she said. 'Anne, but why not? I mean, what's the difficulty? Do you really mean I should not come up to Edinburgh, is there a plague?'

'Darling, do be sensible. I'm serious.'

'But it's been ages! What's to stop us? We promised – or have you forgotten? You can't mean it!'

'Johnny, please don't be angry. I'm sorry but I really do mean it.'

Silence. I waited. I thought the line had gone dead.

'Anne, are you still there?'

'Johnny, please be patient. It's not forever, just for a little while. I'm into exams shortly and I'm finding it hard, much tougher than I expected, it's not plain sailing, you know.'

'But you can't be in exams all the time, that's crazy, you must have time out!'

I did not like what I was hearing.

'You've been in hospitals, Johnny. And, you've been on wards, outpatients and theatre. It's not just books and lectures, you know. Or causes of diseases, pathology and all that. We're starting in the infirmary now, examining real patients, it's the same for all my year. And I'm also into theatre, assisting. There are night ops, and even at weekends.'

My heart sank. How long was I going to have to wait? I had half a mind to go up there anyway. I was not thinking straight. That surgeon at Hammersmith…Mad Marlowe. Medics were a funny lot and I knew Anne would have to study hard if she was to pass her finals and graduate. It would be the best part of another year till then. I didn't want a fight. We'd never ever had even the breath of an argument and I wasn't going to begin now.

'Well, anyway,' I said lamely, 'I'll ring you, okay?'

And I put the receiver down. No. Not to be angry, it wouldn't help. But I felt dismissed. Perhaps she would change her mind. Unless, and until she did, I was back in that snowfield. I was lost.

When I was young I was told you carried your troubles on your back like a rucksack filled with stones, and if you were clever you could discard them one by one. They reminded me of that. They knew I was unhappy, carrying a burden that weighed me down. Mum had heard part of my telephone conversation, and Dad also caught the drift.

'Got to realise,' he observed, putting on his professional voice, 'medicine involves very hard study over protracted time. Concentration and a good memory should see you through, but above all is a passionate desire to learn and to apply your learning, and your skills to help others. So, don't worry, son. She'll get through. Flying colours, shouldn't wonder.'

Mum added: 'Anne will have more opportunity, too, because now Mr Bevan is talking of a health service for everyone. If he gets his bill through Parliament it will mean free treatment for all!'

They meant well. They liked Anne a lot and believed she was clever, just as I did. So I listened when they counselled patience, but they did not understand how I felt inside. Three of my friends had been killed and Anne, my most chosen friend, had closed the door on me. What would be the use of prayer if God, too, had disappeared? Even Amy observed that I was upset, and she tried to show her sympathy.

'Not yourself, Master John, and I'm not surprised. Bin in the war, ain't you. There's lots like you I daresay, not knowing what to do with themselves. Heroes they were, and now in civvy street they can't even get a decent meal. Rationing's got worse.'

What she said appeared to be true. The Ministry of Food spread gloom with announcements that butter and fats would be restricted to wartime levels, while bread was poor in quality and still rationed, as were meat, bacon and poultry.

I wasn't interested. I ate little and Mum said I looked thinner. My eye was better, but for a week I hung about, listless and lacking energy. On Saturday evening I walked over to The Wagon Wheel for a pint. The wireless was still on the bar counter and was reporting how Germany was to be carved up into separate zones to be administered by the Russians, the British, French and Poles. Then another news item attracted my attention. An exhibition of the work of war artists was creating a deal of interest in London. Henry Moore's drawings of families sleeping in the Underground during the blitz were much admired, as were the paintings by Piper and Sutherland of the bombed streets above.

Those images aroused me from my lethargy and prompted me to look out my 'Christmas' easel and oils. I would be an unofficial war artist and try to interpret some of the sketches I had made with 220 Military Government. I was not going to return to Oxford to complete my diploma. What was the use, making prissy studies of the nude Greek statues in the Ashmolean? They had nothing to do with today's world. I preferred to record the plight of refugee families among the ruined towns and villages of North West Europe. At least I could try.

The top room was the obvious place in which to set up my easel. There were three large windows and they would provide sufficient light to work by. They gazed up to the sky where changing continents of cloud were the only distraction. I sorted out my references, the hurried sketches I had made, and there were more of them than I had realised. I knew I could use them and my interest and energy began to return. It was like opening a drawer and finding things you needed, objects that gave pleasure like new gloves, a warm scarf, a freshly laundered shirt.

A letter from Liz – totally unexpected – to say she had been up to Edinburgh and called to see Anne. I was dismayed. She, it seems, can have access while I cannot.

Dear Johnny,

Hope you can read my scribbles, just thought I'd let you know. Went to the funeral service for Walt and the others. An army affair. They awarded some posthumous medals. I met his parents but didn't stay. They don't know me anyway. Then I went on to Edinburgh, to Anne, and I met her flatmate, Kate. Nice kid, I remembered her from school. She made supper just for the three of us. I told Anne I had seen you in London and you were fine. She is obviously working very hard and I thought she looked a bit washed out, pale and not like her old self. Kate said she was overdoing it. I'm back to civvies now and into teaching, well I hope to. I'm on a course for primary. Hope we'll all get together before long.

Take care. Love Liz.

That was the limit, it was so unfair. Girls together. I could not rid myself of the feeling that Anne had changed in some way. I never doubted she would study hard. She always gave 100 per cent. I was at a loss to know what was best to do. I'd better tread carefully. In fact, the only place I trod was over to The Wagon Wheel for a bloody good drink. Every night – until Dad made me see sense. Get on with your painting, he said.

He was right. If I didn't do it now I would never do it. So I looked again through my original sketches and called on remembered images. I would use oils. Full colour and the subjects I selected first included a 'townscape' of Hamburg, a burned-out landscape, then one of the Rhine crossings lit by flashes of the guns showing the convoy of tanks, ambulances, foot-slogging squaddies on the dark river. Then the monastery at Achel, and a group portrait of the deputy Burgomeister at Sittard showing him with wife and two daughters. If I could do it I would also try a big canvas of the pit at Belsen, and another showing concentration-camp victims being unloaded in the barracks square at Ventorf. I had many more references to call on, treatment centres, sheds full of refugees. It was a challenge, but if it came off maybe I could sell. Mum and Dad had lots of friends.

Chapter Thirty-seven

*I*occupied the top room every day for hours on end with turps, boxes of oils and large canvases, which Dad had kindly ordered, and I set to work with my brushes and palette knife. To add to my references a new subject emerged, big trees reminiscent of Cezanne's *Grandes Arbes*, with its incredible medley of colours. My own modest vision would show that ancient of leaves who smiled or scowled and sent shivers down my spine. He was no guardian angel, but there *was* a real one close at hand and she was called Amy. She clattered up and down the backstairs with coffee every morning. I worked, and kept a waiting heart.

It was not until Easter approached that the waiting at last came to an end. A short note from Anne, with an invitation. She was to steal a weekend away visiting her father and would I meet up with her there? On Good Friday. She continued:

> Did I tell you he has joined the Forestry Commission in Northumberland? I suppose that will be my new home. He has rented a place in a village near Alnwick, Eglingham, just off the A697. I've asked Liz to come as well, just a couple of days, she needs cheering up.

I was pleased, but it was very odd. I could not visit Anne in Edinburgh, but I could meet her in Northumberland. I was puzzled but wasted no time with RSVP. With luck I reckoned I could take a train to Eyemouth, then bus or taxi to the address she gave. I just wrote a line: 'Darling, hooray! Good Friday cannot come soon enough.'

✳

Liz said, 'Surprise, surprise! When shall we three meet again, in thunder, lightning or in rain?'

'When the battle's lost or won,' I replied, 'right here in Eglingham!'

It was quite a spacious sitting room, well furnished with French windows to a hilly garden. There was a silver tray by the fireplace bearing four glasses and a decanter.

I said, 'Where's Anne, has she arrived yet?'

'Her father drove up to Berwick, met her off the train. She's upstairs tarting, I expect!'

She gave me a hug. 'So! How's Johnny?'

'Busy. I'm doing some painting. Every one a masterpiece!'

'Keeps you out of mischief!'

'Keeps me exhausted. It's quite hard work. Heavy going.'

'Going?' said a voice. 'Not thinking of going when you've just arrived, I hope!'

It was Anne's father. 'You'll be Johnny,' he said. 'Glad you could come. Good journey?'

I had not expected him to be so tall, but he was. A big man, broad in the chest, well built, with a warm complexion and a shock of snowy hair. He walked with a slight limp, and in tweed jacket and breeches looked like the farmer he used to be. He offered a hand. 'Anne will be down in a minute. Bit tired, I insisted she took a break before her finals.'

Right on cue she pushed the door open and walked towards us…the same big, wide smile. But I was quite shocked. She'd had her hair cut, cropped very short and oddly she reminded me of a photo of Mum in the 1920s, except she was in colour. She had taken pains…bright lipstick, a polo-necked jersey, rose pink, and a navy blue jacket and skirt. Very smart.

'Johnny!' A big hug, a careful kiss.

'Wow!' exclaimed Liz. 'Enter the Dark Lady!'

Dark maybe, but she looked thinner. A moment's awkward silence, then I reckoned another hug was in order as her father turned to put a log on the fire and busied himself with decanter and glasses.

'Anne darling, terrific! You look great!'

But I thought…not really. She was different. We stood there, the three of us, smothered in silence, for once in our lives lost for words. Then Liz grinned and nodded. 'Another policeman!'

179

Anne's father straightened up. 'Police? What's that all about?'

Liz laughed. 'It's what we used to say at home when there was a gap in the conversation. Another policeman being born! Mad, isn't it? Can't think where it came from.'

I felt uneasy. The three of us, so close and yet so suddenly miles apart. I wanted to talk with Anne. I sought more than a hug, and I thought Liz would want to talk about Walter.

Thankfully Anne's father sliced through our spaces with a warm smile. 'Sherry? Or would you prefer beer? Damned if I know what you young people drink these days.'

'Sherry is perfect, Mr Rigby, thank you,' said Liz.

Anne perked up. 'Liz darling, no need to be so formal. Dad is Matthew. Or Matt, that's what Mum called you, isn't it?'

We plumped down on the sofa, Anne on my right, Liz on my left as 'Matt' claimed what I supposed was his chair by the fire. Anne smiled across to her father. 'What was it Mum liked to drink? Gin with something.'

A sad smile. 'Gin and It. Vermouth.' He raised his glass. 'Cheers!'

I wondered what we were really thinking behind and beneath our chat. Perhaps Anne was sharing a moment with the mother she had lost, and her father was remembering the wife he had buried in a faraway place. And how, I wondered, was Liz managing without her Walt?

It was easier over supper. Anne's father said the girl who usually cooked for him was 'unavailable', so he would take us out to a pub. 'Just a short walk,' he said. 'More of a restaurant. Old beams, spinning wheel, swords, shields, that kind of thing. But the food's pretty good.'

A piping hot venison stew and plenty of red wine. Then apple pie with cream. No sign of rationing here. Anne's father told us about his work with the Forestry Commission, which was an official body, a government department. He said he was helping to set up a research unit. His current portfolio concerned social research and woodland ecology. He said, 'We'll be an advisory body with a wide remit. It's early days but on the social side we'll be examining how forests and woodland areas impinge upon society and how forestry affects people's lives. On ecology we will develop strategies on how the management of forests and woodlands can be sustained over the long term.'

It all sounded very interesting. Anne said, 'You've got Johnny's attention, Dad. He's always had an interest in trees and likes making drawings of them. He says they are individuals and should be cared for, like people.'

'So they should, Anne. That's well said, young man. The fact is that although most people don't realise this, trees do have a big influence on our lives.'

Liz was only half-listening. I imagined her eyes did not see trees or woodlands, but were searching for another place. She was without the man she had loved, her chosen friend who had been so brutally taken from her.

Chapter Thirty-eight

On Easter Monday Anne's father drove us all to Powburn then up across the River Breamish into a country of rounded hills and long views of woodland. We got out and walked for a mile or so in the cool upland air. Anne said, 'Johnny, look! Coincidence! There's a sign up that track to a farm or something called Hartside. Your family must have come from these parts – did they?'

I confessed I had no idea, but I realised that after Edinburgh this would be her homeland, her father being based at Eglingham. It was fine country where strong winds ruled. Here, the Cheviots stepped down in a series of sheep-grazing slopes to the flat lands where England ended and Scotland began. As for endings, I did not want to leave, and was invited to stay on an extra day if I wished. Anne's father said I was welcome. Liz said she would have to return to Durham later in the day to her primary-school teaching course.

We walked and talked then repaired to an inn to quench our thirsts. Anne's father said that the land on which we stood was owned by the Duke of Northumberland.

'The Earl still lives in Alnwick Castle. I have to make a meeting there tomorrow with his factor. Anne wants to see the place so I'm taking her with me, sorry I can't take you all. Liz and Johnny, you will have to amuse yourselves. Alnwick is an attractive spot. I'll drop you off there and then we'll meet up later.'

Liz said, 'We could take a turn round the town, look at the shops. Maybe we should find something for Anne's dad for having us.'

I agreed. I thought we might buy something from a rather swell shop that sold fishing tackle but Liz said the trouble was we did not know whether he was a fishing person. In the end we played safe and bought a small flask. It was silver and leather and pocket-size.

The White Swan was where we had agreed to meet up. It appeared to be the town's main hotel. There was a lounge just through the main door. I ordered tea. The waitress said did we want hot cross buns? Of course we did. With strawberry jam if they had it.

'Jam but no butter,' the waitress said. 'It's marge.'

We chatted as visitors came and went, calling at the reception desk nearby.

Liz said she would be mother, and poured. Handing me a cup she added, 'So – what d' you think? She's really doing very well, isn't she?'

She read my blank expression.

'Well, isn't she, Johnny? I know I couldn't do it.'

'Do what? What are you talking about?'

'Anne, of course!' She paused then added, 'Don't you know? Didn't she tell you? Oh my God, you mean she didn't say?'

'Say what?'

She looked away, clearly upset, then murmured, 'Okay, I've gone and blown it. But I was sure she would have said something. She must have told her father, I realise that, but – well I can't believe she didn't tell you!'

'Liz, I've not the slightest idea what you're talking about. All Anne told me was that it was better that I kept away until after her finals, and I was upset. You were allowed but I wasn't. Am I getting chucked, or something?'

'Of course not. You know perfectly well!'

'So?'

'So I didn't expect it would be down to me. She'll never forgive me.'

She was serious. She looked me straight in the face and said, 'It's not good news. I'm sorry, Johnny, but she is unwell. She obviously didn't want to upset you, that's why she did not want to see you.'

'Are you making this up? Anne seems fine to me. Lost a bit of weight maybe, but not ill.'

Whether or not Liz intended to tell me more I don't know, but she did not have the opportunity because Anne, followed by her father, stepped in through the swing doors. She smiled, wrinkled her nose and gave me a peck on my cheek. 'Hot cross buns! I can smell the cinnamon! Any more where those came from?'

Liz got to her feet. 'I'll tell the girl. And I have to enquire about bus times for tonight.' She stepped over to reception as Anne's father pulled up two more chairs to the table.

The summerhouse at the bottom of the garden was perched high and close to a stand of trees. A good place to sit. Liz had left to catch her bus and Anne's father was in the kitchen talking to the girl who cooked and cleaned for him. It was a light, bright evening with skylarks high overhead. She said she did not want to worry me but realised Liz had said something. No fuss, but yes, there was a problem.

'Johnny darling, it's not the end of the world, and I should know because we've been through it on our course. I've got something called disseminated sclerosis. Not much is known about it. It's not all that bad but it makes me feel very tired at times and difficult to do my work. But honestly, not to worry. I can manage, I know I can.'

My heart fell. She told me with that wonderful steady smile, seeking to reassure me, but I sensed that she was not telling me the whole story and I wanted to know more.

'There is no more, Johnny, and even if there was you wouldn't understand the medical jargon with all the fancy words…I'm not even sure that I do. Anyway, I'm having more tests. That's all.'

I took her in my arms, and kissed her. She said again that I was not to worry – but that was easier said than done. With exams, her illness had come at the very worst time.

If Paddy had not been sent home from school I might not have learned the true facts about Anne's illness. Poor lad, he had collected a viral infection that led to glandular fever and that meant he was confined to bed for a month, and probably longer. Mum called Dr Gaynor in from the village. He was a large, heavily built fellow with a white beard that covered almost half his face. When Mum asked which medication she should administer his reply was brief.

'Absolutely none, could make things worse. Give him plenty of water to drink and keep the bedroom windows wide open. Fresh air. Mother Nature's medicine!'

Before he left I told Mum that I wanted a word with Gaynor.

'But not for long, Johnny. He's on his rounds.'

I described for him the little I knew about 'my friend's' condition, and asked if disseminated sclerosis was serious.

'Depends,' he boomed. 'Could be.' He then went on to say not a lot was known about the condition. 'We don't know the cause, could be post-viral. It tends to be progressive – an autoimmune disorder. Occurs when the covering of nerve fibres in the spine and brain are damaged or destroyed. Fatigue and muscle weakness are inevitable. Paralysis can occur but not necessarily. The good news is that there are remissions. One month trouble…the next, right as a Ribston pippin!'

It sounded terrible, but that was all he was going to tell me. It was more than enough and confirmed my worst fears. How on earth could she manage her finals?

When I rang her the following evening she sounded perfectly calm.

'Please, Johnny, it doesn't help to worry. I'm fine, I really am. Just get a bit exhausted at times, but that's work, and Kate's bullying me and getting me to bed early!'

I wished now I hadn't asked Doc Gaynor. But I did try not to worry and returned to my work in the top room and steadily added to my completed canvases. Mum and Dad came to have a look and even thought some of them were impressive. I felt they were being kind and not eager to criticise. When Paddy was well enough to get up for an hour or two he also looked in and I persuaded him to sit for me.

I needed a change from the sombre stuff that had so obsessed me. I started on a near life-size study of him and called it *Boy with a Book*. When Mum saw what I was up to she was really pleased and said she would like to have the finished painting framed.

'There's that art shop, Johnny, where you get your materials, next to the hairdresser's. When you've completed and the canvas is dry I'll get them to come and collect it.'

As time passed I found I could concentrate well enough, but always in the back of my mind there was a space. I was waiting for that all-important call that would tell me Anne's results were out.

It was pure chance that I missed it. I had gone to the shop to purchase more artist's colours and, when I returned, Mum said there had been a phone call for me.

'From Anne?' I asked, 'or Liz?'

'From Anne, darling – I told her you had just gone out.'

'Was it her results? Is she through?'

Mum pulled a face. 'It was a very short call, she sounded to be in a rush.'

'But what was her news? Is she all right?'

I suspected Mum was acting. Very coolly she said, 'I think you should phone her back, but not now. She said make it later.'

'But Mum, come *on*! What did she really say?'

'Well, if you'll take my advice, why not make an appointment right away…with Dr Anne Rigby, MB CH B. You'll feel a whole lot better!'

I could have killed her, it was no time for teasing. Instead, I jumped across, flung my arms around her and nearly squeezed the life out of her. She struggled free and said, 'Dad and I are so pleased for her, she must have worked very hard!'

Pleased? I was ecstatic. She'd done it! She'd been ill but she had *done it*! I wanted to shout it from the rooftops. Dear Dr Anne Rigby MB CH B. I love you!'

Paddy joined in. Very sweetly he came and shook my hand as if it was me who had triumphed. Then it had to be champagne. Glasses were raised. Absent friends. 'To Dr Anne,' announced my dad. 'Good health! And a health to all those she is going to help!'

Chapter Thirty-nine

*D*on't be so stupid, Johnny, she deserves a good rest and the best place for her is with her father until she gathers her strength. And I expect he feels very proud of her and wants to share her success.'

So said Mum, and I suppose she was right, but I was disappointed. 'She promised she would come to Yearsby directly after graduation.'

Mum continued: 'Darling, you can't expect her to be in two places at once, family comes first.'

That evening I rang Eglingham but it served only to increase my frustration. Her father said not to disturb her, she was sleeping. He was going to keep her for a week or at least until she had unwound, as he put it. He added, 'She is fine but completely played out. She will recover, I'll see to that.'

Nothing was going right. Sunny days. Warm days, but general gloom everywhere, and not only Anne was exhausted. The country was as well. We had won the war but were losing the peace. The nation was short of product, short of money. It was back to wartime restrictions on food, clothes rationing, petrol, everything. Attlee was asking America to bail us out. There was nothing cheery on the horizon, unless it was Ebor Images. I discovered the place by accident. I had gone through to town and was wandering around aimlessly and trying not to feel miserable, when I spotted it in Coppergate, a small gallery selling paintings, prints, ceramics and a few pieces of 'modern' jewellery. I thought, what the hell, why not? After sauntering round the two rooms I spoke to the girl at the desk. She said, 'We exhibit work by local artists for a few days every month. If you have anything you'd like to submit we'd be pleased to give you an opinion, sir.'

I grew an inch taller – well maybe just half an inch. No one had ever called me sir before. I quite liked it. Very respectful, even if rather un-Quakerly. Nevertheless, I decided to take her at her word. I had nothing to lose.

'I could bring in a couple of canvases...they're oils, studio work I did from sketches I made during the war. They're not exactly beautiful.'

The girl smiled. 'You must allow us to be the judge of that! We are always open to new ideas, and our directors keep regular contact with the more forward colleges of art...diploma work mainly.'

Back at home, Dad said, 'You should go for it, Johnny. Don't pass up any opportunity. Your mother and I will put the word about. We think some of your work is very good.'

Thus encouraged, I returned to the top room and started painting again. I took the small portable radio from the study with me and worked on to the accompaniment of music and reported events a world away. India was to be partitioned, with Jinnah as the first Governor General of Pakistan. Dior launched his New Look. Then it was announced that the Princess Elizabeth was to be engaged to a young naval lieutenant from the Mountbatten family.

I set aside the two paintings that I felt had come out best. The first showed concentration-camp victims being unloaded from trucks in the barracks square at Ventorf, and the second was a larger canvas depicting the Rhine crossings, a more exciting vision done with palette knife, thick paint, dark brooding blues, greens and black with searchlight beams and stabs of the tracer fire, red and gold. They were both unframed, but I took them down to Ebor and left them with the girl at the desk. If the director liked them, he would get them framed, she said, to be ready for the next 'local artists'.

'I couldn't raise anyone at Kate's place, where is she?'

It was Liz on the phone, asking.

'She's gone home to her father. Eglingham.'

'Is she all right? Has she had the results?'

'If you mean academic results, yes.'

'And?'

'She is a doctor!'

'Wow! Terrific! I must give her a ring. But how is she...did she tell you, y 'know...?'

'Yes Liz, she did, and now she needs to rest, lots of rest to get her strength back.'

'But we've got to celebrate! A party, Johnny!'

'Not yet. She's coming over to Yearsby, at least I hope so, we've got to give her a bit of time.'

Dear Liz – she sounded genuinely delighted. 'I'm so pleased for her! I knew she could do it.'

'Yes. I don't know what she wants to do next. Looking for a job, a posting I expect, but I've no idea, I'll ring you when I know.'

I added that when Anne came to Yearsby the best idea would be for her to come over as well if she would like to. She said if it fitted in with the end of her term she would love to come.

Time – or the concept of time – had always teased me, and now after all the frustration, the dullness, the feeling of being marooned or becalmed in the doldrums, everything seemed to collide. Anne's father rang to say he was bringing Anne over to Yearsby at the weekend. I rang Liz right away and told her she could stay for a day or two if she wished and we could all be together. There was then a message from Ebor Images. It was a male voice. He introduced himself as Tom Willoughby, a director of the gallery.

'Mr Hartside? We would like you to send us a brief CV – where you studied, your qualifications...degree or diploma, that kind of thing. Just drop us a note, will you? We find your paintings most interesting and, if you agree, we will include them in our next exhibition. It will be quite a small affair but we find that the local artists on our list usually sell quite well. We'd better have a rough idea on prices from you, and a line or two on where the locations were that formed your subject matter.'

I was surprised. I had no idea about price, I'd never given it a thought. I decided to have a word with Dad, he had a grasp of most things commercial. He was pleased when I told him what Ebor had said.

'I'll have a word with Bill Glaister at the Grange, he's a bit of an art buff and I believe he has bought from that gallery before.'

My note to the gallery was not difficult to write, and I told them that because of the war and call-up I had not been able to complete my diploma course in Oxford, and did not intend to return. I enclosed our suggestion on price – one at £80 and the *Rhine Crossings*, which I liked the best of the two, at £90. It seemed a bit too much to me, but the gallery's response was that I was asking too little. The price for each of them, they said, should be £150. Dad said they were thinking of their commission. I was astounded. They were not worth that sort of price.

Chapter Forty

A hot, dry day with the promise of hours of sunshine that burns into your bones and leaves a divine longing for you know not what. That was what my Muse said, as I was shaving. The dawn light of an English summer – that was the start of it. Doves belling away. Moist smell of new-cut grass through the window. It was a special day. Anne had come to Yearsby and I was happy. There should have been music – 'sweet sounds that give delight and hurt not'. They would herald the trio that we were – just Anne and Liz and me.

At breakfast Mum said, 'I think it's lovely that you can be together again…make up for lost time, make hay, isn't that what they say? Or is it gather ye rosebuds?'

We laughed. We had already decided nothing would keep us indoors. We took a basket with biscuits, glasses and a bottle of wine and walked from the house over a stile, down a long path fragrant with new flowers and then on to a favourite willow tree where we sprawled under dappled sunshine and shadow. It was time to gather our lives, to find the missing pieces and stitch them together again.

'You first,' I said to Liz. 'Say now, or pay a fine!'

She answered that there were no special excitements. I knew what she was saying. No Walter, she meant. She paused. 'It's not a long course and you don't need many subjects. English, which I had anyway, and maths, and they said music and art would help.' She managed a wry smile. 'Well, I used to like singing, and I can draw a bit. But frankly I think most of all you have to be simply crazy to be with kids. I'm longing for the course to finish…then I can go on to primary school, if I can find one to take me on.'

She sounded wistful, and my thoughts turned back to Whitworth, to our first meeting in the girls' garden. Anne against the sun and the baby wave and Liz with her bright smile. They were like sisters. Then I thought of Walter, but the safety curtain came down. End of show.

Liz said, 'Anne darling, you haven't told us. What was it really like when you knew you were home and dry…one minute a student and the next a doctor? It must have been fantastic!'

'Not much to report,' Anne answered. 'No great transformation, just too tired! The so-called ceremony in the hall was a bit intimidating, but everyone was really happy. My father came and lots of parents turned up…official photos, informal shots, lots of hugging and a bit of weeping. There wasn't much time left over. A dash back to the flat to change, then a taxi with Kate and off to the Union Palais!'

'Come again?' I said.

'The graduation ball in the union. You had to do it, except I got a bit sick – no, not the booze because I wasn't drinking – so Kate and her chap took me back to the flat before midnight. Called me Cinderella Sore Head, but they were very kind.'

I thought it was a sad ending to five years' hard work but she said, 'No, Johnny, it wasn't like that. I loved every minute at uni.'

They turned to me and said it was my time to confess, so I told them about my paintings and the Ebor Gallery and how I was obviously going to be the North Country's Michaelangelo. Then time went out like a tide on the ebb. We listened to the silence as the stillness and the warmth of the day spread its arms around us, three friends who met at the throw of fortune's chance just as, I supposed, most people met and became friends somewhere, sometime between the cradle and whatever was to follow. The warm air pressed us close to the earth. We were loath to stir, so just drank the wine and wished ourselves lots of luck. Liz said we should play a game. I guessed games would be her life in a primary school…tambourines, crayons and chalk and stories and a mop to wipe up.

'There was that game we played at school, Anne, do you remember? Rhymes?'

Anne opened her eyes and smiled. 'Of course I remember. It was usually on wet afternoons.'

It turned out to be a teaser, a daft invention. Each of us had to say a rhyming couplet in turn and see how our line led to the others…a bit like consequences. Liz had a think, then said she would begin.

'Under a willow tree, who loves to lie with me.'

Ah. Distant echoes of a poem I'd heard before. I replied with the first words that rolled into my head: 'I'll lie by your side, and have you for a bride.'

Anne jabbed me in the ribs with her elbow and declared: 'Alas! Alack, no bed, Love's lesson has been read.'

They wanted to continue the theme, so I volunteered, 'Who loves not is a fool, that is the Golden Rule!' Anne responded, 'But when all passion's done, where now the warming sun?'

Liz paused. Anne said, 'Lizzie darling, I think you're stuck…bad luck!'

After a search for words Liz then found some: 'Go seek another tree, that's my philosophy!'

I offered a change of course: 'We're like a musical trio, and terribly *con brio*!'

Groans all round. I said, 'That song – about the willow tree. I can't remember it all, but it was something like this: "I'll hang my heart on a weeping willow tree and never, never think of thee! Fare thee well, for I must leave you, do not let this parting grieve you, and remember that the best of friends must part, must part. Adieu. Adieu. Adieu. Adieu, kind friends, adieu, I can no longer stay with you, stay with you…" '

I forgot the rest of it.

'Don't be so gloomy, Johnny,' said Liz reprovingly. 'No partings! Best friends do not part!'

The wine had made us sleepy and we dozed. When I opened my eyes again there was a whisper of a breeze, and then it happened again. In the leaves above me I distinctly saw the face I had seen before, the ancient with the smile that turned to a malevolent scowl. It was ridiculous but it was real and it unnerved me.

'Sun's dropping,' I said. 'Time to go.'

Surprised, Liz said, 'What's the hurry, Johnny? It's lovely here!'

Anne propped herself up on her elbows. 'I know why Johnny wants to go – it's his devil up there in the tree.'

'Oh, *that*!' exclaimed Liz. 'I think it's all in the mind. Artists are like that, aren't they?'

Anne stood up. 'Why don't you take us to your masterpieces, Johnny? I'd love to see them.'

It was inevitable. The painting they wanted to see was the one I had made from my sketches at Belsen depicting unbelievable carnage. They inspected it closely, fascinated, with exclamations of horror. They turned away then were drawn back to it. Anne shook her head as if denying what she saw. 'We heard about that, and Auschwitz where they said more than a million people were exterminated.'

'And so many of them children with their mothers,' exclaimed Liz. 'How could they do such things…? I can't believe people can behave worse than savages, they must have known what they were doing.'

'They knew only too well,' I replied. 'It was all planned. An immaculate agenda of annihilation.'

My painting was crude, roughly set down. I took no pride in what I had attempted to depict.

'Whenever there is war,' said Anne, 'paintings like yours, Johnny, should be hung on every wall. To be told of inhumanity is one thing, but to see it, to have to confront it, is quite another.'

Then they wanted to gaze upon such obscenity no longer, and I began to wonder all over again, when people knew, did they pray, did they kneel and turn to God, did they cry out or look the other way and pretend it never happened? My tawdry faith took another dive.

We did not linger in the top room. Through the windows the bright day still blazed, shafting light into the dusty corners. It served only to illuminate the sadness that had taken hold of us.

Then it happened. At the turning of the stair Anne collapsed, seemed to miss her footing and fell headlong down as Liz, too late, cried, 'Careful!'

✳

Dr Gaynor took his time. He said she might have lost consciousness, if only briefly, or else she had been reckless, attempting to move too quickly. She should remain in bed, he said, which was where, not without difficulty, we had persuaded her to go.

'Muscle weakness,' said Gaynor, 'is a telltale sign. You say she has just qualified as a doctor? Then she will know this, and should take care. It can happen without warning.'

He did not prescribe medicine. Bed rest, he said. And plenty of it. Then seeing our faces he boomed: 'She'll live! Bruises will be the worst of it!'

I could not know what was in Liz's head. For myself I thought a private prayer would not be out of place. But then the words of that hymn unfairly reached into me: 'Let us with a gladsome mind praise the Lord for he is kind.'

No. No. Prayer would be a fruitless exercise.

Chapter Forty-one

We had no choice. Anne was to remain in bed. She of course declared that she was perfectly well again, she was not an invalid and did not want to be treated as one. Liz and I took it in turns to sit with her each morning. In the afternoons she slept.

When the Ebor Gallery rang I was in the top room. Mum shouted, 'Johnny, please come down, that's the second time. He was quite short with me, he wants to speak with you, he left his number.'

I thought hopefully he might have sold my two paintings, then remembered the local artists' show had not yet taken place.

'Mr Hartside, sorry to trouble you, but do you by chance have any more work you might consider letting me see?' He explained there had been a change of plan. The 'local artists' was to be confined to just one exhibitor and would I call him back as soon as convenient? If I had other paintings and they were considered acceptable the gallery would start the new regime with a solo launch of my work.

I was astonished and, I admit, flattered. Liz cried, 'Whoopie! Go for it, Michaelangelo!'

Anne agreed. 'It's a great opportunity, Johnny, and you have got more you could show, haven't you?'

'Probably half a dozen. I'll have a look.'

Liz wanted to have a look, too.

'I thought you were going to help my mum with flowers. Church tomorrow.'

'Well, I was, but she's already done them. So can I come and see what Michaelangelo has in his locker? I could help you to choose.'

'No you couldn't! You can come and have a look if you wish, but you won't like what you see.'

Back in the top room I sorted out six canvases. They included the landscape of fire-stormed Hamburg with its few remaining buildings burned black and sticking skyward like broken teeth in a massive jaw. Also the monastery at Achel with the few sheep grazing among wrecked tanks and lorries. There was the one with Captain Ramage and Baz loading a stretcher into the back of an ambulance, some concentration-camp victims being off-loaded in the barracks square at Ventorf, and the group portrait I had attempted showing Sittard's deputy Burgomeister with his wife and two young daughters.

Liz called: 'What about this one? I didn't know you had painted Anne…golly! Did she let you, I mean, like *that!*'

She had found the painting set aside in a far corner, the one Clubby Nash had helped me with, the one I called *The Waterfall.*

'It's super, Johnny! Did she really…?'

'No, she did not. And anyway it's private, not for exhibition.'

'Well, I think it's lovely. Very good likeness, even with her hair down, I've never seen it like that before.'

She came across and planted a kiss on my cheek. 'You're so clever! You should do more portraits.' She pulled a face then put her lips to my ear. 'I'll sit for you, if you like.' Then she paused. A stage whisper. 'I'd let my hair down too!'

I told Anne we would just be an hour or so. Liz helped me to carry the six paintings to the car and then into the gallery in town. The director was not present, but the girl took them to the second room and said the director was expected back tomorrow and would be in touch.

As a 'thank you' for her help I took Liz for a cup of tea. 'We'll go to Terry's, haven't been there for ages, the last time was a kids' party in the big room upstairs. Little boys, and girls in white lacy dresses with big pink bows. Tots with their mums. I fell in love with the sheriff's daughter, she was my age, five or six!'

The room was just as I remembered it…the sprung floor for dancing, lots of polished mahogany panelling. Now, there was a flotilla of tables and chairs and gossiping housewives taking a break from shopping. I ordered tea and cakes. Liz wanted to talk about Anne and asked questions

I could not answer. Would she now be able to practise as a doctor? Would a hospital take her knowing she had an inhibiting illness? I told her I had no idea.

'It's a strange sort of illness. It seems there are times when she simply has to rest, just as she is doing now, and other times when she is in remission. One problem seems to be that you can't tell when, or for how long.'

Liz said that she had been terribly shocked. 'I couldn't believe it. I mean, we're best friends, real chums, always have been as you know. Even during the war we managed to keep in touch except when she disappeared to Dominica.'

I wasn't sure whether she wanted to talk about Walter, but I dived in. 'You must miss Walt very much. I loved him, you know, we shared our love for him, didn't we?'

She smiled. 'He was a lad, not always one hundred per cent reliable, but he made me laugh and feel great. It was a good day when he was around. And yes, of course it leaves a gap. We were close, very close at times.'

I thought I knew what she meant. I ventured, 'Did you…?'

She coloured, looked down and lowering her voice said, 'Once or twice. Then the war got in the way.' She grinned, looked me straight in the face and our eyes met. They were blue, or green. Aquamarine. Colour of the sea. Perfect for a girl who had been a Wren.

'And what about you, Mr Michaelangelo? Did you?'

'No, never. Not with Anne, of course not. But, like you, just once or twice, a long time ago.'

She feigned shock. 'Johnny! Really, you surprise me! Who, then?'

'No names. A lady artist.'

She rolled her eyes, tried to suppress a laugh. 'Bloody artists – a bad lot. All the same, aren't you!'

I got to my feet. 'I think we ought to go.'

'I'm paying,' she said. 'My treat!'

We drove back to Yearsby and on arrival another surprise awaited us. We found Anne in the sitting room by the fire, head in a book.

Liz went down on her knees. 'Anne darling, you're so bad! As soon as our backs are turned. Who said you could leave your bed?'

'The doctor.'

I said, 'I don't believe that. Which doctor?'

'Me. I prescribed a little gentle exercise. I'm just a bit stiff, that's all.'

She put her book down on her lap. 'Did you have a nice tea?'

Startled, I asked, 'How on earth…? Yes, we did. Terry's.'

Liz stood up, an expression on her face I could not read. 'How did you know we had tea?'

'Because you were quite a long time, and if I had gone with Johnny instead of you, he would certainly have bought me tea.'

We all laughed. Of course I would – and probably a little present, too.

They went their separate ways, Liz to her teacher training in Durham and Anne back to Edinburgh.

'I can't stay, Johnny, much as I'd love to, I'm expected back in the infirmary to make a start, at least six months, wards 32 and 33. The prof's unit.'

I was disappointed. 'But will you be all right?'

'Yes, I will. Anyway I'm not going to miss out, it's quite a plus to be on the prof's team.'

It all sounded so normal – except that it wasn't. The birds had flown and Paddy had returned to Whitworth. Yearsby was an empty shell and I felt miserable. I should have worked on the portrait of Paddy that I had started and done the remainder when he returned, but it would have to wait. I had no inclination to work, so left the top room and spent days lazing in the sun…a hot, dry month. I strolled down to the willow tree and grabbed at memory, seeking to catch again the chosen two who had – each in her own way – fired my admiration and claimed my heart. Thankfully the leaves above me did not stir, and my thoughts turned to Liz who said she would sit for me. Why not? I had painted Anne by the waterfall.

Perhaps one day I should make a portrait of Liz beneath the willow that she liked so much.

'Darling, do cheer up!' said Mum. 'You should feel very proud to have your own solo exhibition. I'm sure it is most unusual, especially for a first-timer.'

The gallery people were more than kind. They had accepted my six paintings and, with the original two, had given them a room all to themselves. They had also prepared a brochure – *One Man's War*. The paintings were listed, named and priced and a brief CV was included on the back page.

Anne kept her promise and phoned me once a week. Ward work, she said, was fascinating and boring by turns, but she welcomed a change as she also had to put in time in a hospital called The Sick Kids, and in the Women's Hospital. As for the future, she had yet to make up her mind between hospital wards or moving out to a practice somewhere or other. There were times, she explained, when she was not as physically strong and active as she needed to be.

Liz also phoned. She wanted an update on Anne, and asked about the exhibition at Ebor Images. I gave them both a brief account, basically the same letter:

> The private view was a modest affair. Not many people were invited. Some locals came, including my mum and dad, a bunch of teachers and a few service types who had recently been demobbed. Also, two ruffians from the local county rag who, I am sure, only dropped in for the glass of wine. Photos were taken and I had to answer a few questions, but it was hardly an interview. No red pops so far, and it is very difficult to know whether anything will sell. I suspect many people are not eager to be reminded of the war and how they themselves had survived the past six years. Perhaps for many their nearest and dearest had not been lucky.

I sent love to them both and told them how much I was missing them, for it was true. Friends should be closer and there for each other. The show cheered me but apart from that I felt isolated.

Chapter Forty-two

I seemed I had acquired a benefactor. He had come up from London. His name was Durand and he bought five of the paintings. I was astonished. The gallery reported that he was a merchant banker, a collector of mainly 'modern' works of art and a friend of Tom Willoughby, the director of Ebor. He had left word to say he felt there was a market for my work and I should add to what I had already done.

Mum and Dad were genuinely pleased for me and planned a celebratory supper to show me off to their friends. It was a start, they said. Very encouraging. I certainly liked the cheque the gallery sent, but when we calmed down any inclination to run to my easel in the top room faded away. I was out of focus, my mind and heart were with Anne. I was not thinking of form and colour and space on canvas, I had a different ambition in mind. It was not new and had declared itself too early maybe, but I had known where I was going the moment Anne had stepped into that waiting room at Oxendale Halt. Now, the long wait was over. It had to be marriage. Mum must have known this because she really did love Anne as well and probably looked upon her as the daughter she had always wanted but could never have.

I was calm. I was in the study with Mum and Dad. It would be a good opportunity. He had bought a fancy new gramophone. It played only one record at a time but had two loud speakers. Tonal quality – superb. We had Tchaikovsky, the *Nutcracker Suite*, Opus 71a. When it ended I dived in headfirst and told them I had something to tell them, and it was important.

Dad grinned. 'You were never backward in coming forward, Johnny. So what is it? I expect you now want a proper studio. Is the top room not good enough?'

No, I told them. Nothing to do with the top room. I just blurted it out. 'It's Anne. We want to get married.' I said 'we' because I was sure, not just for myself but for Anne as well.

Mum nodded. 'Well I must say, darling, it's hardly a surprise, your father and I suspected this for some time. But you're not engaged yet – are you?' Her eyes twinkled as if to signal 'have you been up to something?'

I told them we were not actually engaged but would be very soon. 'We have waited long enough.'

Dad said, 'Your mother and I are very fond of Anne, she is lovely and a very bright girl, but how do you plan to manage? In our judgement it is too soon. You can't marry when you have no job! You have to get work and earn some money first.'

'I already have earned some money, and given a fair chance I will earn more. And anyway, until I get started, Anne is already earning. Doctors do get paid, you know.'

'Darling, we know, we *know*! But you can't just rely on that. Be sensible, dear. She has a serious condition for which there is no known cure. We hope it won't but it is likely to get worse, and you can't tell how quickly, even doctors don't know.'

I felt hot. I was getting angry. 'That's all the more reason we should wait no longer.'

Dad asked, 'Have you spoken to Anne's father? What has he got to say?'

'No, but I will. He's a nice enough chap, he's no problem.'

'Well, Johnny, I'm sorry if you think we are a problem, but we are convinced you must not rush into this, you really should wait, and after all you can still be friends.'

That did it. I began to shout at them. I told them they did not know how it was for younger people these days, the war had changed everything.

'We've been through a war – remember? And we've survived up to now and we intend to survive in the future!'

'Yes, Johnny,' answered Dad, growing heated. 'You've survived, thanks to us. We provided hearth and home for you…and we'll always be here for you, but not, I repeat *not* if you insist on going on with this so soon and against our wishes!'

'*Soon?*' I shouted. 'Soon? You are a joke, completely out of touch! We're not kids any more…'

I was furious. I turned and left the room, slamming the door behind me. Running into the hall I nearly knocked Amy over.

'Whatever's the matter, Master John,' she exclaimed, 'you're never rowing, are you?'

In the kitchen I caught my breath, and calmed down a bit. I wasn't sure whether Amy had been listening at the keyhole but I told her they would not countenance my marrying Anne.

'Well I never! I don't know, but if that's what you want she'll make you a lovely bride! Can't see why not – she's nearly one of the family already!'

Blessings upon you Amy, I thought.

She said, 'Never you mind, they'll come round to it, you'll see.'

To my surprise she then went to the butler's pantry and emerged with a bottle of sherry and two tumblers. 'Now, Master John, we'll just have a drink. A toast. But don't you ever tell your mam!'

So saying she half-filled the tumblers, raised hers and said, 'Cheerio to lovers! I hope you'll be ever so happy!'

I raised my glass to clink, then immediately put it down on the table. I froze. It was dark cooking sherry, but not so dark that I couldn't see into it…a black, ugly-looking spider was attempting to crawl up to the rim.

I told them I was going to see Anne's father. In fact, I took the train to Edinburgh and at Waverley checked into the North British Hotel. I had money enough from the sale of my paintings, and could easily afford decent lodgings for the night. They turned out to be very smart. I was shown to a quite luxurious room. It was towards evening. I unpacked my case then rang through to Kate's flat. I was delighted – it was Anne who answered. She was surprised and pleased to hear me but said we could not meet for supper as she had a prior engagement. She could come for supper the following day. I slept uneasily and was restless. The trains below my window seemed to be arriving or departing all night long.

After breakfast I took a turn around the New Town and bought some flowers, which I asked reception to put through to the dining room and place on my table. I had noted that the National Gallery of Scotland was a short step along the street from the hotel so decided to take a look. It was a temple-like building. I padded from gallery to gallery. Fantastic! Such portraits! Gainsborough. Raeburn and so much more. Studying masterworks for several hours proved to be exhausting, so back at the hotel I went to my room and dozed until I was woken by the bedside telephone. Anne had arrived.

The table with the flowers, and even a single lighted candle, could not be faulted and the menu was just as good. We had a delicious meal with a bottle of white wine and were then directed to the lounge for coffee. Anne was looking well and had told me how much she was enjoying her spell of hospital work. The waitress brought coffee and a little dish of chocolates, which she said were '*très populaire*' and were called Black Magic. That made me smile. It was a magical evening. I had rehearsed in my mind exactly what I would say, but had barely begun when Anne held up her hand.

'Johnny darling, I know, and I realise what you want to ask because I have known for a long time. You have our future together beautifully mapped out…'

'Yes, so I have! And I think now is the right time. We have been apart so much. Remember that girl…the woman at the station who said were we running off to Gretna Green? Well, of course we weren't. And we won't! We can do much better than that!'

She was shaking her head. 'We're not running anywhere, Johnny, my love. With all my heart I longed for the day when you would ask me, and I've always known what my answer would be. But now…no. It's different. We can't.'

I could not believe what I had heard. She was saying, 'Please, please listen. There is nothing in the world I would like better. But there's this stupid problem, this condition, and we have to realise there is no miracle cure.'

'But other people,' I said, 'there's no reason, I mean, illness doesn't keep them from marrying.'

'Others are not me. This illness is progressive. I have to accept that it can get worse and sooner or later, though I hate the thought, I may have to give up my work. Apart from that we could not be man and wife and that would not be fair to you.'

I was dismayed. I tried to reason with her. 'Anne, please? Marriage is for better, for worse, for everyone. And we could cope, I know we could. You are working in the normal way, and even if eventually it came to the worst I would look after you, I would never leave you.'

She was fully aware of what I was saying, and did not deny that there could be remission, but she still said no. I was stunned. I didn't really know, but I said, 'You could be okay for years and well enough to continue your work, so why not?'

'Look, I know, and only I know what this illness is doing to me. There can be no guarantees. We have to be realistic, Johnny.'

She was adamant. I could not believe it, and I was so disturbed I was not aware of kissing her goodnight. When she climbed into the taxi I could feel a stubborn barrier rising between us, and as the taxi pulled away from the kerb I hardly noticed it was a black night and pouring with rain. The commissionaire held his umbrella over me but I thrust him aside. Rain or no rain I would walk, I had to walk and try to come to terms with what Anne had said. But I couldn't. At the Scott monument I sat down and wept. How could she find it in her heart to dismiss the future we had promised each other?

From that black night a terrible bitterness took hold of me. This was not mere ill luck, there was something more at work, something sinister. The image of the ancient in the trees flared and burned its way into my mind. I felt numb and realised all over again there was such a thing as evil in the world. It visited me… it held me in thrall.

Chapter Forty-three

*M*um and Dad were concerned but I no longer cared what they, or anyone else, thought. Did they expect me to remain at Yearsby for the rest of my life, living like a monk? I returned to the top room thinking to work on the canvas of Paddy I had started but found I could not. Dismay turned to anger. Mum said I should get help, professional help. I knew what her advice would be.

'There's that doctor your father knows – he's mentioned him before. He is a physician but also a counsellor, a psychiatrist, and I think he is a Quaker as well. There would be no harm in seeing him.'

Quaker or not, I was in no mood for that kind of thing…what was the use? There was no therapy that would ease my pain. I began to believe I was possessed like the prophets and fanatics of centuries long gone who were taken hostage by the power of evil. I was haunted by the leaves in the willow, and those other trees. Then there was the image of that spider in the glass – a bad omen that struck fear into me all over again. The love I had lived by with my friends…Walter and Pop and the others at school and through the war, the companionship and energy I found now counted for nothing.

The top room became my refuge, my shelter. I carried my one meal a day up there. I put the unfinished canvas of Paddy on the easel, then I removed it and replaced it with the one showing Anne at the waterfall. Then I took a knife and in desperation thrust it through the canvas as a voice in my head cried Kill! Kill! The blade of the knife shone and I saw the throat of the Polish Officer, then the blade of the knife was soiled red…it was the paint, or else the picture was bleeding before my eyes. At night foul dreams tormented me. I thought I could smell in my nose the stench of the Belsen pit. By day I escaped across the fields to The Wagon Wheel, for that was the only place I could find solace, remaining for hours, propped by the bar, making my bid for oblivion. Time, those consecutive minutes and hours that should signal a day, a night, a year, fell out of place and shot half-remembered lines into me: 'Such a want wit sadness makes of me that I have much ado to know myself.' Schoolroom lessons surfaced with Hamlet clad in black and, like his, my life became eclipsed by darkness. The course it should be taking had disappeared.

There was no word from Anne. I had hoped that just maybe she would turn, would think again. Instead it was the voice of Jack Emslie on the phone that aroused me and dragged me back into the real world. An engineer, he said. He had graduated and was promised a position with an electrical company in London. He did not know about Walter, and was shocked when I told him. He had heard from Len who was proposing to emigrate. Canada.

Ebor Images wanted more. Durand had called them to enquire whether I had further work and if so he would like to have a sight of it. He had clients whom he thought would buy, or even hire. City companies had a new fashion, they sought work by 'artists of promise' to hang on their boardroom walls, reception areas and corridors – almost anywhere to impress their clients. This I learned from a visit to the gallery director.

On returning after the interview Mum asked, 'Where were you, Johnny? I thought you were in the top room, there's someone to see you. I sent her upstairs.'

My heart leapt. Anne. She had come to tell me she had changed her mind.

'She's asking for you, but can't stay long. It's Liz. She called in as she was on her way to Edinburgh to see Anne.'

I found her standing beside my easel holding the painting of Anne. *The Waterfall.*

'Johnny, in heaven's name…what happened to this?' She poked her fingers through the tear in the canvas.

I gave her a peck on the cheek. 'Don't know. Bit of a mystery.'

'Was it damaged at the gallery?'

'The gallery have not seen it. Never will.'

She laid the painting against the easel and stood, hands on hips, staring. She was genuinely upset. 'Are you going to tell me how it happened, because, well…it's criminal!'

I said nothing, and could not meet her gaze.

'Johnny! It's such a lovely painting!'

I plumped down on the stool. 'No, it's not. It's finished.'

'But you could mend it? You *have* to!'

I told her again – no use. It could not, it would not be repaired. 'If you're going to see Anne you'd better ask her.'

'But, she wouldn't…why would she want to spoil it, didn't she like it?'

I said that she had liked it, originally. But not now. Lies. All lies.

'What are you telling me?'

Then, the light dawned. 'No, Johnny, you didn't. How *could* you? Why?'

'Like I said, Anne will tell you.'

She walked over to me, put her hands on my shoulders and looked directly into my eyes. 'Something is very wrong here. How *is* Anne?'

'Don't ask me, how would I know!' Then, I cracked. I shouted, 'I don't bloody well know, there's nothing I can do!'

Tears sprang, stinging behind my eyes. Liz pulled me close, wrapped her arms around me and held me. 'Johnny, Johnny, you'd better tell me.'

She missed her connection to Edinburgh. She was determined to have me explain. I didn't want to talk about it, but I could not simply shunt her away like a truck into a siding, like a baggage not wanted on a voyage. She was Liz, faithful Liz. I pulled myself together, said I could do with a drink.

'Me too, thought you'd never ask.'

We walked over to The Wagon Wheel and I told her as best I could what had happened that evening in Edinburgh. 'She seemed to be perfectly well and obviously able to cope. After all, she is dealing with patients daily.'

'So you don't see why she can't deal with you!'

'I'm not a patient!'

'I'm not so sure!'

'For God's sake, Liz, stop treating me like a kid!'

'Not until you stop feeling so sorry for yourself! You have to see it from her point of view, and she is not thinking of herself, that's not like Anne, she is thinking of *you*. Would you really want the responsibility of having to look after someone who is seriously, and permanently ill? How would you manage?'

I reminded Liz that there was such a thing as remission and that she would probably be able to live a perfectly normal life for years.

'Johnny, you can't bank on that, there's no knowing. From what I've heard these periods of remission may last no more than months, then after that it's probably the wheelchair and permanent help, and that doesn't bear thinking about!'

This was not the Liz I thought I knew…I was seeing another person. Her strength encouraged me. Perhaps I had given up too hastily on Anne, and too easily laid all hope aside.

I said, 'Will you have a word with Anne when you see her? Be my envoy, my good ambassador and try to see if she might change her mind?'

'Knowing Anne, I don't suppose I'll have much success, but of course I'll try if that's what you want.' She pursed her lips, offered me a sad smile and added softly, 'What are friends for?'

Nothing ventured, nothing gained. We deserved another drink. And another. Then as we strolled back to Yearsby I apologised. 'You've missed your train by miles.'

'I know. Can't be helped, there'll be another.'

'Not today,' I replied.

Mum said Liz could stay the night, there was no problem. 'Amy can make up the bed in the nursery for you. Do you need a nightie, dear?'

Liz replied that she had all she needed – her case was in the hall.

'Then what we *all* need,' declared Mum, 'is a good hot supper! I'll tell Amy to lay another place.'

We felt better for that. Liz did not know it but she had come to my rescue – and just at the right time.

Chapter Forty-four

I did not hear from Liz for several weeks. She must have been nearing the end of her teacher training. I returned to my painting and confidence began to return as I took hold of palette knife and brush. I rescued the portrait of Paddy. It was coming along well. Then I worked up several of the landscapes of the hill country and Oxford meadows.

The letter from Liz, when it arrived, would probably contain news I did not want to hear. I was not hopeful. And I was right.

> Sorry to be so long, Johnny. I can't pretend to bring you glad tidings, because frankly I'm not sure. We had a chat, more like the old days and that was good. But I think Anne is in two minds – or even three. In her heart I am sure she wants what you want, but at the same time she is clearly worried about herself. What complicates matters is that she is desperately keen to continue the work she has started and which she obviously loves. I have not done very well, Johnny, and I am so sad not to give you better news. The one surprise – did she tell you she is getting a car!

I'd had no idea Anne could drive. Perhaps it was a positive, more hopeful sign. I decided to ring her and suggested that I could come up the following weekend. She replied that it would not be very convenient. Rightly or wrongly I disregarded it. I was going anyway.

At the flat Kate made me feel welcome and seemed determined to be friendly. When Anne came in from hospital later that evening she seemed quite cheerful and, oddly, looked a bit older. There was a difference.

When we turned to hold each other and when we kissed she was not the Anne who had danced with me in the garden by the sea, it was not the same as when we shared that special day by the waterfall. Some of the magic, the enchantment had fled and it was almost as if I was holding a stranger in my arms.

The Friday morning was 'inconvenient' but the afternoon was clear and Anne said she was free until Monday morning. I was pleased. We could be together. When Kate excused herself, and said she was meeting friends, that was even better. I suspected Kate was being tactful – and kind. She left a teatray with two cups, sugar, milk and digestive biscuits.

Spaces. Pauses. It was like searching for the right words, or reaching for a dictionary when striving to speak a language half-forgotten.

'This car?' I asked. 'You didn't tell me.'

She replied that it was the little roadster, a Riley Rover, that Dr Alex Gordon used to drive. Now, he was leaving town. 'When he knew he was moving on he said he would sell it to me. Actually, he nearly gave it to me...a knock-down price. Sometimes, when we used to go for a spin, he'd let me take the wheel.'

'He was very fond of you, wasn't he?'

'He never said so, but yes, I suppose in a way he was. He was good fun.'

'But is it safe for you to drive, especially when you get so tired?'

'I'm perfectly all right, Johnny, as long as I go carefully. And if I feel too weak I do not get behind the wheel. I'm being sensible – ask Kate.'

Spaces again. But they were shorter as she told me what she planned. 'I'm trying now to decide just what to do. I like the Women's Hospital, and the Sick Kids, too. But on the other hand the idea of joining a practice somewhere does appeal. The work would be much more varied. I'd have to take another course before being accepted, but that could be interesting and not too long.'

She wanted to know about my painting, and I told her the gallery was a good contact to have. Especially for future sales. I did not tell her about *The Waterfall*.

When she carried the tea things back to the kitchen I went to the lav. It was then that I heard a crash and Anne shouting: 'Damn! Damn! Damn!'

I found her on hands and knees trying to pick up the broken shards of the cups and saucers but not doing it very well.

'Oh God, Johnny! *Again!*' She was distressed and wailed: 'It's my hands, my fingers, I lose all feeling in them. I can't help it, it's happened before, last time it was a flower vase. So *stupid!*'

I picked up the pieces. 'No problem, we can replace them.'

'They're Kate's best, she'll be upset. Paragon. Bone china.'

She tried to smile but looked more as if she would cry. I took her hands. 'It's not the end of the world, you can tell her it was me!'

'But you don't understand! I lose all sensation...I can't tell when it's coming on!'

I kissed her hands. 'Come on, doc – we can beat it!'

It was easy to say, but I was far from sure that we could.

The plan was to slip down to Eglingham, just the two of us to see her father and stay for a couple of nights. En route we called in town. Jenners. A replacement for Kate. Minton. And I insisted on buying a set for four, with teapot and bowls. In return Anne squeezed my hand and gave me a kiss. She had recovered and said she would drive the Riley Rover. It was a smart little car, burgundy and bright chrome and with leather upholstery.

We left the city behind and the sun appeared as we motored through Haddington and Dunbar, and Anne was enjoying herself on the long A1 stretch beside the coast with the hazy Lammermuirs on our right. We stopped for a late coffee in Berwick, and I took the wheel to give her a break.

'After the Holy Island,' she said, 'look for the turn off at Belford. That takes us to Chathan and then Chillingham. From there it's easy, just the farm lanes to Eglingham.'

She was a good navigator and we breezed along with the country air and farm smells teasing our noses, mainly from a pig farm with little huts, which seemed to stretch for miles. All went well until, just past Chillingham, she cried, 'Slow down! Slow down, Johnny!'

I had no choice. In the middle of the road there was a woman waving her arms wildly. Probably a hitchhiker, said Anne. We pulled alongside the woman and Anne wound her window down. 'You all right? D' you want a lift?'

On closer inspection the woman turned out to be little more than a girl, probably in her late teens. She slipped a small rucksack from her shoulders and said, 'Newcastle.' She was wearing a man's coat by the look of it and a grubby grey trilby hat.

I said, 'We're only going as far as Eglingham.'

'Okay, man! Just take us to Alnwick, I'll get a lift from there.'

She sounded like a Geordie and there was something about her I did not like. I said, 'Sorry, we're not going that far.'

Anne interrupted. 'Johnny! Don't be so mean! It's only a mile or two and we've plenty of time.' She nodded to the girl. 'If you want a lift, hop in the back then.'

The girl needed no invitation. She plumped down on the back seat, and we drove on.

Near Old Bewick she leaned forward and tapped me on the shoulder. 'What's your name, pet?'

I felt distinctly uneasy, so told a lie. 'I'm Bobby. What's your name?'

'Never you bloody well mind, Bobby. Just stop the fucking car right here!'

Anne, surprised, said over her shoulder, 'What's the problem, d' you need a bush?'

'No, pet,' she replied, 'I need this fucking car. See!'

I heard Anne gasp. 'She's got a knife!'

I pulled to a stop and turned in my seat. She was smirking.

'That's right, pet, I gotta knife – and now I'm gonna get yer nice little car!'

Before I could prevent her she pushed forward, grasped Anne's neck and held the knife against it.

'Now, Bobby pet,' she hissed, 'be a smart lad, switch off and bloody get out. *Now!* Do it quick or the lady's jugular will spoil her pretty dress, know what I mean?'

I knew what she meant and she looked as if she would. I froze. 'Just put it away,' I said. 'Don't be so foolish – and *you* get out!'

'Now, Bobby, my bonny lad, ye do as I say, both of you, or you'll not get to your weddin' an' that would be a fucking shame, wouldn't it!'

There was no wedding, I said. Anne was trembling. The girl held the knife closer and pressed the long blade to Anne's neck. 'I'll count fucking five till ye get the message, then *out*! Ye get *out*!' And in a soft voice she began to sing. 'Bobby Shaftoe's gone to sea, silver buckles on his knee, he'll come back and marry me, bonny Bobby Shaftoe!'

Anne gasped, 'She's mad! Do as she says, Johnny!'

'An' mind ye leave the key!' She flashed the blade, and as she did Anne flung out an arm to push her away, then cried out as the blade sliced into her just below her elbow.

I tumbled out onto the road as Anne struggled clear from her side. Like a nimble cat, the girl climbed over into my seat, fired the ignition and swung the car away down the road with the doors flapping open. She was howling with laughter and started yelling: 'Bobby Shaftoe's gone to sea, but he's *nay* escaping me-ee...'

The car disappeared round a bend. We were stuck. Anne said, 'The bitch! My car, my lovely car!' Blood was coursing down her arm and she was screwing up her face in pain.

We did the best we could, there on the side of the road. She slipped off one of her stockings and we made it into a tourniquet with a stick from the hedge to turn the knot and staunch the flow of blood. We began to walk. We were completely fazed, I was furious.

It was nearly half an hour before a farm tractor towing a trailer trundled towards us. I waved the driver down. He stopped, climbed out and showed no surprise at seeing what he must have thought were a couple of townies.

'You seen a young lass go this way?' he asked. 'Wearin' a daft hat an' one o' my best coats?'

We nodded. 'She has a knife.'

'Aye, that'll be her. Did she hurt you?'

'We need a phone,' I said. 'She's made off with our car, and yes, she has hurt my friend, and we need a doctor.'

He pushed his cap back from his brow. 'She never! The young bugger! Out of her mind...stole yer motor, did she? I'll have the police on her! Where are you making for then?'

We told him and he said he was going to Alnwick and could give us a lift – if we didn't mind getting up into his trailer. It was, as he admitted, 'a bit clarty'.

'Niver bother,' he said, 'I'll tak' yer. Visiting his Lordship, are yer?'

We thanked him and said no. We needed to visit a hospital. And the police. As quickly as possible.

Chapter Forty-five

nne's father wanted her to remain in bed but she said no, it was more sensible to remain mobile and keep her muscles and circulation moving. She knew she was in trouble. The local doctor had stitched the wound in her arm but her back was painful. She had hurt it as she scrambled from the car. As for the Riley Rover, we gave the police the registration number but they said they were not confident that they could track the car down if it was driven out of the county.

It was so unfair. Anne had more than enough to cope with. I noticed she was dragging her right foot. The run of bad luck that seemed to have beset us was becoming too much. I became obsessed all over again with the vision of the face in the tree.

Over supper I broached the subject with Anne's father, half-hoping that he would laugh and blame 'an artist's fevered imagination'. But he didn't.

'There is a long history concerning sprites, tree spirits and woodland goblins that make mischief. It goes back long before mediaeval times when most of England was covered by dense forests, the haunt of miscreants, criminals and murderers. Six centuries ago wise men declared that forests were the haunts of hobgoblins and terrible apparitions.

'One thinks of Odin in Norse legends. He became a God and slaughtered forest giants then divided the world with their bodies before creating the first human beings whom he called Ask and Embla. It is said that he had two ravens called Hugin and Murrinum who flew round the world to tell him all that they saw. Odin himself assumed different shapes – a bird, a serpent, and hid in trees. He travelled like a spirit while his body slumbered.'

Anne cried, 'Really, father, Johnny's imagination is bad enough as it is, don't make it worse! Is that what they tell you at the Forestry Commission?'

'Far from it,' he laughed. 'We are totally scientific. But…we should never close our minds to myths. As a species we need our myths and mysteries…we live by them.'

I did not want to hear more, but he was not to be silenced. 'Trees were the home of gods…the souls of unborn babies whose ancestors lived in the trees. The Greeks believed the first man was made from an ash tree, birch was the tree of health, while willow was the tree of sorrow, tears and enchantment.'

It was clear he was warming to his subject and would have continued had Anne not stopped him. 'I don't want to hear any more. My mother met her death by walking in all innocence into a forest…you're making me scary, we came here for a rest!'

When I went to bed I could not sleep. I was upset as I realised that since the war's ending…since I returned the world had turned upside down.

※

'A little knowledge is a dangerous thing,' said Doc Gaynor. 'And while we need knowledge there is no guarantee that it will solve all our problems.'

On returning to Yearsby I had made an appointment to see him because once for all I wanted to know the truth about Anne's condition. She was so changed. He asked me how she was and I told him. He was not surprised.

'As I have told you, it's a serious disorder. Women are more prone than men. The nerves cannot conduct impulses to and from the brain. Movement and sensation become restricted through weakness, then eventually can be lost completely.'

He confirmed that the symptoms could last weeks or even months at a time, causing sufferers to become increasingly disabled.

'After several years they may not become bed-ridden but are likely to need a wheelchair. The severity of the disease cannot be forecast. Some patients are severely afflicted, others less so, and we don't know why. Neurologists have different views. Regular scans are necessary. Drugs may be recommended. But the best advice is for the patient to keep as active as possible and above all to have a positive outlook.'

I saw more clearly now why Anne was refusing marriage, and I despaired.

✳

Anne phoned. She had returned safely. She said the police told her the car had been found wrapped round a tree on a bend near Newton Aycliffe. It was a write-off. I asked, 'What about that dreadful girl? She really was mad.'

'She should be dead. Apparently she survived. She's in hospital in Durham. Broken nearly every bone in her body except her skull. I'll ring the hospital.'

'Anne, you should do no such thing. She owes you nothing…unless it's a new back and a new car. You are insured of course?'

'Of course, Johnny. But *you* weren't. Not to drive my car. I should never have let you.'

She was right. Another disaster. And why did we take that particular route to Eglingham? That was the mystery – if only we had taken a different way, continued just a little further on the A1. Anne had tried to be sensible and take a short cut. But did someone else, or something else choose the route? The very thought chilled me to the bone.

Chapter Forty-six

Not a good idea. That is what I said, but Liz persisted. Her training course had ended and on her way to visit Anne again she had called in at Yearsby. A walk, I said. Okay. But not down to the willow tree, which was where, she said, we should go.

'But why not, Johnny? It was lovely there with Anne. I thought it was your favourite place.'

'Not any longer. I'm going to chop that willow down.'

'I don't believe it! You're joking!'

'No joke.'

'It's that stupid conceit of yours,' she grumbled. 'That face!'

I replied that I knew it must sound irrational, but there would be no willow tree today. Never again, thank you.

Liz was stubborn, she was not taking no for an answer. She persisted. 'Very well, irrational man, but at least we could walk down, just for once and wave goodbye old willow tree…your time has come!'

She was being silly, but in the end she had her way. We climbed the stile, followed the path and strolled arm in arm until we came to the tree.

'Now,' she declared, in a voice that announced she would brook no opposition, 'we will sit, just for a minute, all right? And we will take a good look and study the old tree's leaves, and we will not notice a thing. No face. Not any more. Gone forever!'

'Want to bet? And don't be so bossy! I'm not one of your nursery kids.'

'Primary, Johnny, primary.' She paused then asked: 'Please? Just for a minute.'

There was no use in arguing. I gave in. We flopped on to the grass beneath the green canopy, the branches almost trailing to the ground. It was pleasantly warm and still.

Not a breath of wind stirred the leaves. I looked up. She was right. No face, no ancient physiognomy scowling.

All I saw was *her* face, a bright smile and those eyes, a deep sea-blue, expectant, inviting, and I began to drown. She put her cheek against mine and murmured, 'Thank you, Johnny. See? The demon has flown!'

Then our lips met. There was no escape, nor did I wish that there should be. We sprawled, then held each other hungrily in a deep silence with only her breath quickening and her breasts shamelessly against mine. Like a ticker-tape message the words coursed through my head: 'Who loves to lie with me, under the willow tree.'

In the Wagon Wheel I bought her a cooling half and gulped down a pint myself. When these things happen someone should throw a bucket of water.

'Lizzie,' I began, 'what was that all about?'

'Nothing really. A celebration! Goodbye, old demon!'

Lovely Liz. A little crazy – she liked to talk in riddles. One word came to mind, and I said it. 'Brazen.'

She shook her head, then brushed an errant strand of blonde hair from her eyes. The blue ocean. Shining. Then she smiled. 'A brazen hussy, is that what you think? Why not? It's a free world.'

'No it's not!'

'Democracy rules,' she answered, then pursed her lips. 'Your move.'

I was not sure that I knew the game – I'd never played it. If this was a friendly we had shifted to a different league. She persisted, clearly amused, and that was better because I liked it when she smiled, and she did. Then winked: 'My queen to your king. It's checkmate – mate!'

I realised she was inviting me to play, so I stepped off the board. Time to change the subject.

'Tell me, what have they been teaching you at that training college? You've learned some new lessons since last we met!'

'Are you angry, Johnny? You can't be. We're from the same school, remember?'

'Yes, but you were West Wing, and I was the cold East.'

She smiled. 'I always thought of you as a warm person.'

'Are you going to tell me what this is all about?'

'Not now,' she answered.

'So, tell me about the teaching world.'

'I don't know whether I'll get it, but I've applied for a post in a small primary. I'm waiting to hear.'

I assumed it was in Durham but she said it was further south. 'You may know the place, it's not far from Middlesbrough. Roseburn, between Stokesly and Ayton.'

I knew exactly where it was. There was a Quaker school at Ayton. I remembered that Pop and I had played in a tough game against their soccer team.

Chapter Forty-seven

*A*nne's letter was optimistic. She was positive. She was moving on and that was good news.

It was my father's idea. He suggested I should contact that doctor in Alnwick who attended to my arm, Dr Manson. So, I did. It's hardly a posh practice, just himself and the nurse. I sent my CV, but he did not want a full-time partner. He said if I wished he would take me on part-time, a trial run. He was really kind. If we liked each other, and if the need arose, he would consider a full-time appointment. So – I've accepted! My father is pleased because I can live at Eglingham and I could do some secretarial work for him.'

There was no further mention of marriage, or her illness. Meantime I had to return to my own work. I completed four more canvases and sent them down to Ebor Images. The gallery was as generous and helpful as ever and put good prices on all four. I tried not to feel smug, but could not resist reminding Mum and Dad that I was now earning a modest living.

Christmas approached. I painted Amy and her friend the milk boy standing side by side, one pouting, the other pert and surprised.

Liz wrote to say she had 'landed' the teaching post she wanted at Roseburn. Her note contained an invitation to me and to Anne to visit St Hilary's for a special end-of-term event. The school's nativity play. Anne was prevented. Her surprising news was that her father had to visit Bavaria of all places on what sounded like a business-cum-holiday trip, and he was taking Anne with him 'as well as his skis!' She said there would be no downhill for her but she was looking forward to the après-ski.

I had never seen a children's nativity play before, and the St Hilary's version was, as one punster put it, truly 'Hilarious'. There came the moment where Mary, mother of Jesus, refused to cuddle her baby. The shepherds had brought a new-born lamb onto the stage, so Mary thrust the rag-doll baby to one side and took the lamb upon her lap with what could only be called a beatific smile. The audience rolled about in mirth, but the lamb was nothing compared to an inspired, chubby Joseph in grey school shorts who shouldered his staff like a soldier with his rifle and sang of a different miracle:

I saw two cods coddling
Down by the deep blue sea,
I saw two cods coddling
But I don't think they saw me…

These were his opening lines – but there was more and it became obvious that he must have heard the song in a pantomime. The most moving performance came from three angels who sang 'Still Night, Holy Night' very beautifully in harmony.

There was lemonade for the children, with mulled wine for teachers, proud parents and Liz and me. Afterwards we strolled out to the playground where cars had been parked. There was a hard frost beneath our feet and the cloudless sky above our heads fairly crackled with stars. 'In such a night,' I quoted, 'stood Dido with a willow in her hand,' and to my surprise Liz added: 'Upon the wild sea banks, and waft her love to come again to Carthage.'

No wild sea banks for us – just the bare branches of a solitary tree, and it was there beneath it that my universe spun as if new stars were being born. Her lips were sweet with wine as we tasted each other with unfeigned hunger. She murmured, 'I think I lost my way, Johnny. It was the war and losing Walt. I forgot my prayers and all that stuff we learned in RE at school, and which I actually believed.'

'Me too.'

We clung to each other, then glancing up she said, 'When you see all this how can you not believe? I mean I have no problem in teaching the kids that there is a God who made it all, and they learn to say their prayers, just as we were taught to do.'

'Do you teach them about angels?'

'Of course! Angels, yes, but not about that stupid demon of yours!'

I stopped her mouth with kisses again. I knew I desired her, but I released her. 'No more demons,' I said. 'And Lizzie, thank you for a lovely evening. I'd better be getting back now.'

She took my hand. 'No, please Johnny, no hurry, you can stay for a while.'

'I'd love to but I'd best be on my way.' I climbed into my hired car. She climbed in beside me and said, 'We have to talk, Johnny. About Anne.'

I said no. She leaned back. 'Then, we'll talk about us!'

'Not now, not here.'

'Well, where? Should we drive to a lay-by!'

'Lizzie, please! Another time. I'm going.'

'A lay-by, Johnny! It's my favourite fantasy. We turn off the main road and into the parking place. He clicks off the ignition with his slim and beautifully manicured fingers. Then, he turns and touches me...my face, tracing my brow, my cheeks, my lips, and I ache for his lips on mine...'

I said, 'Out! Out! Out! Goodnight, Liz!'

She stood beside the car. 'I hate you!'

'No you don't!'

'Johnny, please don't go, not yet. You have to understand, we need to talk!'

I climbed from the car and took her in my arms. 'Lizzie, don't let's spoil everything...we're better than that, and all right, we'll talk, but later.'

Getting back into the car I said, 'I'll give you a ring. Tomorrow.'

'Promise?'

I promised, then I started the car and turned slowly out of the playground onto the main road. I headed slowly back to Yearsby trying not to think but just to concentrate on the empty road and the verges sparkling with frost. And as I drove those school-day words returned: 'In such a night did pretty Jessica, like a little shrew, slander her love, and he forgave it her.'

I forgave Liz and I forgave myself long before I had reached journey's end beneath that resplendent heaven.

Chapter Forty-eight

A sense of guilt hung uneasily about me and one of those 'advices' Quakers were fond of quoting in meetings stuck in my mind.

Every stage of our lives offers fresh opportunities.
Responding to divine guidance, try to discern the right time
to undertake or relinquish responsibilities without undue
pride or guilt. Attend to what love requires of you.

Those last words went to the heart of me. What did love require? And, which kind of love? I had not attended a meeting for worship since those few occasions when, with the QRS, we had found time to sit quietly together awaiting guidance, and a sense of direction to our lives. Love was such a tricky word...a bobby-dazzler like a coat of many colours. One thing was becoming very clear. I was falling for Liz. My need sought to answer the need she clearly felt for me.

A card from Bavaria arrived showing a chalet perched on a snowy slope with a village nestling far below. Anne wrote that her father was working rather than having a holiday so she had spent most of the first week on her own.

I can't walk far but there is a good lift with gondolas which
I regularly ride to a mountaintop restaurant for the
magnificent views.

She added:

My love to Liz when you see her. Hope she is happy with
her school.

✳

It was shortly after the Easter weekend when Liz said again that we should meet. We had both been very occupied and I had completed four more paintings. Then I took a break and drove over to St Hilary's.

'Not the schoolhouse,' she advised. 'We'll go to the staff room in the school. It is hardly used during the holidays.'

A big window looked out onto the playing field…muddy grass and smudgy white lines. There was a single netball post. Two of the staff-room walls bore well filled bookshelves and files. There was a notice board crammed with scribbled messages and three lists of names headed Glenda, Marilyn, and David. For the rest — an empty fireplace and four chairs tucked into an oval table. At its centre was a bowl of fresh daffodils so brilliant that their petals almost trumpeted a fanfare. I guessed Liz had just put them there.

An easy chair completed the furnishings. There was a faint smell of cigarette smoke like a half-forgotten memory.

'If we are having an assignation,' I began, 'it's a rum place to choose!'

'We're not having an assignation,' Liz replied. 'We're having coffee.'

I had not noticed the kettle and mugs, I was too taken with Liz…a new hairstyle with the curls combed out straight and framing her face. She was wearing what I took to be a new spring outfit — a terracotta jersey with a V-neck, and a smart green skirt short enough to show her pretty legs. I sat at the table watching her and warmed my hands on the mug she gave me. She poured her own coffee and perched on the arm of the easy chair.

'You know why we're here, Johnny, but I'll say it just the same. I've known Anne as well as I've known anyone ever since we were kids at school. We shared everything, the same classes, the same dorm in Newsham house, the same games, the same garden. We swapped clothes, and we both had a fearful pash on the lovely A. J. who was our guide and mentor…remember her?'

'And you shared the same secrets as little girls do?'

'Of course, and made up stories about you and Walter! Anne was cleverer than me, I was better at games. But she was and still is my most special friend. I love her, and always will. And because I love her I can't bear to hurt her. That's the last thing I want.'

'So,' I asked.' Is that it?'

'Some of it.'

'What d' you want me to say? That you should no longer see Anne, because we are seeing each other?'

'No, I don't want that…I don't mean that.'

I waited.

'For God's sake, Johnny, tell me what *you* want, don't just sit there like a zombie, it's no help at all!'

She was becoming upset. I told her that I knew what she was really asking. If she and I were to become closer, how far would it upset Anne? I had not given it a run and could not answer. I needed time, for clearly there was a dilemma.

'Liz, the fact is I cannot really tell. I have not seen very much of Anne since Edinburgh, and it's true, I think she has changed. But, you know her so well, surely you are the best to judge?'

I was passing the ball back to her and she did not like it. She banged her mug down on the arm of the chair and wailed, 'Damn it, Johnny, you know I can't! Can you see me going over to her and saying Johnny and I want to go to bed together, is that all right with you?'

Then she really swore. 'Oh! Bugger it!'

I got to my feet. 'No need for that!'

'Yes there bloody *is*! Look!'

She was standing up and I looked. She had splashed some coffee onto her beautiful skirt. A large, dark stain.

'Better get cold water on to that right away,' I said. 'Go on! I won't look!'

'If you think I'm going to take my skirt off here you can think again!'

She was shouting, and it occurred to me that she *did* want to take her skirt off. I got the message but was not going to indulge in a wrestling match. 'All right, Liz, *all right*!'

I attempted to put my arms round her but she pushed me away. Then there were tears. I gave her my handkerchief and she dabbed, first her eyes, then the stain.

'I'm sorry, Johnny!'

'D' you want me to go?'

She sniffed. 'No, of course not. But, don't you see, we have to decide!'

I told her that when I needed to think, to try to find an answer to a problem, I usually managed better with a paintbrush in my hand. 'The two Cs – calm, and concentration.'

'But Johnny, can't you see how it is for me?'

'Yes, I can. And it's the same for me.'

I asked her to find me a pencil and some plain paper, there was bound to be some in a staff room. There was. She brought it to me, and muttered, 'Hey bloody presto!'

I gave her the daffodils from the table and made her hold them like a bouquet. She pulled a face, but obeyed and said, 'Brazen!'

I nodded, and as she sat there, the golden petals against her terracotta I started my drawing. It would make a painting, maybe a half-length portrait. I would call it *April*.

Before I left that room with the sketch of Liz and some colour notes, I realised that we would take the easy way out. I simply said we would have to be the same as we always had been. It would be no different to those times when all three of us were together. I could almost hear her measuring the risk, assessing the folly or the wisdom, the reality of it. She said again, 'I could not bear it, Johnny, if she thought we were, well…you know…'

I said, 'Trust me.'

A sad smile. A long look. A nod of affirmation. I think we both knew that words alone seldom solved a dilemma.

Chapter Forty-nine

To the twelve paintings I had completed, and which had gone on view at the gallery, I added two more, the portrait of Paddy, and the duo of Amy and the milk boy. I had hardly started the one of Liz. She came over on several Sunday afternoons when she was free so that I could work on it in the top room. The sessions were silent, apart from the small wireless set, which I switched on to keep her entertained. She held her pose patiently. It was a seated composition. I arranged 'rest' periods when music gave way to current affairs. She said her children liked to hear about the royal family and had made verses and drawings.

We heard that T. S. Eliot had been awarded the Nobel Prize. She said she could not understand his poetry – 'It defeats me!' She had found, however, that her children loved his *Book of Practical Cats*. She added, 'But Eliot was a religious person, wasn't he?'

I replied that I did not really know but thought he was pretty high church. The mention of religion made me think about our silent sessions. They were reminiscent of a Quaker meeting for worship, and it was she who suggested that for one rest period we should just sit quietly together: 'Like in a meeting.'

When I told her I no longer went to meetings and in fact rarely turned to prayer she was not to be distracted. She was serious. It would do no harm, she said, to sit for a short while together just as we all had done in the meetings at Whitworth. I made no objection. I said okay, provided that, instead of shaking hands to signify the ending of the meeting for worship, we could have a kiss. That was not in the rulebook, she laughed, but she complied. And for good measure she added a hug.

✳

The following month the banker Durand, who had been so influential and helpful in promoting my work in London, surfaced again at Ebor Images and asked if we could meet. I was totally unprepared for what followed. With several of his 'City connections' he told me he was keen to put some life back into British cinema. Their first venture was to finance a bunch of young film tyros at Elstree who were planning an historical costume drama. Part fiction, part fact, it was to feature the 1745 debacle.

'We have formed a company. The film writers are hammering out a scenario, and with two of my directors I will be making a visit north. Amazingly, they have never been north of the Wash and seem to know nothing of a place called Scotland!'

He explained that they were engaging the services of a distinguished American art director. 'He is not yet free to join the team over here, but meantime we require some research on location…the glens, lochs, Aberdeen, Inverness, and so on.'

Casting had already begun for the principal roles – the Bonny Prince, the Duke of Cumberland, and the ill-starred Forbes, Laird of Culloden.

'We'd like to co-opt your help, Hartside, set the ball rolling. We need reference material, sketches of the terrain up there, rough as you like but the colour must be accurate. If you are agreeable we'd pay travel and reasonable expenses for a short visit, so what d' you think? Does the idea appeal?'

I did not think twice, it was a terrific opportunity and, as my dad advised, 'A challenge you cannot afford to refuse!' He was keen to help and offered to stand the cost of a hire car. 'Roads are the only way to get around in the Highlands.'

I wasted no time and hired from the garage by The Wagon Wheel.

Before I left, bag packed and with pads and watercolours in a stout box, a message from Durand said that on my way he wanted me to call at the Gleneagles Hotel in Auchterarder for a final briefing. I was to ask for him there.

I had never been anywhere near Gleneagles, but I recalled when I was a kid hearing the hotel mentioned on the wireless. There was a band that used to broadcast from there. It was called Henry Hall's Gleneagles Band and it played tunes I liked.

✳

It was huge – an enormous building, more like a stately home set in a green park, with 'a nipping and an eager air'. The doorman at the imposing front steps wore a kilt, a dark cape and a bonnet with a feather in it. A true Highlander, I supposed, except we were not actually in the Highlands. I felt quite a toff when he gave me a toy salute and swung the door.

At the reception desk I asked, as instructed, for Mr Morgan Durand. The man lifted a telephone receiver. 'Your name, sir?' I told him.

'We have a Mr Hartside in reception, sir.'

He spoke for a minute or so then replaced the receiver. 'Mr Durand will be down directly. He suggests you wait in the lounge. Tea is being served there should you wish.'

I walked into the lounge, treading softly across the deep carpet. There were guests seated at small tables, with waitresses coming and going between them. I half-expected to find Henry Hall and his musicians but of course they had long since departed. Instead there was just a trio – piano, violin and cello – producing well-bred sounds gently modulated so they would not disturb conversation. Durand strode up and in his brisk and businesslike manner ordered tea. 'We've booked you into Muthill,' he said. 'Small hotel five miles north of here. Hope it will serve for an overnight stop, gives you a flying start for your drive up into the glens tomorrow.'

He selected a cigarette and tapped it on his silver case.

'Can't fit you in here, working to a tight budget, but I've told Muthill to send your tab to me. Two of my directors coming up tomorrow, quite expensive, d' you see?'

Over scones and Assam he told me about the film, which had the provisional title *To be a King*.

'We are bending history a bit, part fact, part fiction if you take my meaning, but we certainly include Drummossie, the Culloden area and that bloody battle. Big feature, several hundred extras, a few bawbees for the local laddies, eh?'

He'd been doing his homework.

'Our writers want to focus on Duncan Forbes, the local laird who was Lord President of the Court of Session…you'll be familiar with

231

the story. We're positioning him as a saintly sort of chap, who made an heroic attempt to restrain Cumberland from that slaughter after the engagement.'

I was only half-listening. At the far end of the lounge I had noted that the figure of a young woman, talking and nodding to her male companion, seemed distinctly familiar. They were taking tea and her back was to me but her hair…it was uncanny.

'Poor old Forbes,' Durand was saying, 'a peacemaker, good politician, bit of a saint but in the end of course he too meets his maker.' He paused. 'You all right, Hartside? Look as if you've seen a ghost!'

I thought I had. Shiny dark hair and the set of her shoulders. I could swear it must be Anne of all people – but if so, what in heaven's name was she doing here? She was a long way from Eglingham – and with a stranger.

I took my chance. When Durand was called to the phone I walked across to the end of the lounge where I had spotted a table on which was an assortment of magazines. It was almost alongside the couple. I selected a copy of *Country Life*, turned a page and stole a sidelong glance. At the same moment she looked up open-mouthed. A look of utter astonishment. Then her cheeks burned. No mistake – it was Anne. She stared, speechless, then recovered.

'Johnny! I don't believe it…what on earth are you doing here?'

'Anne!' I stooped to kiss her cheek. 'I could ask the same of you…this is incredible!'

Her companion sitting opposite looked as if he, too, could hardly believe what he saw. I guessed he was about my age, with a head of hair, silvery or prematurely grey. A handsome, smiling face, a firm handshake as he rose to his feet, tall, relaxed.

Anne said, 'This is Alex…Alex, Johnny.'

'Heard a lot about you,' he volunteered, 'how's the art world?'

An easy manner, almost off-hand. He smiled. 'Pull up a chair, won't you? Do come and join us.'

I was so shocked I simply stood rooted to the spot, then managed 'Thank you, but I'm with someone, it's business.'

A long silence. Questions crowded my mind. I turned to Anne. 'No, no, I don't want to interrupt. You remember Durand?'

'Of course!' He's the one who...the man from the gallery who likes your paintings.'

'Yes, that's right.'

Another silence. She was embarrassed. Then pulling herself together she said, 'It was Alex who sold me the Riley Rover, I think I told you. Doctor Alex Gordon!'

'Yes.' Then I turned my back on him. 'But how are you, Anne, how's it going?'

She shrugged. A wan smile. 'Doing along, as they say up here.'

It was then I noticed a black, rather handsome walking stick propped against the arm of her chair. On looking down I could also not avoid seeing...just a glimpse, her third finger, left hand. The ring was set with three bright diamonds.

The letter was waiting for me when I returned from an utterly miserable, cold, wet reconnaissance among the clouded glens and Drummossie.

Dearest Johnny,

You deserve an explanation, and an apology, which I now give you without reservation. In all fairness I was going to tell you when I got back. When Alex moved on from his house job in the infirmary our friendship did not end there. I did not feel I had to tell you that we kept in touch. I hardly expected to see much of him. Alex has now taken on a consultancy at Perth Royal – a big step for him. I think I told you he was a bit fond of me, well perhaps it was more than a bit. The truth is, he arranged this. He said I was to meet him at the hotel...he had booked for the weekend. So I went up there.

He has asked me to marry him. Very sudden, very unexpected. And I have accepted. Please don't be angry, I have no excuses, I don't know how it will work out. It seems that sooner than he, or I could wish, it will have to be just a friendship marriage. We realise it will be difficult and that there can be no guarantees.

She closed, sending her love. She wished me all the luck in the world and dearly hoped that we could remain good friends 'for always'.

I could not know and, I imagined, nor could she, just how long 'always' would be.

Chapter Fifty

*D*urand had told me to leave my colour visuals of Drummossie and the glens at Ebor Images. The gallery would send them through to him in London. I did so, and under normal circumstances I would have been eager to learn whether they were found to be suitable and, if so, how much I would be paid for my pains. But circumstances were far from normal and when Liz came over for her last sitting I chose my moment. I told her about Anne and the terrible coincidence. Just the facts. When I'd finished she astonished me by appearing almost unconcerned.

I put my brushes down, 'Take five, shall we?'

She came across and after a glance at the canvas she perched on the stool I used when painting.

'I realise it must have been a shock, Johnny, but I confess I am not altogether surprised.'

I could not believe what I was hearing. 'You mean…did she tell you? Did you know?'

She shook her head. 'Course not. But remember when you asked me to be your good ambassador and I did not get a very clear answer for you? Well, I did feel at the time she was not telling me everything. I didn't know what it might be, it was just a feeling. But what stuck in my head was that perhaps there was someone else.'

'You might have told me.'

'No, Johnny, honestly, I couldn't. I didn't know, I had no proof, and anyway I was not going to add to your miseries, was I?'

I could not believe any of this. But I did remember Anne once saying that a young doctor in the medical school had taken her under his wing. I wasn't really worried at the time, and I had not thought much more about it.

'Liz, it's just so unlike her to be secretive…you know that better than I do, but we never had secrets. At least she could have told me…I mean, how long do you think it's been going on?'

She shrugged. 'People change. You said so yourself. Circumstances, pressures, accidents, they all make a difference, and her illness, well that must be part of it. Maybe when it was diagnosed she needed someone to lean on, someone close at hand who could understand and be a support. It's pretty obvious that Alex, or whatever his name is, was just that person and he felt he was in some way responsible for her and came running.'

She put her arm around my shoulders and was shaking her head. 'I can only guess. I thought I knew her inside out, and in a way I still feel that I do. I suppose it's inevitable that people change and who knows the reason why? What's that line – "There are more things in heaven and earth than are dreamt of in our philosophy"?'

Fine words did not help. The truth was that someone had stepped in and taken my place. I had been rejected. And it hurt. It hurt like hell and started me wondering what I had done, where had I gone wrong.

I did not want to talk about it any longer, but Liz asked if I thought it would actually happen. Would they marry? I answered that I had no reason to think otherwise, she had after all made it clear in her letter.

'She said that was their intention…and she was wearing a ring. Three diamonds.'

Liz was silent, then sounded as if she was weighing pros and cons. 'Three diamonds. That sounds like an opening call – in bridge I mean. A pre-emptive opening bid. Its aim is to shut out the opposition.'

I did not know what on earth she was talking about. I had never played bridge, or any card game in my life, but I certainly felt shut out.

'Three diamonds probably means a long, strong suit…seven plus-cards and two honours, but it really all depends on the partner.'

I realised she was trying to distract me, to change the subject, to spare my feelings.

'C'mon, Johnny, you said this would be the last sitting. Are you going to finish me?' And she turned away to take up her position again.

I put my brushes and palette to one side. 'Leave it, Liz. Not now, the light's going.'

It wasn't and she knew I was simply making an excuse.

'All right, Johnny Hartside, in that case *I'm* going!'

She stepped across, took my arm and said, 'The Wagon Wheel?'

I did not feel like it, but I said okay and added, for want of something better to say: 'I didn't know you played bridge.'

'There's quite a lot you don't know about me,' she replied. And she winked one of her blue eyes.

I should have winked back, but I was in no mood and tried not to heed the rising anger that gathered in my gut.

Things to do. Like banking the cheque Durand had sent me. My sketches plus the pictures he had bought so far added up to a good sum. So – who said I could not earn a living!

I rubbed my dad's nose in it and he didn't argue. He sold me the old Star car for a pittance. He was replacing it anyway with an expensive Armstrong Siddeley Landaulette he had seen on his last visit to London.

There was a note with Durand's cheque. The team at Elstree had ambitious plans. When the movie, as he called it, was completed they wanted a meeting.

'Something for you to consider, Johnny,' wrote Durand. 'It's early days, but I advise you to keep yourself available. They'll want to talk.'

I was impressed. But all the talk in the world was not going to shift the ache, the feelings of resentment that had overtaken me.

Chapter Fifty-one

*T*he Sunday afternoon following my return from Scotland Liz
came over to Yearsby to see the portrait I had all but completed.
I think she liked it, but she did not like the letter – the one I
felt I had to write in reply to Anne. It was important that I should
respond, difficult as it would be and my intention was well meant. I
would wish her well, sure in the knowledge that in spite of everything
she deserved a happy life with Alex.

My good intentions did not turn out that way. Dismay clouded my
judgement. I found I could not say congratulations:

> I was shocked and upset that you could behave in such a
> manner. Nor can I understand how you could not find the
> decency, or the courage, to tell me about Alex from the
> start. I am at a loss to believe that you above all people
> could be so devious. You hid behind pretence with a total
> disregard for my feelings and for all that we had promised
> each other. You cheated, and if you expect me to wish you
> well the truth is that I cannot. I have to assume your illness
> is destroying the person I always thought you to be. As for
> remaining friends, I believe you must mean that as some
> kind of a joke.

There was more, but when I showed Liz what I intended she became
very angry.

'Johnny, you cannot send that...you would not be so cruel! What
end will it serve, what difference can it make? It is not like you to be
so bitter, do you think you are the only person in the world to lose,
to be rejected? Grow up! In God's name, are *you* now forgetting who

238

you are? I will not have you send that letter. Leave it. Look away…are you trying to deny all you believe, all your fine words about friendship? For heaven's sake stop and think for one minute of her feelings. She is probably as lost as you feel and she is trying to say sorry!'

I should never have shown her the letter and I tried to take it back from her but she hid it behind her back.

'No, Johnny, you shall not send it! You can't!'

I strode across and tried to make a grab for it but she forestalled me and started to tear the letter to pieces. That was too much. Now I was angry. I seized her and we fell to the ground, and as we struggled we collided with the stool and then the easel and they both went flying. She was stronger than I expected and we started to fight. We twisted and turned, cried out and we raised our fists against each other. I was furious and attempted to hit her as she shouted, 'No, Johnny…*no!*'

Worse might have followed had not I heard footsteps on the bare boards and Mum shouting, 'Stop it, you two! Johnny, whatever d' you think you are playing at! For mercy's sake…we could hear the racket downstairs!'

I got up, then dragged Liz to her feet. We were covered in dust. 'It's all right,' I gasped. 'No worry, just a bit of fun!'

Brushing herself down Liz said, 'Sorry, Mrs Hartside. Very sorry, it was my fault.'

I said, 'No, no! It was my fault. We fell over.'

My right knee felt as if it was twice its size and I saw Liz was holding her elbow. I had hurt her.

'Liz dear, you'd better come with me, get yourself cleaned up. And Johnny, please, no more of this.'

Our struggle had been childish and pointless. I calmed down, then suffered an anxious week, waiting, consumed with shame and holding myself ready with explanations to a bewildered mum who, as it transpired, was too tactful to ask questions. I thought hard, then penned a second letter in place of the first:

Dear Anne,

I don't know what to say but you will understand if I do not
offer congratulations. It was a shock. I had no idea you and
Alex were so close – you might have told me. But I wish
you luck and hope you will be happy if you are sure this is
what you really want. Take care, and don't overdo things.
And sometime, if you feel up to it, let me know how you
are.

A hopeless letter, but I could not think of what else I might say.
To forgive is not easy and on the other hand I had not been open to
Anne. I had not told her how love once lost had found another home.
Except that now I was not sure that it had. There were fences to be
mended.

The initiative had to be mine. At very least – a phone call.
  'Lizzie, it's me. Are you all right?'
  Silence. I tried again. 'I sent another letter – one I think you would
approve.'
  'Yes, so I heard. She told me. She was relieved to hear from you.
She honestly does not want to lose touch, she said, friends are for always
and she means it.'
  'Is she all right?'
  'She sounded well enough.'
  'What about you, Lizzie? I'm sorry if I hurt you, I didn't mean it, I
was upset.'
  'I'm bruised, you brute! Don't you dare hit me again!'
  'Friends?'
  A long pause. Another of her policemen being born. Then her voice
warmed. 'Friends,' she replied.
  'Next weekend,' I said. 'Will you be free?'
  'Could be. Why?'
  'That talk we never had.'
  'Okay. You mean – brazen?'
  'Absolutely! Saturday, then. I'll come over.'

For a Quaker who had been taught peace and reconciliation I was out of line. I was not doing very well. As my form master at Whitworth once wrote of RE on my school report – 'Could do better.'

Chapter Fifty-two

W hen Durand called at Ebor Images I went down to see him. It was almost inevitable that he would ask whether I had produced more canvases and I told him work was in hand. What I really sought was more information about the Elstree team and what they wanted of me.

'Not really my bag, Hartside,' he replied. 'But I imagine they have more work for you – part-time I should think.'

'But I know nothing of film-making.'

'Then you'll learn. Probably a freelance arrangement as a gofer to Assistant Art Director, but don't quote me, just keep your fingers crossed until you get the nod.'

When opportunity knocks it was best, as I was learning, to answer without delay. Lady Luck could be asking to come in. As for my ill-luck with Liz, that had to change. I had hurt her and I was ashamed and did not know where my anger had come from. I had seen enough of violence in Europe to last a lifetime. Now, I had to make my peace with Liz and ask her to forgive.

On Saturday morning I drove over to St Hilary's and the old Star purred along quite smoothly. Liz had said she would wait for me at the schoolhouse, not the staff room. She had put on the style for the occasion. A cherry-red buttoned jacket, a pleated skirt and at her neck the rainbow scarf that Mum had bought for her on that long-ago trip to the coast. She offered coffee but I said no, we were going to take a drive in the old Star. We had the whole day before us.

'Okay! An excursion? Where to, mister?'

I had no idea. I had made no plans and not even brought a map.

'Deep country,' I answered. 'And somewhere nice for lunch.'

'I'll settle for that.'

North and west, I said. We'd find a peaceful place. Kiss and make up.

'Like under the willow tree?' she said.

'No more of that!' I replied. I told her the old tree was to come down – if Odd Job had not already carried out the execution.

She pulled on a wide-brimmed hat and a dandy pair of gloves and settled herself beside me. I started up and drove across to the A68 and away we went, bowling along towards Castlerigg and Reedon Mill under a sky piled with fleecy clouds and enough patches of blue to make a Dutchman's trousers. The car was fun to drive, a touch noisy, but there was plenty of life left in her. I told Liz the last car I had driven was the Riley Rover. She nodded. She had heard from Anne all about the mad girl with the knife and our narrow escape.

'We won't be stopping for any hitchhikers, then,' she shouted.

I said we would turn off the main road. A choice of routes, I thought, and hopefully we'd find the right one. I recalled Ma Neatly and her advice in meeting to find the right way forward. Her words of long ago returned. 'All that glisters is not gold,' she warned. First appearances could be deceptive.

We had driven for an hour or so when Liz placed her hand on my knee. She was grinning. 'Shall we find a lay-by and have a breather? I should have brought a flask.'

'Not a lay-by, none of your fantasies today!'

I had spotted a turn-off. Two miles to Gunnersby. A nice name, I liked it.

Liz started her crazy game again. 'Gunnersby, a lovely place, to visit would be no disgrace!'

I replied, 'Okay, I've got a hunch, we'll find a little pub for lunch!'

It was a long, winding lane with high hedges on either hand, almost a tunnel, the road steadily climbing with barely room for another car to pass. But there were no cars, no vans, not even a farmer's pony and trap. We were in deep country, a sheltered, private place. A bit of luck. A good choice. I saw rooftops ahead and slowed down. It was hardly a village…no more than a handful of cottages crouching round a green with a flagpole. At the far end I spied what I was hoping for. The sign read 'The Smiddy Arms' and showed a crudely painted anvil.

We pushed open the door and found a dark space, shadowy and partially lit by a fire, which crackled and sparkled in the hearth. A solitary figure sat beside it, an old man glumly contemplating the glass of beer before him. At the opposite end there were a few tables and chairs and a door marked toilet. It was a place thick with silence, where you felt you should not raise your voice.

'Coffee?' whispered Liz.

I agreed, but we were out of luck. The old fellow clambered to his feet and shuffled round to the bar regarding us as if we had flown in from another planet. There was no coffee, he said, only beer and spirits. We had to settle for a shandy and a lemonade. And more silence. Liz put her mouth to my ear. 'D' you think he'd do sandwiches?' I guessed the answer before I asked. Alas – no sandwiches.

We did not delay, we drank up and decided to move on. We needed food. We would find another village further up the valley. Liz disappeared through the door marked toilet. I paid, went out to the car, and waited. When Liz rejoined me she said glorious Gunnersby was not for us…or for anyone else for that matter. The toilet, she declared, was men only. 'You know, just a kind of trough against the wall.' She grinned. 'Difficult, but I managed! Let's get out of this place!'

She walked round the car to the passenger side. I heard her shout 'Oh *no*! Johnny, look at this!'

I got out and looked. The front nearside wheel. A flat tyre. Flat as a pancake down to the rim. It was no longer funny. Gunnersby was a disaster, the wrong choice, and what was worse, the Star carried no spare wheel. So – it was back to old grumpy. Perhaps he had a foot pump, but when I asked he said no.

'A puncture? Aye, well, you could try the lady, top of the lane, yonder.' His face registered distaste. 'She might help yer. Used to be a farm. Hillside, it's called.'

There was no other option. I was furious, it was a disaster. But Liz calmly corrected me.

'It's an adventure! Come on, Johnny, at least it's not raining and it isn't very far!'

So, we walked. Hillside looked much larger than the cottages. A square house like a Georgian manse. Old stone, with a slate roof. The white window frames were newly painted as was the front door on which hung a bright brass knocker.

'Shall we?'

I nodded. We rapped and waited. There was probably no one at home. I was wrong. The door opened. On the threshold stood a handsome woman wearing a blue-and-white-striped apron over her dress. A cheerful nod. 'Good afternoon,' she said. 'Do come in.'

It was as if she had been expecting us. We followed her into a sitting room, which was not unlike ours at Yearsby. It was smaller but beautifully furnished. The cream walls were hung with paintings in gold frames, there were dark beams overhead, and two plump, white sofas facing each other with a table between on which were several leather-bound books and, I noted, a folded map.

Hands on hips the woman regarded us with a bright smile. 'I'm Christina,' she said. 'Have you had a good journey?'

I calculated that she was about sixty. She had a 'town' voice, no trace of an accent and I could not believe she was a local farmer's wife. Recovering from initial surprise I apologised for intruding and explained that the landlord at The Smiddy Arms had suggested she might be able to help us.

'It's our car,' I said. 'A flat tyre.' If by any chance she possessed a foot pump we could perhaps borrow it and manage along a mile or two to the nearest garage.

'How very trying for you. I do have a car, but, alas, no pump, I'm afraid! In fact, I also need a garage. It's miles away and I have rung them but of course, being Saturday afternoon, they are closed. It will be Monday – with luck.'

I thanked her and said we would return to The Smiddy Arms. He had no pump, but he surely had a car.

'A van, I think. But you would be wasting your time, I doubt very much if he would get it out – unless you were the Princess Royal, or the Queen herself!'

She turned to Liz. 'But you're not a princess, are you, dear!'

We laughed and it broke the ice. 'D' you know, he's the meanest man on God's earth!'

In fact it was no joke. We were well and truly stuck, and apparently miles from anywhere. Liz volunteered: 'Perhaps he has accommodation, more and more pubs do these days.'

'Yes, dear, he does put people up when he feels like it, hikers and the bicycle brigade. Quite a lot come in the summer.'

Then she explained: 'When you knocked I thought you were looking for accommodation and must have found me in the book, *Country Comforts*, the new one by Alan Sowerby. I don't really advertise in the magazines, too small, and in any case I've only been open since last autumn.'

I looked at Liz. A broad smile, and she was nodding. I should have guessed. Christina was bed and breakfast.

Chapter Fifty-three

I can happen only once in your life when all the pieces fit, when luck steps in and literally seems heaven-sent. A cup of tea and a chocolate biscuit, that was the start of it. And comfort. We sank back into a soft-cushioned sofa with a choice of Indian or China served in beautiful cups by a total stranger we had met only half an hour earlier. And there she was, perched on the arm of the sofa opposite.

'I have not had many young people so far,' she began. 'Usually older couples, touring, retired, with time on their hands. But honeymoon couples…' She paused and looked from Liz to me. 'I have a feeling that you might be on your honeymoon. Would I be right?'

We answered in unison. No, I said. Yes, said Liz.

Eyebrows raised. She looked at us both and struggled to prevent a smile. Silence. Another policeman being born. She glanced at Liz's hands, then raised her head to study one of the dark beams above.

'I take it, Mr Hartside, that you are not husband and wife.'

I nodded.

'I'm afraid I have only the one room at present, the other is being redecorated.'

It sounded as if she was very politely saying no room at the inn. I said – but not with any enthusiasm – 'I think we should try the Smiddy, you mentioned that he does take people.'

Liz gave me a sharp nudge in the ribs, pulled a face and was clearly signalling 'No!'

Christina picked up the teatray. I could not read the expression on her face, but as she turned to the door she said, ' I'll be in the kitchen. Let me know if you need any help with your luggage.'

※

'Liz, I am not sure this is right, I don't think she wants us, she is clearly embarrassed.'

'She has read us like a book and I like her. She is a businesswoman and we are business, can't you see that? I am not, repeat *not*, going back to that Smiddy place, I'd rather spend the night in the car!'

In the end it was no contest. The only available room won. It was at the top of the stairs and it was beautiful. A door with a latch led to a narrow, short corridor with a chair and a bookcase and two more doors, one to a bathroom and the other to the bedroom. Snowy white quilts, a nursing chair, an old-fashioned mahogany dressing table, a wall of white cupboards and two windows. One looked over a small garden and beyond to a paddock where I could see two sheep grazing. They were large black sheep.

Liz came to the window and looked, then laughed. 'Do you think that's us? You know, really wicked!'

I kissed her, then said I would go downstairs and have a word, but before I could do so there was a knock on the door.

'May I come in? I thought you might need your luggage.' She handed Liz a brightly patterned silk dressing gown and, smiling, said, 'No hurry. We'll eat in the kitchen tonight. Nothing very special. Savoury mince – I do hope you're not vegetarians!'

Liz said, 'That's very kind but really, it's not necessary.'

'I think it is. And by the way, in the bathroom cupboard there are toothbrushes, I always keep a few spares, you'd be surprised how forgetful some people can be!'

It was the way that she said it. There was more to this lady – much more – than savoury mince in the kitchen.

'My friends call it harlequin mince because it has so many colours! Green peppers, carrots, onions, mushroom, courgette and sometimes a dash of tomato purée.'

We were both very hungry. It was delicious, and we tucked in. Food, I thought, makes friends, and that was true, but over supper round that kitchen table a bond was formed by something rather different. Christina told us that when her husband died she gave up her life in London and decided to make a change, to start afresh.

'My family came from this part of the world, so I thought…why not? Back to my roots and, what was just as important, I found this lovely house. My husband would love to have retired here but then not all your dreams come true. We were army, generations back, and he was very keen. In the Paras, 1st Airborne Division, and he did very well until, along with thousands of others, he copped it. September twenty-fifth – but that won't mean anything to you.'

For a moment her steady smile disappeared, then she stood up and said, 'Let's take the coffee through, shall we?'

So we returned to the sitting room. Liz said, 'I had a friend, a special friend and he too was 1st Airborne. He died of his burns after Arnhem.'

Christina looked incredulous – then shocked. 'But, my dear…how dreadful for you. Was he quite young?'

Liz nodded. 'About my age.'

She put an arm round Liz's shoulders and stroked her hair. Shaking her head she said, 'It was one of the most cruel actions that almost succeeded, that could have succeeded, but…such a terrible loss of life. The full story has never been told but my husband would have known. If he had survived he would have taken a colonel's pension – or even a brigadier's.'

As I listened I thought how strange it was, the whole day somehow turned upside down – and more than that, coincidence running deep like the fateful Rhine at Arnhem Bridge. I longed to take Liz in my arms and carry her to the quiet, white room upstairs and hold her and love her. But memories of the man she loved and which she had pushed aside cruelly surfaced again.

'I think we should have a nightcap,' Christina said. 'Brandy. Would you like that? Cheer us all up!'

She turned to Liz. 'We will never forget. But we must thank the Lord it's all over now, my dear, and hope such a tragedy will never happen again.'

✳

The silken dressing gown with its colourful pattern of dragons was useful after all. Liz took a bath, and said she had cleaned her teeth, then it was my turn as she floated past like a geisha girl to claim the bed by the window. I had not expected we would be coy, or shy, and I longed to share her bed, but I could tell those memories had returned to trouble her. Now, the need I felt, the hope I had cherished, had to be put aside. Just a goodnight kiss. Sleep well. Lights out, like the dorm at school.

Chapter Fifty-four

At breakfast we sought Christina's advice.

'Fairholme,' she declared. 'That's if you fancy a good walk. About two miles. It's a much prettier village than Gunnersby, and there's the remains of a castle, more like an old watchtower and some sunken stones which are said to mark the site of a Cistercian monastery.'

Liz said she was not feeling particularly 'historical'.

'If you prefer of course you are welcome to stay in. I'll be busy in the kitchen. I'm having the builders next week but there is no problem. There are lots of books if you want to read.'

There certainly were. One wall of the dining room where we'd been served breakfast was lined with books. History. Trollope, Wordsworth, a selection of art books – the Phaidon Press – with Manet, Monet, most of the Impressionists, and old red-covered editions of *Who's Who*.

Liz voted for a walk, so Christina lent us a Barbour, a heavy tweed overcoat and a pair of garden shoes, which fitted Liz well enough.

'It's Sunday, Johnny. Remember, after meeting? Walking with friends as A. J. used to say!'

We found the watchtower. It was little more than a tall circle of granite walls rough-hewn, weathered by the centuries and mixed with rubble, but it was worth discovering as it commanded a brilliant view across a wide valley. Beyond it in a haze of blue was the promise of still higher hills. It was a windless morning…a stillness in the air. The world had come to a full stop. We clambered into the tower and sat down on a cold stone slab. We held each other and snuggled. No words – we wanted none. We waited and it was as if we were in a Quaker meeting again. I wondered if Liz was saying a prayer in her head. Because

I was. You could call it a vote of thanks, and I thought that maybe…just maybe a whisper of faith was trying to return.

Back at Hillend the amazing Christina had made soup, a vegetable broth, which we scoffed, seated at the end of the long, polished table in the dining room. On a sideboard I counted eight crystal decanters. They were all empty. A row of sentinels, retired I guessed after serving in many an officers' mess. Proud toasts. Beakers of Port…bubbles winking at the brim, I said. Then, Liz winked and I understood.

We climbed the stair to our white room and closed the door on a silent world. Not even the ticking of a clock.

She perched on the bed and she knew, as I also knew, it was time – our time. She needed no silken dragon gown in which to hide.

I folded her in my arms. 'Lizzie, Lizzie!'

We kissed and we became breathless. She whispered, 'I want you to undress me, shock me. Will you, Johnny? God forgive me but I've been waiting so long for you to fuck me!'

I needed no invitation. That lovely word, the ages-old word, as ancient as the tumbled tower, and how often spoken, moved me. I murmured, 'Tell me again!'

She struggled to be the temptress she had no need to be, and breathed: 'Fuck me, please, please fuck me, Johnny.'

Gently, as slowly as I dared, I answered her command until, little by little her clothes lay on the floor and she lay naked on the bed. Then I covered her mouth with mine so she would not cry out.

When night came, and striving not to show indecent haste, we said goodnight to Christina and let our coffee grow cold. Then we climbed the stair again and we were glad to have no luggage, no clothes to delay or deter us.

'Brazen!' she declared. 'I'll be your geisha girl. Now it is my turn!' She reached to remove my jacket. 'I mean to have my way with you…try as you may, sir, I'll have no refusal and I'll do as I please!'

Quaint words! A girl with her fantasies, striving to eliminate the past. More bad words, but I found them touching as they turned in my mind and stirred my heart.

We did not draw the curtains at the windows but let the night come in, the darkness and the starlight, to see our nakedness as she offered her lips, her sweet breasts and her limbs. When we came together she wept a little and I was deeply moved. I knew now, as we explored our new-found land, that this was meant, and we were beautiful.

✳

We slept in and were late down. We did not deserve breakfast. Christina saw how we were but made no comment and did not seem to mind. She said brunch was available – eggs and crusty bread with honey or marmalade. She had phoned her garage and, pouring coffee and coming to sit with us, she said, 'I think they're attending to your car now, they'll see to mine later.'

I had left my wallet in my jacket and stumped upstairs to get it. Money for the garage man, and our bill. Liz followed me, straightened the quilts on the beds, then gazing from the window she said, 'The black sheep, they're still there, Johnny!'

She reached up and put her arms round my neck. 'I wish we could still be here, I don't want to go, darling, ever, ever.'

I kissed her and tasted honey on her lips. Then a last look round the room, our special place, bright now with sunshine slanting through the window by her bed.

I had expected a heavy bill but was surprised. The charge was for only one night, not two, plus the cost of a new tyre. Christina refused to take more. So we said our many, many thanks to a wonderful woman who had become a friend. Sadly we made our farewell and walked back to reclaim our car outside The Smiddy.

As we drove away Liz said, 'I wonder which night we paid for?' I replied that I was sure it was the second one.

When Gunnersby was well behind and we turned south for home, Liz dozed close against me, her hand on my knee. When she woke she said, 'I didn't tell you, Johnny, but what d' you think? Christina said something quite strange…she felt she had known me all her life! And that's not all. She gave me a parcel with a note. In it was that silk dragon dressing gown. You can return it, she said, when you come back to see me again. On your honeymoon.'

Chapter Fifty-five

*A*s autumn closed in, views diminished. The edges of each day hardened with desire. I longed for Lizzie, impatient for her voice on the phone, and when she rang it sent my pulse racing. Our need for each other could not be quenched.

For me the Ebor Gallery provided a brief diversion. They owned a small studio flat in a mews behind Coppergate and let it to me. I was midway through moving my canvases and painting materials down there when Lizzie's letter arrived.

Darling,

I don't suppose they meant to disappear forever, but I expect it was Anne's idea to get right away. Her letter said that she and Alex flew out to the Caribbean of all places, to an island called Mustique. The postmark said St Vincent, so it's somewhere in the Grenadines. I quote: 'We arranged it through a resort company. They did all the organisation and put us into the island's only hotel. Mustique is tiny, just four square miles! A chaperon took charge of us like a mother hen. We were flown to St Vincent to meet the minister, a delightful West Indian lady who asked us many questions about ourselves. We were there for the whole day, taken to the consulate to get the licence, there were forms to sign and then it was more forms to sign in the register office and get them stamped. After that we were shepherded back to the hotel in Mustique to establish residence – a minimum of four days is the rule. Then the minister flew in from St Vincent and two witnesses were arranged: a waiter and a waitress from the hotel. We were married on the beach under the palm trees. The service was Church of England. Back at the hotel we had champagne and were then taken in a small boat for a tour round the island! This was followed by the wedding breakfast that night, on the beach. Flares and candles were lit, it was superb. We had an entire ocean at our feet and the world was ours! You would have loved it. We spent three days in Barbados, then on up to Dominica to my mother's grave.'

Dearest Johnny, please don't be upset, but I felt you would at least want to know when and where they were married. I still hold on to the hope that one day we can all be friends again.

I suppose I was glad to know, but it wasn't as easy as that. Promises not honoured were gone, were like flowers left in an empty room to die. Close the door on them. Then only the perfume remains, soft, fading, like the wraith of a figure receding at the corner of a half-remembered street. Now, it was Lizzie who was not simply 'my most trusting and assured good friend'. She was a part of me. I dearly loved her and she it was who gave me the will to look to the future with hope.

In London I returned to Tavistock Square where the QRS were still operating a post-war service for volunteers overseas. A bed for the night was no problem, and nor were the Elstree boys I had come south to see and where the interview took place on an echoing film lot. They agreed to pay me a retainer, which meant I would be at their beck and call should they require me on occasion to assist their distinguished art director. The money was welcome. It would be an extra lifeline to add to what I hoped to earn from the sale of my 'serious' work.

Back home Sundays were the only time Lizzie and I could be together. I set aside my brushes. We made love in the little studio flat and unashamedly chose afternoons as our bedtime.

Sometimes I awoke in the small hours and if sleep would not come I would leave our bed to sit in the adjacent room so as not to disturb

Lizzie. Around four one morning the big window beckoned, and gazing out I saw a sky blazing with stars, the large ones, the small ones, the ones that winked and those that simply beamed a steady, brilliant light. I thought I saw the entire universe, sparkling, crackling with an astonishing energy, and imagined beyond the visible stars were pillars of flaming gas trillions of miles high spitting out a succession of new-born galaxies. And I thought I saw a multitude of stars gathering together to form a gigantic cross, but when I blinked in sheer disbelief it disappeared. I was so deeply moved my cheeks were wet – then I felt a hand on my shoulder.

'Come on, Johnny-head-in-air, come down to earth, come back to bed. This is no time for weeping.'

The following Sunday as we were making supper, Lizzie surprised me. She announced that if a vacancy occurred she would apply for a post at Whitworth School. The juniors, she said. 'And perhaps I could assist with PE for the girls.'

'The boys as well,' I said. 'I imagine the old place will have gone co-ed by now.'

When Founders' Day at Whitworth came round and former scholars returned to revive memories and grumble about the changes that had taken place, we returned with them and with our most chosen friends – Pop and Walt and Cumberland.

After meeting for worship we walked on the Green again, Lizzie and me, and Anne in a wheelchair with Alex pushing. Then Lizzie stirred in the bed and folded her arms around me.

'Johnny darling,' she said, 'what is it? You were twisting and turning and it was terrible, you were shouting your head off in your sleep!'

It was of course the impossible dream. Or was it wishful thinking, a trick of the unconscious? In the broad light of day it could never really happen.

Marriage, nevertheless, seemed to be in the air. In that late November Princess Elizabeth married her handsome naval officer at Westminster Abbey. A Hartnell dress it was said. Very beautiful. And more than 2,000 guests attending.

In the following May, Sundays changed their colour. Change was the story everywhere, with Russia creating trouble in Berlin and the Jews proclaiming a new state in Palestine.

We gave it all scant attention. We were still too busy trying to come to terms with the direction our lives were taking. It was also on a Sunday that she said it. She told me quite casually as we were making supper.

'By the way, Johnny darling,' she said, 'term ends next week. We'll have more time. So I've rung Hillside at Gunnersby to make a reservation and take that silk dressing gown back to Christina.'

'Funny you should say that, Lizzie. I was thinking of ringing her myself!'

※

It was early June, and fair weather. A popular time for weddings, when people made their promises.

We were driving north once again up the A68 to Gunnersby. As we passed a solitary van she said, 'I rather like that, Johnny!'

I looked, and on the side of the van, in bold letters, I read 'A promise means nothing until it is delivered.'

The Beginning